OUT OF NOWHERE

Patrick LeClerc

Firedance Books

First published in the UK by Firedance Books in 2012.

Copyright © 2012 Patrick LeClerc.

The right of Patrick LeClerc to be identified as the author of this work has been asserted in accordance with sections 77 and 78 of the Copyright, Designs and Patents Act 1988.

All characters in this publication are fictitious and any resemblance to real persons, living or dead, is purely coincidental.

Cover design copyright © 2012 Rebecca Kemp.

All rights reserved.

This book is sold subject to the condition that it shall not, by way of trade or commerce, be lent, resold, hired out or otherwise circulated. No part of this publication may be reproduced, stored in a retrieval system or transmitted, in any form or by any means, without the prior permission in writing of the author, nor be otherwise circulated in any form of binding or cover other than that in which it is published and without a similar condition including this condition being imposed on the subsequent purchaser.

ISBN: 978-1-909256-09-5

Firedance Books

firedancebooks.com

Acknowledgements

I'd like to thank Gary, for herding the cats and enduring my outbursts, Ray, Tim, Kevin, Steve, Ren, Louise, Janet and Julie, who suffered through the early drafts, and my lovely wife Rebecca who stayed with me even when I chose to add "writer" to a description that already included "short, angry and often fired."

Last, I'd like to thank the EMTs and Paramedics I've worked with, who inspired much of this story.

Chapter 1

THE HEAVY STEEL DOOR WASN'T LOCKED, but, like every utility room door I'd ever encountered, it was stuck. Grunting in pain, I pushed down on the handle with my good hand and slammed my shoulder into it. It yielded with a screech of protest and I staggered into the room, managing to close it before collapsing against the far wall. I sat on the floor with my back against the cool bricks. I couldn't hear any sound of pursuit, but hearing anything over the blood pounding in my ears would have been a trick.

My left wrist was broken, no doubt about that. Any pressure on the forearm brought waves of queasy grey pain. I'd also turned my right ankle in a spectacular tumble down an iron staircase. It would have been worse if the guy I'd been wrestling hadn't broken my fall. I wasn't sure if he was dead or just unconscious, but he was unlikely to come though the door any time soon. A few of my ribs were probably cracked, or at least bruised; I felt a cramping stab every time I tried to breathe deep. Other than that, a few cuts, scrapes and bruises, but nothing I couldn't recover from. My lungs worked like a bellows. A shallow, painful, tentative bellows, maybe, but a bellows just the same.

I'd managed to keep a grip on my pistol. I clutched the .45 in my uninjured right hand like a heroin addict clutching his next hit. The slide hadn't locked back, so there was still a round in the chamber. How many left in the magazine I couldn't say.

I really wished I could. I replayed the last few minutes over and over and tried to count, but I couldn't swear how many shots I'd fired. Certainly three. Maybe six. I argued with myself until it seemed too much like *Dirty Harry,* and gave it up as a bad job. I certainly wasn't feeling lucky.

There was a full magazine in the pocket of my jacket, but changing magazines would require me to move, which hurt, and a large part of me argued for just making do with whatever was left in the gun.

My wiser if less kind self overruled that thought. It was possible that I was down to my last round, and if they burst—no, let's be honest—when they burst through that door, a single bullet wasn't going to do the job.

I steeled myself, remembering my training. It's just pain. Pain is only sensation. Messages from the nerves, dispatches from the front. Like a cool breeze off the ocean or the smoky bite of a good whisky or the touch of a woman. A sensation to be savored, proof that life still beat in the breast. It was all in how you chose to interpret those tiny electric impulses. Take the pain. Let it wash over you and enjoy it just to spite it. You know what you need to do, just do it.

I pressed the magazine release with my right hand, dropping the spent clip. My mind still rebelled at the thought of rummaging in my pocket with a broken left hand, so I engaged the safety, tucked the pistol under my arm and dug out the full magazine with my right hand. I slotted it clumsily into the butt of the weapon one-handed, then took the grip in my hand and pressed the magazine home on my knee, sighing in relief as I felt it click into place.

Since I knew there was a round chambered, I didn't have to try to operate the slide one-handed. I took aim at the door, resting my shooting arm on my raised right knee. I'd have preferred a two-handed grip, but having my injured wrist anywhere near the weapon when it recoiled didn't bear thinking about. Now any attempt to move it elicited a twinge not unlike someone stepping gently on my left testicle.

By the time I finished moving, my breathing was ragged, I was running with sweat and the world was fuzzy and grey through a haze of vertigo. Just my body's way of letting my mind know that while it would follow orders, like the jaded, cynical old soldier it was, it wasn't buying any of the Zen bullshit about pain that my oh-so-gullible brain was selling.

I tried to slow and deepen my breathing, as much as the pain in my side would allow, and the dizziness and nausea ebbed enough that the world swam back into sharp focus.

It was largely wasted on the room. It seemed to be a custodian's office. Cheap desk, broken office chair with torn Pleather upholstery, an olive drab file cabinet covered in stickers—Harley Davidson, Teamsters, Aerosmith, Lynyrd Skynyrd and some Harry Crumb artwork—and a selection of mops, brooms, and cleaning supplies on a steel shelf against a wall. Posters of naked women, expensive cars, and naked women draped over expensive cars. Calendar six months out of date featuring a stunning blonde in a bikini holding a socket wrench. Holding it wrong.

Yep. Definitely a janitor's office.

I concentrated my focus over the sights of my pistol, wondering if there had been some point during the past few days when I could have made a decision to avoid all this.

I heard my pursuers creeping up to the door, like Sandberg's fog, on little cat feet. I thumbed the safety off, blowing out a deep breath, calming myself for the confrontation.

Had I been in a worse spot than this? I must have been. There was the time Cromwell's cavalry had me cornered in that old stone barn. I had a musket ball in my leg and only a massive wheel-lock horse pistol.

But at least that time I'd had room to move, things to work with, even if I had to count straw and lanterns. Tools that fit my innate underhandedness. Here there was only one way in or out, nowhere to hide. Not an ideal venue for a quick-thinking coward. More for a stalwart hero, full of stiff-upper-lip, diehard fatalism.

A good place for a last stand, but I've never been a fan of last stands. I always like to think I have a few more stands in me.

Lewie Puller would have liked it. Probably would have said how the setup saved us the trouble of going out and finding the sons of bitches. But he was a head case. And apparently bulletproof. I don't ever remember seeing him take cover, but all through Central America and the Pacific and Korea he never got wounded. I didn't feel comfortable in a uniform until it had mud and grass stains on it, and I still caught my share of incoming.

I always got better though.

I hoped I'd have the chance this time.

I watched the door over the sights of the pistol, trying to control my breathing to reduce the rise and fall of the muzzle. Soft footsteps approached the door.

I concentrated on my sight picture, pushing all the pain and worry to the back of my mind. Wait for the target. Nothing exists but my target and me.

Suddenly, a movement in the corner caught my eye. A twisting and morphing of the shadows into something...

Solid?

Chapter 2

'Paramedic 20,' the radio crackled, 'respond to 248 Broadway for the man down.'

'Lovely,' I muttered. 'Try to drive slow so I can actually drink some of this hot.'

'20, received. Broadway for the fall,' Monique said into the mic. 'You really think you need that fourth coffee?'

'I'm old and tired,' I said. 'I need the caffeine to keep up with you.' Maybe exaggerating a bit, but to a girl her age, thirty was old and tired.

'In your dreams, old man.' She shot me a wicked grin, a glitter in her eyes that said while she had the face of an angel, her mind was willing to entertain offers from the other team.

It didn't take long, maybe four ounces of coffee, before we pulled up on scene. The patient sat in a dirty snowbank on the sidewalk in front of a run-down boarding house known for cheap rooms, a relaxed attitude toward references, indifferent housekeeping and very good prices on heroin. He looked out of place, a well groomed white guy dressed Eurotrash chic in a black sweater, slim cut jeans and a black leather trench coat that suggested a career as a pimp or a Gestapo officer. His face was white as a sheet, a sheen of sweat on his forehead, his right foot turned at an unnatural angle. The engine crew was already on scene, three of America's Heroes administering the 'stare of life.'

'Think that's him?' Nique asked as the crowd of firefighters all pointed at the man sprawled on the ground.

'That's why they paint fire trucks red and put all those lights on them,' I answered. 'So paramedics can find the patient.'

Nique pulled the ambulance over and we got out.

'Hey, guys,' I addressed the lieutenant. 'Watcha got?'

'Thirty-two-year-old male subject, complainin' of lower extremity ankle pain after experiencin' a fall.'

'As opposed to his upper extremity ankle?' Nique whispered with a grin as she passed me on the way to get the cot.

'I always listen to their report. Makes them feel loved.' I smiled back, before turning to the lieutenant and pitching my voice appropriately for someone who's spent twenty years with a bucket on his head next to a blaring siren. 'Cool. I think we got it, you guys can clear up.'

Due deference shown to the almighty Fire Department, I could now turn my attention to my patient. 'Hello sir, I'm a paramedic. How you doing?'

'I... I think I broke my ankle,' he gasped. 'I slipped off the curb and twisted it.'

He had an accent, but I couldn't quite place it. I'm usually good at that, but this guy's stumped me. It sounded a little Eastern European, but it wasn't Polish or Russian, and didn't feel like Czech or Hungarian.

'Is that all you hurt?' I asked. 'You didn't hit your head or anything?'

He shook his head, 'No. Just my ankle.'

I knelt, carefully removed an expensive Italian loafer and gently palpated the twisted limb. It was displaced, very swollen and clearly broken. I concentrated on the feel of the leg through my fingertips, extending my perception deep beneath the skin, sensing the jagged fragments of bone, the lacerated venules and capillaries oozing blood into the tissues, the inflamed flesh squeezing the nerves, frantic with messages of agony.

'OK sir, I'm gonna have to wrap this up before we move you,' I said calmly. 'It's probably going to hurt.'

My partner was already walking up with a bath blanket, an ice pack and a roll of tape.

I sent a small trickle of healing energy though my fingers, quieting the nerves a bit before we moved him. Not much, just enough to take the edge off. I wrapped a folded blanket around the joint, immobilizing it with some two inch tape. Better than trying to strap the thing to a rigid board.

He held his reaction to a small grunt as we lifted him onto the cot. One of the firefighters tried to grab the patient's shoulders for Nique, but it made me proud to see her step in his way, cutting him off while appearing not to notice. Looking like she did, she could have completed an entire EMS career without lifting anything over ten pounds, while three cops and an engine crew would watch me carry a burning piano down a spiral staircase without comment. I respected Monique because she never abused that power. She didn't make a big issue of refusing help, she just did her job well and efficiently and flashed that smile at anyone who might be thinking about getting offended and they'd just melt.

We got the patient in the truck and Nique got a quick set of vitals while I felt around his ankle. If we left it as is, he was looking at some serious surgery and about a half pound of hardware to fasten all the fragments together. 'Hmmph,' I commented.

'BP's 140 over 84, pulse is a hundred,' Nique informed me. 'Line and some morphine?'

'Yeah, he's real dislocated. I don't feel any crepitus,' I lied. 'But I don't have a pedal pulse. I'm gonna medicate and reduce it.'

'You got it,' she replied. Most partners would have questioned what I was suggesting, but we had built enough trust that we were beyond that; another reason I loved working with Nique. She quickly hung a bag of saline. 'Toss me the narc keys and I'll draw you up some Vitamin M.'

I spoke calmly to the patient while I assembled my IV supplies. 'Sir? I'm going to start an IV and give you some medicine for the pain. Are you allergic to anything? Any other medical problems?'

'No,' he replied as I tied a tourniquet around his arm and looked over it, shopping for veins. I swabbed a likely candidate with an alcohol pad.

'You're gonna feel a little pinch.' I held the skin taut and slid the needle in, seeing the flash chamber fill nicely. He was young and healthy and had nice veins, so I didn't have to cheat to guide the IV, but I did let a little energy through my fingers to take some of the sting out of it. I quickly hooked up the line, let it run to check it and taped it down.

'Your morphine, sir.' Nique handed me a syringe. 'There's ten milligrams in here.'

'Cool. I'll give him four, then reduce it. If I need more post reduction, I'll let you know.'

'Sounds good,' she said. 'Anything else I can do for you?'

'Not unless you want to piss off your fiancé. Just a nice easy ride to the hospital.'

'I could tell him you just asked me for a nice easy ride,' she leered as she got into the driver's seat.

'He knows me better than that. I'd never ask for nice and easy.'

I opened up the valve on the IV tubing and let it run as I slowly pushed the morphine, flushing four milligrams in over about a minute. 'You might feel a little strange,' I told the patient. 'That's normal, but if you start to feel sick, let me know.'

I moved down to the foot of the cot. Keeping my balance like a sailor on a pitching deck, I knelt by his foot and unwrapped it. I laid my hands on either side of his ankle and concentrated.

First, I just quieted the nerves, helping to take the edge off the pain. 'This is gonna hurt, but the morphine will help, and I need to get the circulation back. Ready?'

He nodded.

I carefully rotated the foot back into its rightful alignment. I coaxed the bone shards into place, and knit the torn tendons and ligaments, but stopped short of fixing it completely, since after that fall and that pain, something had to look bad for the ER.

I don't know why I can do this, I just know that I can. I also learned early on that people distrust what they can't understand, even a good thing they can't understand, so I made sure never to fix anyone too much.

Do that too often and the villagers with pitchforks and torches show up.

'There we go,' I said, and made a show of checking for a pedal pulse. 'Aaaand, we're back. Damn, I'm good. How you feeling now, sir?'

'Better... better,' he replied, with a bit less grateful awe than I'm used to.

I looked up from his foot and noticed something in his eyes, some hint of suspicion, like he knew something was wrong. Or not wrong enough.

I felt that dry-mouthed falling sensation that comes when someone with a more aristocratic accent than you tells you to fix bayonets and advance across an open field toward some heavily armed and ill-disposed foreigners. To hide my concern, I kept up my banter. 'Have you at the ER in two minutes. They do good work. Probably be in a cast or a brace for a few weeks. How's the pain? Need any more morphine?' Maybe he'd chalk up the suspicion to the drugs, or even forget it.

'No, thank you. It is much better.'

'You sure? I'm just gonna throw it out. Lotsa lucid kids in China would kill for this,' I joked.

'Again, no,' he replied. 'I prefer to keep a... clear head.'

Something in his tone made my hackles rise.

Was that the sound of a mob? Was that smoke?

* * * *

We dropped the patient at the ER and I tried to shake off my premonition. There's a fine line between vigilance and paranoia. I reached for my rapidly cooling coffee.

'P-20. Paramedic 20,' the radio crackled. 'Respond to 300 Haverhill St, outside in the alley for the stabbing. Ambulance 34 is on scene now. They'll update.'

'20,' I answered. '300 Haverhill. Meet the BLS outside for the stabbing.'

'Ambulance 34 is Katie and Tina today,' said Nique. 'So at least we have competent EMTs.'

'If there aren't too many uniforms around for Katie to keep her concentration.'

Nique shrugged. 'If it's serious, she'll focus. If it's not, who cares?'

'Fair enough,' I said.

We drove through the city toward the call, just around the corner from where we'd picked up our friend with the twisted ankle. 'Busy part of town today,' I observed.

'People probably saw all the red lights earlier and got jealous. All the cool kids are going to the ER.'

'Early in the day for a stabbing,' I said.

'If it isn't some guy who cut his finger on a beer can and called 911 with broken English and dispatch screwed up the call.'

'So young and yet so cynical,' I said.

'I learned from the best.' She smiled back.

We pulled up on scene behind the BLS truck. About ninety percent of our calls can be handled by Basic Life Support: Emergency Medical Technicians who can splint, bandage, give you oxygen and drive you to the hospital. As medics—Advanced Life Support—we can start IVs, give medication or fluid and use the cardiac monitor, so if the guy was stabbed badly we might need to step in. Stab wounds can be deceiving. You get stuck in an organ or an artery gets cut and you can bleed out internally without showing much, and act perfectly normal until blood loss gets critical.

We pulled out our bags and walked over to the alley. The fire engine was just pulling up, a police cruiser already on scene.

Out Of Nowhere

Down the narrow alley, the dirty snow strewn with broken bottles and crushed drug vials, the victim sat on a stoop as the two EMTs checked him over.

He was completely out of place here. A fortyish white guy wearing an L L Bean barn coat over a hideous sweater, the kind only a WASP would be seen wearing in public. Relaxed-fit khakis and topsiders. Probably drove his BMW here from Hamilton. Katie was checking his blood pressure while Tina bandaged a cut on his face.

Two burly cops stood just behind them, waiting to interrogate the victim. I was impressed by the fact that they were waiting instead of stomping all over the EMTs' questions, until I recognized Carlos.

Carlos had worked with us years ago on the ambulance. He'd fought in Iraq, then gone on the truck, and finally, utterly unsuited for any kind of civilized job, gotten into the police department. He understood that our job came first. Once we had stabilized a patient, then he could slap them around all he wanted.

'What's up?' I asked.

'Mr Foley here was minding his own business, not buying any drugs whatsoever,' said Carlos, 'when he mysteriously got cut.'

'I hate when that happens.'

'They're probably all set with you guys. It looks like just a shallow cut on each cheek.'

'Somebody trying to send him a message?'

'He's too scared to tell us anything. I think he'll swear he cut himself shaving.'

'Tell him he should just get one of his dentist buddies to write him a script for Vicodin instead of trying to score in alleys.'

'No point in telling him,' said Carlos' partner, Nelson. 'You white folks don't listen.' Nelly was about six and a half feet and two-hundred-and-fifty pounds of muscle, a shaved head and skin the color of mahogany.

'Sean ain't white,' said Carlos. 'He's just pale for a Puerto Rican.'

'What does that make me?' asked Nique.

'You look that good, don't matter what color you are, *chica*.'

'So Carlos,' I said, 'you still keep your EMT certification up? I know you do, so you can get that stipend. Why don't you pick up a few shifts on the truck for old times' sake?'

'Tried to. Said I couldn't carry my gun.' He smiled. 'I just don't feel safe in this town.'

Tina looked over at us. I raised my head.

'Watcha got?'

'Forty-two-year-old male, lacerations to both cheeks, no other complaints,' she replied. 'His vitals are fine.'

'You guys comfortable with him?'

'Sure. He just needs a ride to the ER for some stitches and a tetanus update. You guys can clear.'

'Thanks,' I replied. As I turned to go, I spotted something. A smear of fresh blood on a doorjamb off the alley, a crimson handprint on the stairway railing.

'Hang on. I think we may have a second victim.' I nodded toward the blood. Nique followed my gesture.

'You guys take this patient to the hospital,' she said. 'We'll go see if we can find another guy who needs to buy a safety razor.'

'Hey, Trigger Happy,' I called to Carlos. 'We got a blood trail here.'

He moved quickly to the door, hand on his pistol. Nique and I stepped aside. Always let the guy with the gun and the vest go first.

The door opened into the hallway of an apartment building. Searching each apartment would take forever.

Fortunately, we could just follow the trail of bloody handprints up the stairs to a door.

Carlos and Nelly stood to either side, Carlos hammered on the door. 'Police! Open up.'

'No Ingles,' came the reply.

Carlos rolled his eyes. *'Policia! Abre la puerta!'*

The door opened a crack. A young woman stood in the gap, a baby in her arms. 'Nobody here—' she began.

Carlos pushed past her. Nelly followed, gently but firmly steering a toddler out of the way. He scanned the room, then nodded to us and we walked in.

The blood trail led to the bathroom. Carlos strode to the door, ignoring a torrent of indignant Spanish from the woman whose home we invaded.

'Policia,' he said, knocking on the bathroom door with his nightstick.

Out Of Nowhere

The door swung open to reveal a wiry Hispanic man, pale under his dark skin, stripped to the waist, his shirt wadded up and pressed against his abdomen, trying in vain to staunch the seeping blood.

Nique swung the bag off her shoulder and I unfolded the stair chair. 'Have a seat here, sir. We'll take a look at that belly.'

'I'm all set. I don't need no ambulance. I don't need to talk to nobody.'

'You're bleeding pretty bad—' I began.

Carlos stopped me with a raised hand. 'Look,' he said to the victim. 'I know you're dealing smack. You know I know. And we both know that you and that scared shit white dude who was buying got cut by somebody who don't want you dealing on this corner. You don't need to tell me any lies, because we already know what happened, and that other guy is gonna sing like a bird just to keep his name out of the paper. So, you can sit on the chair and play nice with the paramedics, or I can ask them to step outside for a minute because you don't have all your injuries yet.'

The man wisely decided to comply. Nique grabbed a pulse while I took the shirt away from his abdomen.

Three inches to the left of center, a clean slit two inches long oozed blood. The man's flat stomach was beginning to feel firm around the cut, filling with blood. It was the wrong side for his liver, but maybe his spleen. That could bleed like crazy. I tore open a big gauze dressing and pressed it into place. I put some pressure on it, sending some energy through to slow the bleeding. I wrapped some gauze bandage around his waist to hold the pressure and cinched the strap of the chair over the dressing for good measure.

'Strong radial pulse,' said Nique. 'Rate's a little fast, but not too bad. One hundred, one ten. How's the wound?'

'Not so deep as a well, nor so wide as a church door,' I replied. 'But 'tis enough. 'Twill serve.'

Nique looked at me with a raised eyebrow.

'Shakespeare. It's bleeding bad. Maybe his spleen. Don't think it's his bowel. Doesn't smell bad.'

She tied a tourniquet. 'I'm gonna line him up here, so he doesn't go out while we're carrying him down the stairs. His veins aren't flat yet.'

'Good plan.'

'Hey, I don't want no needle, man,' he protested.

12

'Dude! You have a sleeve full of Latin Kings ink and a knife wound in your belly. An IV is gonna hurt a lot less than that.'

Nique deftly inserted a 16 gauge IV into the man's vein. To be fair, it was a big needle. But he had nice veins and if he did need rapid volume replacement, the bigger the better.

'Ah, *puta*!' he shouted, straining against the straps of the chair.

I put a hand on his throat and pushed him back into the seat. '*Mira!* I said. 'Listen up. We don't help you, you're gonna die. You're gonna bleed out. It may not hurt that much or look that bad, but your belly is filling up with blood. I've seen it. You need fluid, you need an OR. You talk to her like that again, you might need a dentist. *Comprende, pendejo?*'

He nodded in silence. I released his throat.

'See, Nelly,' said Carlos. 'I told you he's one of us.'

Violence among the gangs who controlled the drug trade was hardly new. Turf battles, real or imagined insults, too much youth, anger, drugs, money and testosterone without a constructive outlet or any real ambition. People got cut or shot or beaten for being in the wrong neighborhood, talking to the wrong girl or guy, wearing the wrong colors. But that was just business as usual. This attack was different. It had been done in broad daylight and seemed both brutal and carefully focused. Sure, it had been a bad wound to the dealer, but it was one stab. Nobody stabs somebody once in anger. This was a message. Don't deal on this corner, or we'll cut you. We don't really care if you live or die. That's how little you matter. And then a clear message to the buyer. Somebody was using a precise and careful application of violence in place of the usual messy and haphazard fashion common to street gangs.

I wondered if somebody had translated Sun Tzu for gangbangers. There promised to be interesting times ahead.

* * * *

We dropped our patient at the ER and cleared up. The rest of the shift was fairly routine. We treated a legitimate chest pain, a cry-for-attention chest pain by a guy whose girlfriend left him, and a beautiful example of how not to slice a bagel; we saved a prostitute unresponsive from a heroin overdose who signed herself out of the hospital and walked out, looking to score, before we finished our paperwork.

'Hey, wait,' Nique called after her as the patient walked past the tiny, battered EMS desk. 'That medicine we gave you is gonna wear off before the heroin does and you'll go right back to not breathing.'

In response, the woman flashed a hand at us, palm outward, in the universal sign of dismissal, her head held high and her expression haughty as a runway model; assuming stained halter tops, threadbare mini-skirts, scabbed knees and no panties was the hot new look in Paris and Milan this season.

'Bitch,' Nique muttered. 'See if I save you again. Shoulda just left her there.'

'Now, now,' I smiled. 'Where's your sense of compassion?'

'Used up about three calls back,' she replied. 'Next time I find that bitch unresponsive I'm intubating her.'

'You'll probably get your chance. Given her line of work, shoving a tube down her throat probably wouldn't bother her all that much.'

She chuckled and her brow unfurrowed. 'OK, I'm good. All sunshine and bunnies again. Maybe we can come up with some kind of incentive program for our repeat customers.'

'What, like a card you punch? After six transports you can turn it in for clean needles?'

'That could work.' She smiled. 'Seriously, why do we do this?'

'Fifteen bucks an hour?' I replied. 'Actually, I just do it so I can hang around with you for twenty-four hours a week. You're so damn sexy. I told 'em they could cut my pay if they bought you a tighter uniform.'

She laughed at that. 'Oh, that did it. I feel better now. You're the only one who gets to talk to me that way, you know.'

'And I'm honored,' I said.

It was true; for whatever reason, I could make comments and she'd laugh where the same thing from other guys would draw her Gallic ire. I wasn't sure if I should be subtly insulted that my inappropriate comments were seen as witty and nonthreatening.

Our rapport confused me a little. Nique was funny, smart, a good medic and drop-dead gorgeous. We clicked well as partners, had a good enough time that the twenty-four-hour shift flew by, and got on well outside of the truck, but for some reason our flirting stayed in the realm of friendly banter, both of us understanding that it wouldn't go any further.

I couldn't put my finger on why.

Chapter 3

'It's probably because you're gay.' Peter, my Tuesday partner, delivered his expert opinion as we drove through the snow on the way to a call. It was a good distance out, mutual aid to the town of Riverdale, just downstream along the Merrimack from Philips Mills.

'So why am I not attracted to you?' I asked as we slowed at a red light. 'Clear right.'

'Well, that's just crazy talk,' he said. 'Since I am an incarnation of masculine sexuality. Oh, yeah, do that, lady. Do exactly that,' he added as a soccer mom in a minivan pulled out in front of the ambulance, then panicked and stopped in the middle of the road. As he steered around her, I gave her a charming smile and a salute.

'Keep drivin' like that, ma'am,' I nodded benevolently. 'Job security for us. Look,' I turned back to Pete and the discussion at hand, 'it's not like I don't know she's attractive, it's just that there's none of that automatic lust instinct with her like with any other hot blonde. Watch this guy on the right, he's gonna cut out—'

'Thanks, man, I got him.' He hit the siren.

'I'm just sayin' it's curious is all,' I continued. 'I'm seeking insight and wisdom and you give me gay jokes.' I shook my head sadly.

'Dude,' he replied with a grin, 'this is EMS. Default conversation between male medics is limited to the hotness of particular women, what you want to do to them, sports or gay jokes. There is no provision for hot chicks you don't want to bang. My hands are tied here.'

'I just hoped we could break new ground, explore theories of attraction. Act like the intellectuals we obviously—oh, no. No. You did not just do that, you arrogant fucking douchebag asshole!' This last directed at a well dressed man in a Lexus who pulled out around the car that pulled over for us. 'Yeah, they pulled over for you, dickhead.' I addressed his offended look as we passed him.

'As an intellectual, you do realize you left out "cocksucker"? What was that address again?'

'Ninety-five I think.' I scanned the houses. 'Oh, wait. Up there.'

'The one with the engine blocking the driveway?'

'We can hump the cot over the lawn.' I shrugged. 'There's not much snow.'

The patient was in bed, where her family had found her unresponsive. A firefighter was performing artificial ventilations with a bag valve mask. There was vomit down the bedspread, but the patient's color was good.

I took her pulse, strong and slow, while Pete started snapping electrodes onto the EKG leads. I got out my stethoscope and had a quick listen to her lungs. Plenty of air was getting in and out, but she did sound a bit junky.

'What happened here?' I asked the husband. 'Did you find her like this or did you see her pass out?'

'She just kind of gave a little shudder and stopped moving,' he replied. 'Is she going to be OK?'

'Her pulse is good.' I started with the good news, to keep him calm until I finished getting info. 'And we're working on the rest. When did she vomit? Before she seized?'

'She vomited when we put in the OPA,' offered a firefighter, holding up the large, curved, plastic oral airway device for inspection.

Ya think? I said to myself. *She pukes when you shove a big hunk of plastic down her throat? Really?* 'Yeah, patients with a pulse generally don't tolerate an oral,' I said out loud. 'If you feel the need to put something in, use a nasal.'

Her EKG and oxygen saturation were all very reassuring, and I thought I saw her chest rise in between the firefighter's ventilations.

'Stop bagging for a sec,' I said. 'I think she's breathing on her own.'

Sure enough, she was. I still didn't know what was causing her unconsciousness, but blood and oxygen were circulating, which is a good start. I began shopping for an IV site while Pete took a blood pressure.

I soon had the tourniquet on and a likely target lined up. I just got the needle in, watching the flash chamber fill and sliding the catheter forward, when she spasmed, sending my tape and saline flush flying. 'What the—?' I looked up and saw my friend the fireman bagging again.

'OK, stop that. She's breathing. It's like CPR; you can stop when the patient asks you to.'

He retreated a step, but maintained his ready and eager position, still clutching the bag mask. I figured if I wanted to keep him out of the way, I'd keep him busy.

'Grab me a non-rebreathing mask out of the O2 bag, could you?'

Look of eager incomprehension.

'The green bag. Over there.' Glued to the patient, unable to remove my finger from the IV still sitting unsecured in a vein, I fought down my frustration. 'Yes, that bag. Grab that mask. No, no, that's a nasal cannula. The mask. No, that's a pedi mask. You can tell because it's too small for her face and says 'pediatric' in red on the package. No, that's O2 supply tubing.' I struggled to remain calm as, with the expression of a Labrador retriever who expected the command to fetch a stick and was instead asked to solve a quadratic equation, he tore the plastic from yet another unasked for but previously sterile device, 'Look, maybe you could just toss the bag over where I can reach it.'

'I got it.' Pete's voice cut through my rising impatience. 'All set, man.' He placed the mask on the patient, then handed me the tubing for the IV and some tape, already ripped to the right size.

'Thanks,' I told him, 'you're a lifesaver.' Only he and I knew I was talking about the life of Engine 4's newest recruit.

He took the spent sharp from me and checked a blood sugar from it. 'One four five on the sugar. BP's 210 over 104.'

'OK. I got this line secured. Let's roll.'

We got the patient downstairs and into the truck. Before he closed the doors, Pete asked, 'Sure we don't need an extra pair of hands? I could ask the lieutenant if he can spare a guy?'

I glared up at him, murder in my heart, until I saw the wry half-smile that showed he was screwing with me.

Once we got under way, I did a more elaborate assessment, extending my senses down deep into the patient's nervous system, looking for the anomaly that had to be there. I found it in a clot occluding one of the vessels in her brain. I sent a psychic nudge to the platelets to unstick them a bit, and hoped.

Out Of Nowhere

Trauma is easy for me. I can patch holes and fasten bones together without much difficulty. It's like carpentry or pottery. Other mechanical issues like blockages are possible but harder. Disease is hit or miss; I have to try to convince the cells to act right, to repair themselves, which sometimes works and sometimes doesn't. I felt pretty good about this one.

The nice thing about a stroke, it can resolve on its own and isn't likely to prompt anyone to stone an underpaid ambulance jockey in the town square for using his Dark Arts; or call the tabloids, which might well be worse.

'What do we want to call this?' Pete asked through the passage between the driver's compartment and the back.

'Unresponsive. I'm leaning toward stroke. Doesn't look like an OD, and her blood sugar's fine. Pressure's high, pulse is slow-ish. Let's head to the Hole. They have a decent CAT scan, not like the one at the General that goes offline if a tech breaks wind.'

'Holy Trinity Hospital it is.'

We dropped our patient at the hospital, by which time she was showing some improvement. Pete smiled as he climbed into the passenger seat of the ambulance.

'Building bridges with the hose-draggers?'

I shook my head, 'Ya know,' I began, 'don't get me wrong. I'm glad that someone who isn't me is willing to run into a burning building and pull people out.' Or stop a fire spreading. I'd just as soon not see another Great Fire of London. 'But do we really need three speedbumps in turnout gear surrounding my patient, doing nothing? Or even worse, misapplying the minuscule iota of medical training they did get at the academy between lectures on how to put wet stuff on red stuff? It's not like that axe jockey from the last call is gonna get disciplined for sucking as an EMT. If a private ambulance crew was that clueless, we could choke them on scene, and get a medal for it.'

'They're bullet proof, man,' he replied. 'You need to come to terms with that.'

'I know. Part of me wants to show up at a fire and get in their way, but the lesson wouldn't take. They'd hit me with an axe and get three cheers and I'd get arrested.'

'They're not all that bad.'

'No,' I admitted. 'The guys here in Philips Mills are generally OK, but they actually fight fires. They don't want to do my job, so they stay out of the way. It's the Cat Rescue Specialists in Riverdale that make me want to climb a bell tower with a deer rifle.'

'I hear ya. Just let me do my job and I'll let you do yours.'

'I was gonna say "If the patient isn't on fire, get the fuck out of the way," but your way's more likely to win friends.'

'Speaking of winning friends, and of you being gay, some guy came by the base asking for you yesterday.'

'Looking for me?' I asked. 'He look like a cop, a bill collector, or an angry husband?'

'Said he was a patient. You and Nique fixed up his ankle and he wanted to thank you. Didn't know your last name, but your first is on your tag and he described you well enough.' The half-smile was back. 'Since he noticed you and not her, I'd say that's compelling evidence he bats for the other team. Tall guy. He had a foreign accent. Russian or German or something.'

I tried to stay calm despite the alarms sounding in my mind. 'Nobody said anything to him, did they?'

'Of course not. We figured you might owe him money or were banging his wife. Or his husband, since this is Massachusetts. We don't throw our own under the bus.'

Maybe it was just a grateful patient who wanted to say thanks, but that didn't happen to us very often. Or at all, that I could remember. Sometimes a card would arrive at the base, or maybe some cookies, but I'd yet to see a face-to-face thank you. If he'd come by in a bid to meet Nique I could see it, since she had a body that would make a dead man kick the lid off his coffin. I, on the other hand, was a fairly unremarkable working class medic whose only talent was career-limiting sarcasm.

And the ability to heal with a touch, but that was a secret.

That was supposed to be a secret.

As I drove, I felt the old fear like a heavy ball in my stomach. Attention was never a good thing. Sure, nobody had been burned or hanged for witchcraft around here in three centuries, but fear of the unknown and the natural pigheadedness of human nature had a tendency to rear their ugly head.

The nice thing about being a cynic is that you are rarely disappointed.

Chapter 4

WE MADE IT THROUGH THE REST of the shift, and as I drove home in the morning, I tried to think what the foreign sounding patient could have noticed. He couldn't know I'd healed him. He'd been in a lot of pain, and it's not like he stumbled onto an x-ray table. It could have been just a dislocation, for all that he knew.

Hell, that was one reason I stayed with EMS. Very often nobody knew the real severity of an injury until they got to the hospital. It was easy to nudge a patient back to the healthy side of the fence without raising eyebrows. One of the few jobs where I could use my gift and not attract attention.

I trudged up the stairs to my apartment, fumbling for my keys. These twenty-four-hour shifts in the lovely metropolis of Philips Mills were wearing on me, and I wasn't as young as I used to be.

I opened the door and looked down into the stern, dignified gaze of a large black and white cat. He stood in his usual spot as guardian of the house. I squatted down and scratched his head. 'Morning, Buddy,' I said. 'Permission to come aboard?'

I walked in, dropped my keys on the table and picked up the mail. I was tired, but nerves weren't going to let me sleep anytime soon. I fed the cat, then went to the liquor cabinet and poured myself four fingers of single malt. Drinking at eight in the morning doesn't count, I told myself, since it's after work. I checked my email, nothing exciting; somebody wanted a ride to fencing club tomorrow, three people wanted to help me claim my foreign lottery winnings and two more wanted to sell me generic Viagra. The concern was touching, but my thoughts kept sliding back to the man who was asking questions about me.

Out Of Nowhere

I couldn't place his accent, but I knew I'd heard it before. It remained just beyond my mind's grasp. I wracked my brain through half the glass of whisky, then decided I needed a visual aid.

I pulled down an atlas from the bookcase; I always find that looking at maps helps me put things in perspective. I flipped open to Eastern Europe and ran my finger over the page, letting my mind drift back, hearing the speech of each country. I stopped when I realized I was tracing the route of our retreat from Moscow.

It was disheartening in more ways than one. Somewhere along the long, frozen road, I'd realized that my zeal to fight for liberté, egalité and fraternité had turned into the cynicism of an expendable foot soldier in servitude to the Emperor's ambition, a blood sacrifice on the altar of Napoleon's ego.

I shook myself. The mind was wandering and getting me no nearer to enlightenment. I shivered at the memory of marching on numb feet until I realized that the apartment really was cold. I'd turned the heat down before I left on my twenty-four.

I was tired and preoccupied. That was enough for today.

I turned up the heat, finished my drink, and had a hot shower. I still got all excited that heat and hot water were available at the turn of a knob. I felt sorry for people who took indoor plumbing and central heating for granted. I toweled off and went to bed. The cat curled up on my feet, and between the glow of alcohol, the steam of the shower, and the warm weight of the long-haired beast on my ankles, I drifted off to sleep.

I woke in the early afternoon, pulled on jeans and a sweatshirt and made a pot of coffee. As I wandered around the apartment in the old converted textile mill, looking out over the city, I reflected on how lucky I was to have found this job. I really didn't want to have to leave.

EMS was good. I was happy there. I could practice my art without the weight of a blade on my hip. The faces changed often enough and the workforce moved around enough that I could maintain my anonymity as easily as mustering out of the Legion and joining the Black Watch after six months, a boat ride and some work on my accent.

I finished my coffee. I shaved, studying at my reflection. It's never easy to dispassionately assess oneself, but the face in the glass still looked about thirty, like it always had, as far back as I remember.

That was a long way, but not all the way. I had no memory of my childhood, of my true age. I suspected memory was only good for so far back. Events in the past are viewed like objects in a pool. Sharp and clear near the surface, increasingly blurred and obscured as they settle to the depths. The bigger and more important events fade slower, but they do fade.

I sat on the couch and the cat hopped up on my lap, beaming at me with large amber eyes. I scratched his head, smiling back at him. He was, almost certainly, the world's oldest cat. I had long since grown tired of watching those around me grow old and die, and he certainly wasn't going to lynch me for urging his cells to do a little housekeeping and maintenance every time I patted him.

I didn't have a good explanation for my own longevity. I couldn't heal my injuries like I could other people's. I healed faster than normal, and I healed from injuries that a normal man couldn't. I suspected my cells just repaired and renewed themselves. Whether it was a case of not aging or of very slow aging, I couldn't say.

I eventually gave up. I couldn't figure what that foreign patient could have noticed, or where he could be from, and the self-examination was making me maudlin.

There would be time enough to worry. Tonight, I'd go to fencing club at the local college and get some exercise. It would be nice to pit my years of encounters survived and dirty tricks learned against the crowd of brash young fencers. Perhaps I could even use my prowess to impress some athletic lass with an interest in swordplay and loose moral standards.

Had to get some living in. My next ambulance shift would be here soon enough.

Chapter 5

OR TOO SOON.

We grabbed the bags from the ambulance and entered the house. Looked around at the empty foyer. We could see a den beyond. Wood paneling, fishing pictures, photos of a man in a World War Two era Marine Corps uniform, with a First Division patch and the Fourragère, so it had to be 5th Marines, a black and white wedding photo, and a worn recliner upholstered in faded brown plaid facing an old console TV. I assumed the engine crew, the visiting nurse, and probably the patient were in the house somewhere.

'You think they need three firefighters and a nurse in there to work him, or could they spare somebody to point us in the right direction?' Nique wondered.

'Draggin' hose and wipin' ass they can do,' I replied. 'Helping the medics find the patient, not so much.'

'Ambulance!' she called.

'Marco!' I shouted. So far, nobody had ever called out 'Polo!' in answer, but I held out hope. Nique dug me in the ribs with an elbow as a firefighter, probably the probie, since he was running, pounded down the stairs and waved us up. He started to lead the way, then got an eyeful of Nique and held a hand out.

'You need help lugging that?' he asked, indicating the bag on her shoulder.

'Thanks,' I replied, handing him the cardiac monitor. 'You're a prince.' I walked past him up the stairs.

'I don't think he was talking to you,' Nique grinned. 'Pretty sure he was flirting.'

'Hey, I'm comfortable in my sexuality,' I replied. 'I can accept his flirting.'

I heard raised voices in the bedroom as we reached the top of the steps.

Out Of Nowhere

'Hey, guys,' said Nique, addressing the wall of turnout gear coats in the doorway, 'watcha got?'

The sea of Nomex parted for her smile and I caught sight of a short, wide, middle-aged woman in a scrub smock with whimsical puppies printed on it. She was arguing with an elderly man who was sitting on the bed in a t-shirt and boxers, his skinny arms covered in shrunken tattoos, blurred and faded to the point of being unrecognizable.

'What's going on today?' I asked.

The nurse drew herself up as if posing for a statue entitled 'Indignation.' 'Mr Harris needs to go to the hospital.'

'I told you, I'm not goin',' the man said, exasperated.

'Mr Harris.' The nurse rolled her eyes, which isn't something I'd care to see again. 'You can't walk unassisted.'

'I walked out of the Goddamn Chosin Reservoir, I can walk in my own damn house!'

'Mr Harris, the doctor's orders are for you to transfer to the wheelchair with assistance.'

'The doctor doesn't know shit!'

'There's no call for that kind of language,' the nurse said.

'OK,' I interrupted before things got even uglier. I addressed the nurse. 'Do you have a med list? Great. Could you give that to my partner and I'll talk to the patient. Thanks.' I directed her toward Nique with my most charming smile. She seemed to thaw a bit. Probably didn't get smiled at very often.

I squatted down beside the bed. 'Hi sir. I'm Sean, I'm a paramedic. What's going on today?'

'He needs to go—' the nurse began, but was cut off. I imagine Nique asked her a question. Or punched her in the larynx. Either way, I was happy.

'Sir—' I resumed.

'I'm not going to no hospital.'

'Alright,' I said calmly. 'Let's not get ahead of ourselves. I just want to see what the problem is today and see you get headed in the right direction. That may not be the ER. You know where you are and what date it is?'

'I'm at 139 Elm St and it's January 15th,' he rapped out with his jaw thrust belligerently forward.

'Good enough for me,' I replied. 'Now, you don't have to do anything you don't want to, but let's work through this, alright sir?'

'Frank,' he corrected.

'Frank. Pleased to meet you. You fought in Korea?'

'How'd you know that?' he asked suspiciously.

'My grandfather was at Chosin,' I lied. 'You a Marine?' I had seen his photos; not that I needed to after hearing him invoke that name. I could never make up my mind which was colder, the retreat from Moscow or from Chosin. Probably Korea, but the spiritual chill was less. At Chosin, we brought out our wounded, most of our dead and most of our gear, hobbling out on frozen feet just the same, but with heads unbowed. By that time, I'd learned the trick of acquiring a pair of boots a size too big and doubling up on my socks, so I didn't get frostbite too bad.

'Baker Company, Fifth Marines. What outfit was your Grandfather in?'

'Fox Company, Seventh Marines,' I replied. 'He used to talk about it once in a while. Tell me, is it true the rifles used to freeze up? He said they had to thin the oil with aftershave or something.'

'Hair tonic,' Frank corrected me, like I knew he would. I recognized something in his eyes. A familiar look, one that told me he was watching something half a century and half a world away.

'That's right,' I smiled. 'He used to say every time he went to the barber shop he'd start shivering.'

He grinned. 'I'm not surprised. You never forget that cold.' He gave me a much friendlier look. 'Is your grandfather still alive?'

I nodded. 'He's in Florida. I guess he'd had enough of snow. We generally go down there for Christmas and he comes up to see the rest of the family for a week in the summer.'

'Next time you see him, tell him Frank Harris from Baker Five asked if his balls have thawed yet.'

I chuckled. 'I will.'

'I walked out the whole way. I couldn't feel my feet by the time we got to Wonsan.'

'So, what's going on today?'

He looked down and grumbled a bit before answering. 'I been fallin' a lot lately. I'm not gettin' around like I used to. My kids want me to go into a home.'

I nodded in sympathy. He was a proud man; it couldn't be easy to admit he couldn't be independent. I noticed a glucometer on the nightstand.

'Diabetic?'

'Yeah,' he sighed.

'How's your sugar running?'

'It's pretty good.'

I smiled. 'So how's it running?'

'180, 200,' he replied.

'Your fingertips getting numb?'

'Yeah.' He stared ahead. 'Vision's getting blurry. Feet gettin' numb too. Worse than Korea.'

'How often you check your sugar?'

'Couple times a week,' he admitted.

'How often did you clean your rifle?' I asked.

'OK,' he sighed again. 'I read you.'

'Now, your sugar isn't something they're gonna fix at the ER, but you should call your doctor and get it under control. You do that, and maybe you can stay independent.'

'Mm,' he answered.

'So, I'm gonna make you a deal,' I said. 'You show me you can get up and walk to the bathroom, and you call your doc and make an appointment to discuss your blood sugar, and then I'll sign off on you staying home. Deal?'

'Deal.'

He managed the trip, and called his doctor while Nique and I talked the visiting nurse down from her hysterics. No, he doesn't have to go. No, we don't have to take him, this is America, he has rights. Sure, call my supervisor, I hope foul language doesn't bother you.

We did eventually clear up with a refusal of transport, and some very sour looks from about 300 pounds of angry nurse.

'You were really compassionate with that guy,' Nique observed.

'He's a proud old war hero, he's lost his wife, obviously, and now diabetes is eating away at him. On top of that, Nursezilla is telling him he needs to have help to get up and take a piss. I'd be surly too.'

'You think he'll be OK at home alone?'

'I think he wants to be. I think he's not ready to be in some Elderly Storage Facility. Too bad he's a diabetic. I friggin' hate diabetes.' I do.

There's not a damn thing I can do about it. Neither I nor medical science knows how to tell the islet cells to start making insulin again. It's frustrating.

The radio shrilled, its piercing tone cutting short our conversation.

'Medic 20, respond to 300 Broadway, Dugan's Lounge, in the rear parking lot for the man down.'

'Joy,' I muttered. '20 responding,' I said into the mic.

'Drug interaction between alcohol and gravity, you think?' Nique asked.

'Probably. It's six at night so the regulars will have been there long enough to tie one on.'

'Eh,' she said, 'lightweights if they're already in the parking lot.'

'Maybe,' I conceded. 'Or real hardcore drinkers vomiting in the alley to clear the decks for round two.'

'Oh, that's disgusting.' She winced. 'How do you even come up with stuff like that?'

'That's just halftime at a Danet family reunion,' I grinned.

'There's more like you at home?' she asked. 'You're not some random fluke to embarrass a decent middle-class Franco-Irish family? It must be that Irish blood. My Mémère told me to watch òut for your kind.'

'Hey, I'm the white sheep.'

I pulled the ambulance down the narrow side street past the bar and into the potholed parking lot. There were many, many bars in Philips Mills. We used to joke that nobody dies of thirst in this town. Each filled a niche, served a certain population. Medics, EMTs, cops and firefighters generally drank at the Harp, which had Guinness on draught, good food and halfway decent live bands on the weekend. Plus the local college students tended to hang there, so there was always some relatively clean, young, freethinking tail, unlike most of the dives in town. Dugan's fell at the other end of the scale of bars with Mick names. Working class who didn't work, swilling Bud, Miller High Life or Keystone from bottles, or generous shots of low-end vodka, scotch or bourbon. Food was stale chips and seldom-cleaned bowls of peanuts that half the patrons confused with the ashtrays. No entertainment unless you counted spontaneous disjointed spoken word pieces and fistfights. We actually got called there once at closing time because a guy died and nobody noticed until they tried to throw him out so they could lock up.

Pissed 'em off when we wouldn't take him, as he was long since cold. The bartender was horrified he had to wait for the Medical Examiner. Actually asked if we could write a note for his loanshark to excuse him for showing up late.

We drove over to a group of raggedly dressed men in a corner of the lot, clustered around a man on the ground. They looked like the usual Dugan's crowd, shaggy haired, skinny white guys dressed in dingy quilted flannel and blue jeans grey with dirt, ball caps and work boots. Pretty much like the crew at a construction project but not as clean.

A few turned and waved us over. People always feel the need to point to the guy on the ground, like they think we'll take some random bystander instead. For once, there were no police, firefighters or nurses to get in the way, just a bunch of drunken white trash.

'You comfortable with this?' I asked Nique.

'Coupla drunk scrotes?' she said. 'No problem. You?'

'These are my people,' I replied. 'I speak fluent drunk.'

I put the truck in park and hopped down, heading around the back to pull the cot as Nique got the bag out of the side door.

I was at the rear door of the ambulance when I heard the tone of the crowd change. I didn't exactly hear a scuffle, just a deliberate, concerted movement, which means trouble in any crowd, and more so in a crowd outside Dugan's.

I took a few quick steps around the truck and saw two men break from the startled mob, unwashed alcoholics falling back in confusion as the pair, dressed the same as the rest but cleaner, better muscled and with a glint of determination in their eyes and knives in their hands, came at me.

At me. Not us. I noticed that part.

The closer of the two was almost on top of me as I rounded the truck. He lunged with his blade, and out of instinct I sidestepped, caught his sleeve and banged his wrist against the side of the ambulance. I put my whole weight into the move, dragging him off balance and slamming him against the truck. I drove a knee into his groin and, still clutching his wrist with my left hand, threw a few short, hard rights into his temple, his neck, his kidney. He went slack and I started toward the second man.

That guy shoved Nique aside and headed toward me, wary, knife held ready, low and close to his body. He knew what he was doing, which was bad. I was unarmed—no time to scramble for his buddy's weapon. I had to hope I could hold him off, keep the blade out of my vitals until I got a clear shot, or Nique got away, and hope he wouldn't have any more friends in the crowd.

I looked at Nique to see if she was hurt. I saw no fear or pain in her expression, just the offended shock only possible in a very pretty girl of French descent ignored and rudely pushed aside by a man.

She hit him.

It was a telegraphed punch. Possibly the least cunning fist ever thrown in or near Dugan's, a place not known for subtle and strategic pugilism. If the guy was halfway competent, which he certainly looked to be, he'd see the blow coming and avoid it or hurt her very badly.

Except he wasn't looking. He made the mistake of ignoring Nique. Few men do. Underestimate, yes, but ignore, well, that took a certain singleness of purpose. His eyes were on me and only me, so he failed to see the windup or the delivery.

For all its lack of guile, it was one of the most emphatic punches I'd seen in a long time. She cocked not just her arm, but her whole body, and uncoiled in a fluid, vicious snap like the strike of a cobra. Nique was a strong girl, used to lifting overweight patients and hefty gear all day, and she put a step, a twist of the hip, and all the strength of her shoulder, arm and wrist, as well as a large measure of Gallic indignation, behind her blow. It caught him, by careful aim or Divine providence, right in the jugular. Her fist met his neck with the sound a filet mignon makes when the butcher slaps it down on the counter.

The man dropped like a puppet whose strings had been cut.

She looked at me, her face a study in righteous indignation. Her retreat to the truck was quick and efficient but dignified. She was leaving because she chose to, not because she was afraid to stay.

I'd been in enough retreats that I wasn't concerned with the image I projected. My eyes darted back and forth like a hunted rat, scanning the crowd for threats.

I heard the first man moan and try to crawl, so I hastily applied a size nine combat boot to his solar plexus. As he folded up and retched, I snatched up his knife, brandishing it at the mob as I beat feet around to the driver's door. The drunks still on their feet seemed as surprised by the events as we were, so I imagine they weren't directly involved, but you can never be sure how a man's going to respond to seeing a fight after a bellyful of Keystone and Mad Dog 20/20, so I wanted them to see the knife and take it into consideration.

I got into the ambulance without further violence, dropped the knife in my jacket pocket, and peeled out of the lot.

'Medic 20 to Operations,' I called. 'Be advised, dispatch PD to this location. Patrons attempted to assault crew. We'll stand by on Broadway.'

'Received, P 20. You guys OK?'

I looked at Nique. She nodded.

'We're OK. Thanks for asking.'

'P 20, head back to quarters. Police and Ambulance 36 will head over. 36, wait for PD. Do not enter the scene before the Blue Canaries.'

Nique turned toward me, her voice quick and loud, still riding the adrenalin of the encounter, 'So what the hell was that? I thought these were your people.'

I shrugged, fear and anger draining away, leaving me shaking. 'Dunno. Maybe they heard you make that Irish crack.'

As we drove away, Nique looked at me. 'You're bleeding,' she commented.

'What? Damn.' I saw blood running down my left wrist and over the steering wheel. I inspected my left hand and saw a clean slice across the pad on the pinky side of my palm. I hadn't noticed in the heat of the moment. I must've gotten that when I grabbed my attacker's knife hand. Now that I saw it, it hurt.

'Pull over in that parking lot,' she ordered calmly. 'I'll clean it out and wrap it up.'

I pulled off the main street into the lot of a corner *bodega,* and climbed through to the back of the truck. Nique grabbed a bottle of sterile water from the cabinet, broke the seal and poured it over my cut hand. I flexed my fingers, just to make sure they worked. No tendon damage, which was good.

'Looks like it went down to the fat pad,' she observed. 'You're gonna need to get that stitched.' She quickly dressed the wound with a four-by-four pad and some roll gauze. 'How's it feel?'

'Not bad,' I replied. 'It didn't hurt until I saw it.'

'You should get it looked at anyway. I'll drive.' She grabbed a container of bleach wipes from the cabinet. 'After I clean up the mess you made in the cab.'

'You sure you're OK?'

'I'm fine,' she said. 'Since I didn't let them cut me.'

'Silly of me not to think of that. Where did you learn to throw a punch?'

'I've been doing Tae Bo and Cardio Kickboxing for years,' she answered. 'An ass this phenomenal doesn't just happen.'

That explained why the punch had such nice form but so little guile. I prefer a sneakier and less pretty knee to the groin, myself. Can't argue with success.

We drove over to the ER where I got my hand stitched and my tetanus shot updated. The doc confirmed that there was no damage to the tendons, gave me a note for a week off, since I shouldn't be wearing sweat inducing gloves, obsessively washing my hands and lifting fat bastards with that cut on my palm. The stitches would come out in a week.

I would heal a lot sooner, but I didn't tell him that. If he insisted, I was willing to not work for a week.

Chapter 6

I SLEPT IN THE NEXT DAY. I made a pot of coffee and let my body wake up slowly. After half a cup, I felt confident to make breakfast without hurting myself too badly. Fire and knives are dicey enough without a bandaged hand, but I wasn't spending a week off eating cold cereal. A man has to have standards.

Peeling and cutting up potatoes and onions for homefries was the only challenging part. Bacon, eggs and toast were easy enough to do one-handed. I blanched the potatoes in water before frying them in some bacon grease from the cup I kept in the fridge. When the homefries were well under way, I placed two more slices of bacon in a second pan. Once they started to crisp up, I moved them to the side and dropped two eggs in the pan, letting them float in the fat. I put a slice of oat nut bread in the toaster. Gotta eat healthy.

When it popped up, I put it on a plate, arranged the bacon, eggs and homefries around it, then poured the excess bacon grease from the pan back into the cup. Never waste bacon fat. I'd learned that long ago, when starvation was a bigger concern for the average person than obesity. And it makes everything taste delicious. Butter flavored cooking spray is humanity's worst idea since racism.

After eating, I dug out the knife I'd snagged from the scene of the assault. It wasn't a common lock knife or even a hunting or combat knife, not any that I recognized. It was a knife-fighter's weapon. The blade was six inches long, broad and single-edged, with a cross guard and a wire-wrapped leather grip. It wasn't highly polished steel, but dark, with the rippled pattern of watered steel, which I hadn't seen in a very long time. Along the back edge, near the hilt were some... symbols. Letters, maybe, but not that I recognized. I couldn't even identify an alphabet.

Was the attack connected to the foreign patient who was asking about me?

I was sure it had to be. Not prove-it-in-court sure, but sure enough. A vaguely familiar accent I couldn't place, a man looking for me, and then an attack with a knife with writing I didn't recognize, all in the space of a week.

We don't get attacked very often. Even gang members don't generally mess with us. They know we don't really have any agenda against them, and sooner or later every gangbanger will get shot or cut or one of his buddies will, and none of them wants the ambulance to be hesitant to get to his street. Once in a while a domestic-violence call might suck us in to the chaos, and drugs or alcohol or psychosis can make patients unpredictable enough to prove a threat, but that isn't what happened at Dugan's.

Those guys were stone-cold sober. That was a planned ambush.

* * * *

I killed the morning fairly unproductively. I didn't have enough information to do anything more than make wild guesses.

That afternoon, I gave up and went by the local college and stopped in on the fencing class. I was technically a part-time student, since I took a class a semester, just to keep boredom at bay, and I knew the instructor from the fencing club. He was always happy to have an extra assistant to poke with a foil. I just wanted a distraction from thinking about the attack.

The concentration required to fence generally helped clear my head. It gave me the strategy, concentration and physical exertion, as well as the rush of competition I always enjoyed, without anybody needing to die.

I served as a practice partner for the class, and hung around to spar with Bill, the coach, for a bit. A few other students did the same.

'Not tired of being hit by now?' asked Bill, saluting and donning his mask.

'Just so long as I can hit back,' I grinned.

We came *en garde,* and after beating his blade against mine a few times, feeling me out, he lunged. I parried and threw a quick riposte at his chest, but he just managed to stop it, retreating back a step. I followed him with a strong feint, then disengaged under his parry, catching him in the shoulder.

After that, he tightened up his guard, stopping everything I threw and flicking his point out in rapid, deceptive attacks. He quickly racked up a few points on me.

I answered back, scoring one point through guile and another through pure luck, as he tried to beat my blade, missed and advanced, allowing me to pretty much lean forward and lay the point on his chest.

That annoyed him, and he shifted into higher gear, landing two more touches in rapid succession. Bill is a better fencer than I am. I'm not really a fencer at all. I'm a swordsman. For all that I love fencing, it's just playing tag with blunt swords. My years of training were all geared toward keeping sharp steel out of me and putting it in the other fellow. My instincts are less about lightning flicks of the point and more about firm, decisive attacks and overly secure parries. I'm good enough to beat novices, and hold my own with experienced fencers, but a master can land five touches on me without breaking a sweat.

In a real duel, those five touches would be scratches that would hardly slow me down, let alone stop me shoving a foot of steel through him, but a touch is a touch.

Now that he had me panting, he drove me back, holding his guard close and making swift attacks, steadily advancing. I parried frantically, giving ground, not really launching any offense of my own.

Not seeing any ripostes, he pushed harder. As he came on, instead of retreating with a quick parry, I used a wide Italian lowline parry, sweeping his blade down and out with my guard while keeping my point in line with his body. I stepped into his attack as I blocked, driving my own point against his side.

'*Touché*,' he said, after a pause. He removed his mask. 'Now what the hell was that?'

'Counterparry with opposition in *tierce*,' I replied, stepping back and returning his salute.

'You could be really good, you know,' he sighed as he shook my hand. 'Your timing is dead on, your instincts are all good, but you parry too wide and hold it too long.'

'I learned Italian style,' I shrugged. 'Old habits are hard to break.' Which was true enough.

'For Christ's sake,' he said. 'Your name is Danet. Your ancestor codified French swordsmanship and you learned *Italian?* Nobody fences Italian anymore.'

'My fencing instructor was old school,' I replied. 'He came from a different era.' Again, true, but not the whole truth.

He shook his head in disbelief, 'What am I going to do with you?'

'Use this opportunity to learn how to stop an Italian counterparry.' I grinned. 'Look, I'm too old for the Olympics. I work too many hours to travel with a school team. I'm just here to play with swords. No point trying to make me a real fencer.'

I fenced a few students, just to see if ages of painfully acquired dirty tricks could still defeat the speed and strength of youth. Results were mixed. As we eventually cleaned up, I noticed a textbook in one of the students' bags.

'There's a class on ancient languages here?' I asked.

'Oh, yeah,' she replied. 'Professor Deyermond teaches it. It's really interesting.' She lowered her eyes. 'If you're into that kind of thing, I guess.'

'Where's Professor Deyermond's office?' I asked.

'At the library. You can probably still add the class, if you want. It's not all that full.'

'Thanks,' I said. 'I'll see about it.'

Chapter 7

I MADE MY WAY TO THE LIBRARY directly from the gym. I did shower as a courtesy, despite my eagerness to talk to somebody about the inscription on that dagger, and walked into the building with wet hair, my fencing bag over my shoulder and a sloppy, one-handed, post-shower rebandaging job on my left hand.

Behind the checkout desk sat an attractive redheaded undergrad doing her work study with a level of enthusiasm usually reserved for prison chain gangs. Her thumbs flew with blinding speed over the keypad of her cellphone. I asked her where I could find Professor Deyermond.

Without any perceptible loss of thumb speed, she looked up at me and tossed her head to indicate the rear of the building. 'Back wall,' she said, going the extra mile.

I thanked her and gave an ironic exaggerated bow, but it was probably wasted as she had already returned her attention to her phone. I made my way through dusty stacks to the back of the library.

This was where they kept the books nobody read. Ancient languages, philosophies and politics that had gone out of fashion, history that nobody wanted to remember; probably so they wouldn't feel so stupid when they repeated it.

I hadn't realized there were offices back here, but there were two brass plates screwed onto one of the doors, indicating a shared office. I could imagine a professor of ancient languages requesting such a place. They tend to be an odd bunch. Linguists who deal in current languages are generally alright, since they talk to living people. If all you study is what a handful of bureaucrats and philosophers left behind in a tongue nobody has heard in a millennium, you get a bit rusty on social interaction. I prepared myself for an elderly, pallid, bespectacled gentleman in a tweed jacket with elbow patches. The door was slightly ajar, after the fashion of doors that open onto the offices of the absentminded, so I just gave a courtesy knock and stepped through.

It was a typical shared office; a window directly across from me opening onto the pleasant rolling green of the quad; a desk facing each side wall, so nobody had a good view of either the door or the window; bookcases and posters on the walls. Cats figured heavily in the posters on the side with the unoccupied desk, as well as Mel Gibson dressed as Hamlet and Sting in a puffy shirt on the grassy courtyard of a romantic castle, apparently reading. Someone was sitting sideways to me at the other desk.

'Excuse me,' I began, 'I'm looking for Professor Deyermond—' and I stopped dead.

'That would be me,' came the reply.

I was right about the glasses, but that was all. Regarding me over the rims of those glasses through the most amazingly green eyes on the planet, in place of a pale, greying old man muzzily annoyed that I'd intruded on his session with Plutarch, was a breathtaking blonde in her late twenties.

To be fair, she did exhibit a few signs of absentmindedness. She was poring over two books at once, making notes in a third; she held a pen in one hand, and had another tucked behind her ear. An impressive mass of loose golden curls was rumpled from the hand she was running through it as she worked, and stray wisps trailed over her forehead. She was dressed modestly enough in the finest academic tradition: a grey cardigan over a white blouse, the top two buttons undone and the collar gaping slightly as she bent over the book. A glittering pendant on a silver chain hung down just to the top of the shadow that teasingly hinted at cleavage. Long, shapely legs emerged from a knee-length black skirt, sheathed in black stockings and ending in black, low, fairly sensible shoes.

When she saw me, and my sentence died without any sign of continuing, she raised one perfect eyebrow, took the pen she had been chewing from between her teeth and curled her lips into a smile that was warm and inviting, but had mischief in it. Her glance flicked from the fencing bag slung over my shoulder to my clumsily bandaged hand.

'If you're looking for books on fencing, there's a nice copy of Talhoffer two rows back, but I can save you some time and tell you you're probably holding the wrong end of the sword.'

At that moment, something happened. A tightness in my throat and my chest and, to be honest, my loins. I knew Dr Deyermond was probably not the most beautiful woman in the world, but that's a hard thing to judge, especially across centuries. Cleopatra, for example, would need the services of an orthodontist if she were to vie for an emperor's affections today, and with a six-week aerobics class and a decent salon, Lady Godiva might have set western civilization back a century with that ride of hers. That said, I couldn't remember the last time I had been so attracted to someone.

For a man of my talents, long-term relationships don't work. You can only stay young so long while people age around you before they start becoming suspicious, and while I could always shore up the youth of my companions, like the World's Oldest Cat, humans never accept such things with good grace. So I'd had a fair number of lovers over the centuries; but something about this woman had my pulse racing like at no time I could remember.

I dragged my attention back to the task at hand. 'Sorry,' I smiled. 'You teach a course in ancient languages?'

'I do. I studied ancient languages and the theory of language development for a long time. How trade, travel, writing and so on affected the evolution of languages.' She shrugged. 'But that's not as lucrative as it sounds, so mostly I teach English Lit. Were you looking to take a class on ancient languages? It's only the second week of the term. I could add you.'

'Actually, I was looking for help deciphering an old inscription. Or at least nailing down the period and region.'

Her smile remained in place, obviously hiding her disappointment that I wouldn't be attending her class. 'I may be able to help. Where is this inscription?'

'It's on a knife. An archeological find, probably a ceremonial weapon,' I lied.

'Where was it found?'

I was ready for this one. 'In the ruins of a country manor in England. The family was minor gentry going back forever, long tradition of soldiering and diplomatic service, so this could have been dug up in a bog on the estate or carried back from anyplace the Brits went.'

Her smile widened. 'Which narrows it down to...?'

'Pretty much the whole planet,' I admitted. 'I can usually get at least a basic idea about languages, but this is totally new to me. I was hoping you could point me in a direction.'

'I'll try,' she said. 'Do you have a photo of the knife or a rubbing of the inscription?'

'Nothing quite so good,' I said, digging out my notebook. 'I have a freehand copy.'

'Let's see.' She pushed aside her books. 'I've been staring at this for too long anyway. Too much epic poetry is bad for you. Almost as bad as too many romance novels.' As I crossed the room to her desk, she stretched, uncrossing those long legs, rolling her head to ease her neck muscles and arching her back. While I'm sure this relieved the tension of sitting hunched over an obscure *Chanson de Geste,* it also showed off how white the skin of her long neck was, and how her firm breasts strained the fabric of her blouse when she moved that way.

I swallowed hard as I handed her the paper. 'It's not very exact. I figured I'd compare it to some books and see what looked close. I didn't expect you to be so helpful.'

'Please.' She took the sheet from me. 'By this time of day I'm happy to talk to somebody born in the last century.'

'A standard I shall do my utmost to live up to,' I replied with a grin.

'Sorry, that sounded wrong.' She blushed, just a bit, but enough to make my pulse speed up. 'Again, I plead too much time with dead scribes. Well, dead scribes and very young college students. My finer manners sometimes take a beating.'

'No problem. I completely sympathize. I'm a paramedic, so when nobody's bleeding or unconscious, I'm not sure how to act.' I extended my hand. 'Sean Danet.'

'Sarah Deyermond.' She took my hand with an elegant, palm-down, fingers curled grace that would have passed muster in the court of Queen Victoria. It seemed so natural that I wasn't sure if she was playing or not. I resisted the urge to click my heels and kiss it.

'Now, let's see if I can help you.' She studied the paper, her brow creased. One by one, she went through the classic stages of thinking. She adjusted her glasses, tapped her pen, chewed her pen, looked at the page from a slightly different angle, and ran her free hand through her hair. At length she made the face that people do when they're trying to figure out how to break bad news. 'Are you sure this isn't a fake? There was a lot of phony medievalism in the Victorian era. Maybe some gentleman wanted to make it look like there was a pre-Roman society living on his estate and commissioned the weapon. Any smith could have put these mysterious symbols on it.'

'It's possible,' I conceded. 'I didn't recognize the writing, so I thought I'd look into it.'

'Sorry.' She looked like she meant it. 'I wish I could be more help. I mean, you can check the stacks if you want, but if there were anything close to that here in this library, I should at least have a clue. I spend enough time here.'

'Not at all.' I smiled. 'Thanks for saving me an hour of poking around to not find anything.'

'Well, I'm happy I could do that, at least. See you around?' It really seemed sincere.

'I'll make a point of it,' I replied, bowing my head as I made to leave.

She rolled her head again, working out the kink in her neck and pushing my buttons. I hesitated in the doorway. She looked burned out on research. And she had sounded sincere about seeing me around. And for whatever reason, she had me snorting and pawing the ground.

'Actually, I have that hour you saved me, and you look like you could use a break. You want to grab a cup of coffee or something?'

She looked a bit surprised, but not unpleasantly. 'In all honesty, I could really use a bite to eat and a beer. I wouldn't mind the company, if you don't have anything you'd rather do.'

'My car's in the student lot,' I offered.

'Mine's closer,' she replied, 'but I think a walk would do me good. Let's take yours.'

'Alright, but I'll warn you. You may feel the need to throw yourself at me when you check out my sweet set of wheels.'

'I will try to restrain myself,' she said, smiling, 'emotional creature though I am.'

We arrived at my car. It was a ten-year-old Chevy Impala, which I bought second-hand, and while the registration said it was green, in January the color was really grey beneath a fine patina of road salt. I haven't ever been much of a car guy. They get me around and they are generally less fragile than a horse, but you can't eat them when they break down on a long journey in the wilderness.

'Your chariot, my Lady.' I opened the passenger door and brushed some crumbs from the seat, noting happily that the interior was less cluttered than usual. No woman wants to rest her shoes among a pile of empty Styrofoam coffee cups and crumpled paper takeout bags.

I tossed my fencing bag in the trunk and came around to the driver's seat.

'So what does this car say about you?' she asked.

'That I'm cheap, but low maintenance and reliable, I hope.' My car responded by starting readily despite the cold. 'I call him Vlad, by the way.'

She looked at me quizzically for a moment before laughing. 'Vlad the Impala?'

'Fewer people get that than I hoped,' I admitted, pulling out of the space.

* * * *

We ate at a small brew pub a mile from the campus. I'd driven past it and been intrigued, but hadn't been inside before. It was a nice, quiet place in a converted mill building, all age-blackened wood and exposed brick. Part of the nascent American Foodie movement, they had a small selection of beers brewed on the premises and simple, dressed up bar food. Sandwiches, soup and salads, but all fresh and well seasoned. What Europeans have been doing all along while America had its love affair with fast food.

We ordered pints and sandwiches and started the usual get-to-know-one-another conversation. I already knew that she had an unusual affinity for epic poetry and good beer. Made me happy I got to her before Malory; all that courtly-love drivel he put into *Le Morte d'Arthur* was just a ruse to help him get into as many skirts as he could. One of the great brawlers, lechers and convicts of the fifteenth century, revered by professors in tweed and dreaded by schoolchildren everywhere. But I mostly disliked him because he wrote about a sixth century Briton, a war chief, and didn't get one damn detail right.

Not that I could have believably corrected him.

I kept my own fiction more vague and uninteresting but, unlike

Malory, I made sure it fit with known facts and appearances. Over a brown ale and a grilled chicken pesto sandwich, I spun a tale of a middle-class upbringing: French-Canadian father, Irish mother, mediocre student, brief enlistment in the reserves and five years chipping away at a History degree while working on an ambulance.

The key to a good secret identity is to make it mundane enough that nobody feels the curiosity to dig deeper, but give it enough details to cover and explain what people do see. There were hundreds of people along the Massachusetts-New Hampshire border with the exact same story. It also covered any mannerisms I might have picked up in far too many years in uniform, or historical facts that seemed too obscure for a humble ambulance jockey to know.

'So, why study history?' she asked, smiling over the rim of her glass. 'Seems like a strange choice for a medic. Why not biology? Work towards a degree you can use?'

'I see I've given off the mistaken impression of ambition,' I replied. 'I'm too lazy for Med School, and have no desire to drag hoses or wipe other people's backsides, so that's firefighting and nursing out. Other than that, there's no logical next step for a paramedic, so I study what interests me. History is just stories about people. People who lived a long time ago, maybe, but stories just the same. How about you? I confess, you're a lot younger and prettier than I expected in an English Lit professor. Not that I'm complaining, mind.'

She blushed attractively. 'I guess I like stories too. I always liked stories but in Grad School I realized what those stories could tell us about how people lived.'

Oh boy, I thought, *if she really believes in the princess in the tower, best back away slowly.*

She must have caught something in my expression. 'Don't get me wrong, I don't think the works actually show life as it was. That'd be like basing your opinion of our culture on Lifetime Original Movies and Danielle Steele novels.'

OK, maybe she was too smart for Malory.

'What the works tell us,' she went on, pausing to lick some errant sauce from her thumb and push my pulse up a few more points, 'is what people wanted to read, to believe. To fantasize about.' She smirked, looking at me over the top of her glasses with those big green eyes.

'Don't you wonder if people back in the fifteenth century fantasized about the same things we do?'

I took a breath, covering my agitation with a deep pull that emptied my glass. I wasn't sure how much of it was deliberate, but she was pushing my buttons, playing me like an artist. Was she just flirting, or was she really interested, really giving me an opening?

I decided to push back, just a little. 'Right now I'm having a good lunch and a good beer with an attractive, intelligent blonde. I bet most guys are fantasizing about being me.'

She dropped her eyes and blushed again. *Bullseye.* She was interested and, strangely, not used to being told she was beautiful.

In my experience, very pretty, articulate women don't tend to remain available for very long, but she certainly didn't act like she was in a relationship, nor did she exhibit any of the signs of the recently liberated. I had noticed the lack of a ring on her left hand, but that didn't mean much. I could make a snide observation that it didn't mean much these days, but it really never had when the cards were actually on the table. All that matters, all that has ever mattered, is whether she wants to play. Single, married, engaged or living in sin, a woman is either happy in her situation, in which case you won't get anywhere, or she's looking for something, in which case all's fair.

Now, the existence of a husband, lover or protective father might increase the risk to life and limb, but it doesn't change your actual chances any. And I've risked life and limb for far less reward.

Like trying to keep North Africa French or India British.

Although it must be said that both England and France have better restaurants today because of our noble sacrifice.

I decided to try a direct approach. I leaned forward across the table and flashed my sincere and charming smile, the one I've put centuries of practice into. 'What about you? Is there a handsome prince in the wings? Or even just a jealous boyfriend who's going to take advantage of my injury to challenge me to a duel?'

Her smile remained, but it lost some of the bantering quality and took on a hint of sadness. 'There's been a shortage of handsome knights riding to the rescue for quite a while now,' she sighed. 'I work on a college campus with about six thousand women between the ages of eighteen and twenty-two, most of whom are away from parental scrutiny for the first time. I'm not even a blip on the radar. This is the closest to a date I've been on in forever.'

There it was again. Just like working with Nique. For some reason, I project an aura of non-threateningness that makes women open up even when I'm actively on the job. 'Well, then you're surrounded by some very clueless men. Any straight male with a pulse should notice you.'

'Thank you.' She smiled. 'It's really nice that you did notice.'

We finished our meal and I drove her back to her office. 'Are you busy later?' I asked, as she got out of the car. 'Or can I call you sometime?'

'Why, Mr Danet,' she said playfully, 'what kind of girl do you think I am?'

'It's more what kind of girl I *hope* you are,' I grinned.

She laughed. 'Actually, I really do have papers to grade tonight. Honest. But give me your number; I should be free later in the week. I'll see if I can hunt around for any more info on that inscription for you.'

I gave her my number, not asking for hers. Put the ball in her court, don't push too hard. 'I will count the minutes until I hear from you.'

'Thanks. It really was nice meeting you. I'm sorry I couldn't be more help with that writing.'

'Not at all. I'm glad I stumbled into your office.'

'Me too.' She smiled warmly. 'I'll be in touch.'

Chapter 8

I WALKED INTO THE APARTMENT to the sound of a ringing telephone. I'd normally ignore it, but part of me, probably the part located between my knees and my sternum, urged me to pick it up, hoping it would be Sarah.

'Hello?'

It wasn't. 'Sean! You sound good. I hope you're doing OK,' came the too-friendly voice of my supervisor, Marty Genovese. This couldn't be good.

'I'm feeling fine, except for the hand.' *You know, the wound I received in the line of duty.*

'Yeah, we all hope you're recovering quick. Anyway, I talked with Kathy from HR and she says you don't have any more earned time, so she was wondering when you thought you could be back to work.'

Back to... *Oh God, I hate private EMS.*

'Dude, I got cut with a knife on the job,' I explained, slowly for ease of comprehension. 'I have stitches. I can't carry some three hundred pound welfare cheat with fake chest pain down three flights of Philips Mills switchback stairs. What the hell?'

'I know. I hear ya,' Marty oozed. 'That's what I told the chuckleheads at HQ, but you know how they are. I went to bat for you, and the upshot is, we'll hold your job, but you aren't gonna get paid any more until you come back, or your Long Term Disability kicks in. I told 'em that was ridiculous, that you're good people, got hurt on the company business, but what are ya gonna do?'

This last phrase came out *whaddayagunnado?* Marty was a walking caricature. His dad was a professional Italian, an exaggerated stereotype, like a guy named Murphy who owns a pub and acts like every day is St Patrick's. He was a big fish in the small pond of local politics, playing to the old neighborhood, and Marty had grown up on a steady diet of schmoozing and gangster movies. It was natural that his supervisory style was like a bad Tony Soprano impression.

I mean, it wasn't even a bad Michael Corleone impression, as much as he wanted it to be.

Anyway, it was very important to Marty that I know how he was the one in my corner, because, you and me, we understand one another, but the suits, well... whaddayagunnado?

I sighed. 'So what am I supposed to do here?'

'Now, do I look out for you or what? I filled your shift tomorrow, so you're all set there. If you can work Friday instead, that gives you three more days to heal, and you don't lose any pay.'

'You do realize I have a doctor's note?'

'All that means is they can't fire you for taking time off,' he replied. 'They don't have to pay you. Or you could go answer phones in dispatch, but you don't want that, do you?'

Well, he was right, there. I didn't. They didn't want me to do that either, since I'm fine as a medic, off on my own with just one partner, but don't play well up at headquarters.

'So who'm I working with on Friday?' I conceded.

'I got you a good partner,' he said, like he had somehow made the open shift wink into existence. 'It's with Monique.'

'Cool. How'd a shift opposite her open up? No heterosexuals wanted to work on a Friday?'

'Jim Burton offered to swap. He's working your shift with Pete tomorrow.'

'The spaz?' I asked in shock. 'Pete will kill him.' Seriously. He might. Jim was way too wound up, got too excited, ran in before looking far too often, and said totally inappropriate things to patients, even by my lax standards. If he pulled that stuff with Pete more than once, Pete would just back over him in the garage.

'Well, he's more afraid of Monique,' said Marty. 'I guess she had words with him a few shifts ago. I saw her jabbing him in the chest with a finger while she explained things to him, and now he wants off the shift.'

So, I didn't say, *your favor to me is letting me solve your manpower issues since you have a crap employee nobody will work with, and you haven't got the balls to fire, you fucking Guinea cliché.* 'Cool. I'm happy to work with Nique. Thanks for being there for me,' I said. *Don't say it,* I prayed, *don't—*

'Fuggeddaboutit,' he said, 'Just remember who's got your back.'

One day, I thought, *I will ask a favor.* 'Thanks, boss,' I said and hung up, disgusted.

Hurt on the fucking clock, attacked on a call and good old FirstLine Ambulance was going to play cheap with my pay. Typical.

If I worked for a hospital service, I'd have more sick time than I could use in a year, and they'd write off my treatment. A fire service and I'd have my Union rep down there right now making waves on my behalf, and a reporter from the local paper penning a story with a headline like 'Fatcats Deny Pay to Injured Hero.'

I sighed and walked over to the liquor cabinet.

This was tough. I needed to work, because as amazing as my powers might be, they didn't make me any money, and this was one of the few jobs that I could work easily, so I did want to keep it. And my hand really wasn't all that bad. But dealing with the corporate side of the job grated on me.

I will admit to a blind spot as far as money is concerned. In theory, I should have been able to put away some money and let it accrue interest and be all set, but that never seemed to work out. After ages as a soldier I just got used to spending my pay, taking the necessities like food, clothing and quarters as part of the job. Not much point in opening a nice traceable bank account when I might have had to walk away from it. I had a few emergency stashes of cash in case I ever did need to go on the run, but I didn't touch those for anything else. Better to be a week late on the rent and sweet-talk the landlord, or have the lights cut off, than have to go on the lam without any funds.

There were, I reflected, dropping into my favorite chair with three fingers of whisky, different kinds of courage. There was the kind you needed to stand fast with a bayonet fixed and one round in your musket while the points of the enemy lances got closer and more distinct and you felt the pounding hooves vibrating in your chest, and you held your fire for the perfect moment because the only thing that would keep you alive was the well timed volley and there wouldn't be time to reload. That took courage, and discipline and trust in the men to either side of you because if one man ran, the whole company would disintegrate. But that was quick courage, courage for a few moments, after which either a wave of euphoric, exultant relief washed over you, or you were dead. Either way, you didn't need to be brave very long, and if you lived there'd be medals and bagpipes and starry-eyed women.

Then there was the long, slow kind of courage. Courage that kept you dragging to work day after day, not stabbing your spaz partner or calling the boss on his shit or storming into HR with a machete. Just to keep the job so you could collect a pittance to keep the bill collectors from the door and keep up a carefully constructed facade.

As easy as it might be to say in a warm living room with the booze blazing a trail down to my stomach, spending the night in a shallow trench scraped into a frozen hillside in Korea while angry Chinese soldiers swarmed in the darkness with grenades and burp guns was looking better than enduring one of Marty's famous pats on the back and greasy smiles.

Christ.

I was halfway through my drink and my mood was mellowing from anger to general disgust when the phone rang again.

Fuck you, Marty, I'm not interested in another favor, I thought, letting the machine pick up.

Hi, Sean, this is Sarah. Deyermond. I was just wondering—

'Hello!' I lunged across the room, dislodging the cat and nearly spilling my drink. Pity to do that to a whisky that survived twelve years in a sherry cask on a Scottish hillside, but this woman did things to my brain. 'Hi, I was on the other side of the apartment,' I lied. 'Screening my calls,' I admitted.

She laughed. 'Well, I'm free earlier than I thought and wondered if you still wanted to grab some dinner? If that sounds like something you'd like to do?'

What would I like to do? I thought. *Well, for starters, I'd like to run my fingers through those long blonde curls, and kiss those full, pouty lips and that white neck, and then I'd like to tear your clothes off and touch and kiss and caress every inch of your body. I want to feel you and smell you and taste you. I want to kiss my way down over those perky breasts and soft smooth belly and over the curve of your hips and down those long, perfect legs and back up. I want to lick and tease and stroke you with my lips and tongue while my hands play over your breasts and buttocks until I hear you scream with desire and then, after I've done all that, just to prove that my feelings aren't more than nine-tenths pure lust, I want to make love to you and then hold you all night.*

'Dinner sounds great,' I managed.

'So,' she said, a bit awkwardly, 'is there somewhere you'd like to meet, or...?'

I considered my finances, what with my good buddies at FirstLine messing with my pay, and thought of the kind of meal I'd like to buy her. 'You know what?' I said, 'Let me cook you dinner.'

'Really?' She sounded surprised. 'You want to cook for me?'

'I'll be honest. I can't afford to take you to the kind of place you deserve, but I am a decent cook. Unless that sounds too forward. Or too broke.'

'No, no. Not at all. It's kind of sweet. Where's your apartment?'

I gave her directions.

'Great. Eight-ish?'

'I'll see you then.'

I went through my kitchen and did a quick inventory, seeing what I could make for two. One of the perils of cooking for one is that you often don't have enough of any one given thing to make a meal for two. I was in luck tonight, since I'd recently stocked up, figuring on being home for a week, nursing my injured hand. I took out some chicken breasts and started marinating them in a little balsamic vinaigrette dressing.

I actually am a good cook within narrow parameters. I've always considered food one of life's great pleasures, and the best way to ensure you'll have access to your favorite meals is to learn how to cook them.

I chopped together a quick salad, then cleaned up the place a bit. At around seven-thirty I took down a saucepan, poured a good splash of olive oil in the bottom and set it on a low heat. I chopped a clove of garlic very fine and scraped it from the cutting board into the oil with the back of my knife.

I have definite views on garlic. The garlic press is a tool of the devil, garlic powder is for the lazy, and the jarred stuff is an abomination. If you can't be bothered to chop it, you don't deserve garlic.

When the garlic started to go translucent, but before it caramelized, I took a half stick of butter and broke it up into the pan. As it melted

I peeled and chopped up a tomato. I took a stick of good French bread that I'd bought on the way home, figuring on a few days of sandwiches, cut some slices, dipped them in the garlic butter and then put them aside on a rack for the oven. I scraped the tomato into the pot, followed it with a dash of salt, a handful of parsley and a splash of wine. I simmered it, letting the tomato dissolve into the sauce.

I heard the doorbell, buzzed Sarah in, then turned on the oven, spooned some tomato on the bread, sprinkled some cheese, parsley and basil on it, then opened the door to her knock.

'Hi.' She smiled. 'I stopped to pick up some wine, but they wouldn't sell me a six-pack of it, so I got us some beer. I hope that's OK.'

'I'll try to carry on, somehow,' I replied. 'Come in, let me take your coat.'

I ushered her in and took her jacket. She had put a lot of effort into looking casually gorgeous. She wore a pair of dark jeans and a deep purple blouse that went very well with her coloring. Unlike earlier at her office, she was wearing makeup, but it was carefully toned down. Her hair was shining, brushed and completely devoid of pens.

I took the proffered six-pack, complimented a very nice French manicure—which drew a raised eyebrow—and waved a hand to indicate my humble domain.

'Make yourself at home for a sec, I need to put a pot on the stove, then I can give you the two-dollar tour.'

I set a pot of water on high heat to boil, and turned back to find her studying my bookcase. It's an eclectic collection, to say the least.

'Is this really a signed Mark Twain? And are you really keeping it out in the open?'

'Probably a forgery,' I lied, 'but it's the only copy I found with those shorts in it, and it's some of his best stuff. I want it where I can read it at a moment's notice. I got it cheap at a yard sale.'

'Holy crap,' she exclaimed. 'You have a hundred-year-old printing of *The Three Musketeers*! In French!'

'Sentimental value,' I replied, which was true enough. I liked Dumas. Missed the old bastard. 'My Mémère gave it to me when I was younger. She found it in a box in the attic. I was always interested in swashbucklers, and she figured it would get me to learn French. It was her father's or uncle's originally. I knew it was old, but have no idea when it was printed.'

She finished her examination of my bookcase and I showed her around the apartment. It didn't take very long. She glossed over my record collection, smiled at the pictures on the walls, and won big points by dropping down to scratch the cat under the chin. He turned to me as though to say 'this one's alright.'

The oven timer chimed. I pulled the bruschetta out and set the tray on the table, found two pint glasses and a bottle opener and decanted two of the beers she'd brought. I dropped some pasta in the pot of boiling water.

'Dig in,' I said, 'I still have about ten minutes of cooking. Some things need to be done *à la minute*, can't leave 'em to simmer.' I put a pan on the stove, drizzled some oil into it.

She raised an eyebrow again. I liked the look, and seemed to be good at provoking it.

She took a bite of the bruschetta. 'Oh, wow. That's good.'

'Thanks. Within my limits, I'm not a bad cook.' I took the chicken breasts out of the marinade and laid them in the hot oil. 'These need about four minutes a side.'

'Did you ever work as a chef?'

'Hmm? Oh, no. Way too much stress.'

She laughed. 'Aren't you a paramedic? Don't you guys deal with life-threatening emergencies?'

'Well, sure.' I turned the chicken. 'But they can't send my IVs back if they don't like them.'

She laughed again.

'Seriously, though, I work best on my own. All day on my feet at a hot stove with a manager behind me? I'll take ten minutes in a syringe-strewn alley with a stabbing victim.'

'So you don't play well with others?' She smiled. 'You don't seem tough to get along with.'

'I don't take direction well,' I said. 'I have a job where I can pretty much do whatever I need to get the patient to a better place, so long as I can justify my actions after the fact. I become impatient when somebody's backseat-driving my decisions.' The timer chimed and I took the pasta pot off the stove and dumped it into a colander.

'Make sure to shake the strainer so you get all the water out,' she said.

I turned to see her grinning evilly over the rim of her glass. I felt that tightness again.

I dropped the pasta into the sauce to finish, fished the chicken out of the pan, laid it on the plates, then added the pasta.

'*Bon appetit,*' I said. 'Let me know if you like it. Please, be honest.'

She took a bite, closed her eyes reverently as she chewed, then swallowed and said 'That's delicious.'

'My thanks.'

'I'll have to have you over for dinner sometime.' She took another bite. 'I have a wide variety of take-out menus, and all the best places on speed dial.'

We finished dinner and retired to the living room. We talked for hours. It was an interesting contrast of worlds. I told stories about my colleagues, the ragtag band of misfit adrenaline junkies who worked the ambulance because they were unfit for normal employment, and the spectrum of patients from the homeless, the drug-addicted and the shot-up gang members to the pushy home health aides from the Visiting Nurses Association and bosses who thought a fly-by-night ambulance company could be run like the Gambino crime family. She laughed in all the right places and responded with observations on working in a detached little world filled with young idealists and jaded professors, a place where people really could read Karl Marx and Lord Byron and actually think they were on to something.

She was very funny, and had a dry, quick, cutting sense of humor. She'd learned to look at stupidity and naiveté and arrogance and find humor in them rather than screaming and tearing her hair out. She was smiling over her drink, those big green eyes shining over the top of her glasses. We were sitting close, and I figured the chemistry was there. I set my own glass on the coffee table.

I leaned in and kissed her. Lightly, just by way of reconnaissance. She tilted her head as I came in.

I felt a tiny spark as our lips met, which roared into blazing life as her lips parted under mine and I tasted her tongue. She grasped the back of my head and moved in close, pressing her body against me. She made an attempt to put her half-empty glass on the table, missed by a foot, and wrapped her arm around me, holding tight.

Feeling her nails through my shirt, I kissed her along the jaw from her ear down the side of her neck, then swept her up with a growl and carried her to the bedroom.

My head was spinning with desire, blood pounding in my temples. Sarah moaned in my ear, then bit the side of my neck. I took a deep breath, inhaling the scent of her hair.

We landed on the bed, and managed to undress almost without letting go.

It was intense. I was more turned on than I had been in a long time, and she reacted with an urgency that surprised me. I put forth my best effort, and she seemed to appreciate it.

Being a good lover is all about being able to read a woman and respond. Being able to read a body's rhythms below the surface is helpful.

Cheating? Maybe. But nobody's complained yet.

We fell asleep tangled together, her head resting on my chest, a lazy smile on her lips. I drifted off with a warm glow in the pit of my stomach.

Chapter 9

THE AIR WAS STILL BITTERLY COLD. I hunched my shoulders in my parka and wiggled my toes to keep the blood moving. I'd thrown away my Shoepak boots, which trapped the sweat when you moved and let it freeze when you stopped, and just wore a pair of regular leather boots a size too large with an extra pair of wool socks. I was cold, but not frostbitten.

The fighting hole was too shallow, but it was deeper than most on this inhospitable hillside. I had worked long and hard scraping and chipping at the frozen ground, and pushed the rest of my squad to do the same. Work kept you warm, and a deep enough hole kept you alive.

Private Hackett snored quietly in the bottom of the hole, his legs in his sleeping bag, sitting up against one wall of the pit. Ever since a team got overrun and bayoneted in their bags, we were ordered not to climb in and zip up. We were ordered to keep our boots on as well, but that must have come from some rear echelon idiot who'd never been north of Virginia. You need to take your boots off and dry out your socks. Wet socks will cost you toes.

It was my watch, but since it was too dark to watch, I was listening. Other companies had been hit, and we assumed we would be sooner or later.

I heard something at the base of the hill. I couldn't make out anything in the darkness, but only humans were dumb enough to be out on a night this cold, and only the Chinese were motivated enough to be out probing instead of hunkered down in their blankets.

I dug out a grenade, squeezed the handle to loosen it, since they'd been freezing up. Didn't pull the pin yet, but made sure the spoon would release when I threw it.

Silence.

Had I just imagined the sound? I flexed my fingers in my gloves, wiggled my toes, waited. Listened and waited as the chill seeped through my parka.

Suddenly I heard the blast of a whistle and the shuffle of feet and the enemy made a plodding charge up the hill through deep snow on frozen feet.

I prodded Hackett with my boot, then hurled the grenade and ducked back down. Hackett came blearily awake, reaching for his Thompson.

'Grenades,' I told him. Muzzle flashes would give us away. Until the artillery got some flares up, we couldn't see anything to shoot at anyway.

We each grabbed one, pulled the pins, knocked the spoons against the frozen walls of the pit to loosen them and threw them, together.

We ducked back down and heard the explosions. Now there was gunfire and screams in English and Chinese. I took a third grenade and stood to throw when the first of the flares popped overhead, bathing the hill in harsh white light.

Chinese soldiers swarmed up at us, their legs churning as they tried to run through the deep snow, shoulders hunched in the unconscious crouch every infantryman adopts in the face of fire. Most carried submachine guns, but only a few were firing. Our holes were hard to see, most of us showing as little of ourselves as possible and the flare had just spoiled everyone's night vision.

I quickly estimated their number at around a billion.

The nearest were only about twenty yards away. I threw my grenade, saw it land among the closest enemy, dropped down into the hole and grabbed my rifle. When the explosion sounded, I got just high enough to aim over the lip of the hole and started shooting.

This close, I didn't have to really aim. Squinting through the rear sight actually kills your peripheral vision. Under fifty yards, I just had to look over the sights, take a second to line up and squeeze. They were headed straight at me, no need to lead them. Just don't rush the shot.

I fired at a tall guy hunched over a burp gun, running directly at me. He spun around and fell, his limbs flopping loosely, his weapon pinwheeling away. I lined up and dropped another man, then fired at a third, whom I couldn't have missed, but who kept right on running, his weapon chattering full auto. I fired again. Nothing. My third shot hit him in the forehead. His hat flew off, he jerked straight up and toppled over. I shifted my aim to another man, but I saw tracers from a machine gun further up the hill scythe him down. To my left, Hackett's Tommy gun stuttered in short bursts.

I fired a few more shots, then swore as my M1 ejected the spent magazine with a metallic *pang!* As I grabbed another clip from my bandolier, Hackett made a noise between a grunt and a wet cough and fell against the back wall of the pit.

I put a hand out toward him and the world exploded.

A club of light and noise hit me, sending my helmet spinning off into the darkness. I felt hot, stabbing pain in my right shoulder and fell into the pit, dazed.

Disoriented, I groped blindly, my hand coming down on a bloody parka. Hackett was unconscious, his breathing slow and snoring. I stayed down, sending energy to explore his wounds, stop his bleeding. I heard the enemy attack pass around the hole, running and shooting and screaming. A soft, heavy weight landed on my legs, then remained horribly still.

I tried to control my fear, with Hackett's rasping breath in my ears, an icy cold settling on my right side where my parka was torn by fragments and my blood had frozen on my skin, and the heavy, still warmth of a dead Chinese soldier lying across my legs.

I woke with a start, my heart racing, and looked around. I was in my bed in my second floor walkup in Philips Mills.

Sarah was on her side, wrapped up in my blankets, which she'd managed to pull half off me, exposing my right side from shoulder to hip. She was snoring quietly. The cat lay draped across my knees.

I took a deep breath, slid out from under what she'd left me of the covers and threw on a robe. I took my longest t-shirt out of my bureau, laid it on a chair near the bed, and made my way to the kitchen. I walked softly, making sure not to wake her.

The dream had been vivid. Nothing so vivid in a long time. Maybe talking to that Korean vet brought it out.

Or maybe being hunted and helpless, waiting in the dark for a knife between my shoulder blades reminded me of that night.

This couldn't be as bad as that night above the Toktong Pass, could it? And I'd survived that. Except that I didn't have any hand grenades now. Even if I did, chances are the neighbors would object to me throwing them at strange noises in the dark.

Out Of Nowhere

That night had been bad. I'd patched Hackett up and we kept our heads down as the assault raged on past us. Someone called in an artillery strike all around us which stopped the second wave of Chinese, and the rest of the company threw the survivors off the hill. We limped up after dawn and rejoined the platoon.

It might sound cowardly, playing dead in the bottom of a hole while the enemy swarmed up after your buddies. Hell, it might be cowardly, but if we'd gotten up and started shooting, dazed, wounded, and half-blind from a grenade explosion in the middle of a Chinese company and started shooting, they'd have killed us in seconds. If we'd tried to retreat up the hill to the rest of the unit, either the Chinese or some panicked Marine would have shot us. There's a time to fight and a time to hug the ground.

Enough thinking about that. Now it was time to concentrate on the fact that there was a beautiful woman in my bed. The hunters in the cold dark night would keep.

I made a pot of coffee, picked up the beer glasses left by the couch, and started hunting around for breakfast for two. Maybe after breakfast I would think of something to do about the man with the ankle. I needed a name for him. Gimpy? Von Gimpy? Gimpsky! Maybe Sarah would have an idea on how to pursue that inscription.

In addition to survival, one thing soldiering had taught me was not to worry about things you couldn't control, but about what you could. I opened the fridge.

Two eggs. Well that wouldn't work. Three slices of bread for toast... not promising. Plenty of milk at least. Well, it could be cold cereal.

Aha, I did have the makings for pancakes. Who doesn't love pancakes? But no syrup... OK, blackberries. Not in season, but I could make that work, and whipped cream. I was in business.

A little water in a pan on low, add some butter, dump in some blackberries, spoon some sugar over them, cover and let simmer.

I heard footsteps coming from the bedroom. I turned to see Sarah come into the kitchen. She looked good in an oversized Boston Celtics t-shirt, give her that much. The tattered remnants of the nightmare melted away.

'Hi gorgeous,' I said. 'Sleep OK?'
'Like a baby. What smells good?'

'Homemade blackberry syrup,' I replied. 'In the mood for pancakes?'

'I could be persuaded.' She kissed me lightly. 'I'm gonna go freshen up.'

'I have a new toothbrush in my work bag. Stole it from the hospital in case I needed it but I haven't used it. It's still wrapped up.'

'Thanks,' she said, retrieving her purse from the couch, 'but I brought my own.' She must have caught something in my expression; she flashed her trademark twisted smile. 'Because I'm just that slutty.'

I laughed.

'I'm not naive. When I accepted your dinner offer, I thought this might happen. We're both adults, we had some chemistry.' She shrugged. 'Although, you had me worried for a sec.'

'How do you mean?' I asked as I cracked an egg into the mixing bowl.

She shrugged again. 'Well, I felt a connection but after the literature, the cooking, and the fact that you're good-looking, well... When you complimented my manicure, I thought "Oh God no, he's gay".'

I burst out laughing. 'Oh, man. I hope I reassured you.'

'Definitely. But for a second, I wondered if I'd waxed for nothing.'

'If I'd complimented you on a nice job with that, would that have pushed your suspicion further toward or away from gay?'

'That's a good question.' She laughed. 'I'll think about it while I clean up. You keep cooking for me, you're gonna have a hard time getting rid of me.' She gave me a quick kiss and walked into the bathroom. I heard the shower running.

I finished cooking, plated the pancakes, drizzled the syrup over them, dropped a few uncooked berries on top and finished with a spritz of whipped cream.

How many guys can beat up armed thugs and still garnish?

She came out of the bathroom and sat down. I put a plate in front of her. 'Coffee?'

'Please.' She looked at the plate and then up at me. 'OK, where'd you learn to cook? Honest this time. Your mom didn't make breakfast like this.'

'I had a friend who was a chef. I picked up a few things.'

'How long were you sleeping with this friend?' The smile took the sting out of the accusation.

'What do you mean?'

'Come on. The chicken and pasta I can see, but this is a booty breakfast. This is what you cook to build up somebody's strength for round two. Not that I'm complaining. Who doesn't love pancakes with fruit and whipped cream?' She picked up a fork. 'No judgement, I know you had a life before this week, but I don't need to worry about a jealous ex who packs knives, do I?'

'Nothing so dramatic,' I said. 'It was a long time ago. I dated a chef, she knew I liked good food, she taught me a few tricks.'

'Any that involve cooking?' she asked. There didn't seem to be any jealous psycho vibe coming from her.

'I used to use that same joke. We dated for a while. It didn't work out. Her memory pales in comparison to you.'

'Sweet talk will get you nowhere,' she said. 'But you're cute, you can cook and you're not bad in the sack.' She finished her breakfast. 'These pancakes have restored my energy.' She stood up from the table. 'If, in fact, that was your nefarious plan, it worked.'

She walked toward the bedroom with an exaggerated sway of her hips. 'You coming?'

'Just breathing hard,' I muttered, rising to follow her. 'For the moment.'

Chapter 10

FRIDAY I RETURNED TO WORK. I endured the usual ribbing: the box of gloves in the ambulance cut in half and labeled "Right only"; the set of cutlery with my name on it, the knife replaced with a plastic one, "Hold this end" written on the handle.

I love my co-workers.

I shook my head and walked out to the garage to check out the truck. Nique was already there, going through the jump kit, shaking her head and rearranging it to her liking.

'Hey, you,' I said as I walked up. 'Nice to see the place hasn't fallen down without me.'

'Sean!' She hugged me, then stood back at arm's length, looking into my face with an expression of deep concern. 'How're you feeling?'

'Doing fine,' I replied. 'The hand is OK, just wearing the bandage to protect the stitches.'

'You OK to work? Really?'

'I'm fine. Honest. I'll flash my bandage at the hose-draggers, get them to do my heavy lifting. They're gonna be there getting in the way anyway. Other than that, it's my left hand; I can start IVs, take vitals and everything else with the right.'

'I heard Marty gave you the "going to bat for you" speech.'

'That he did,' I replied. 'Because he's got my back. Unlike the suits.'

'This company has suits?'

'Well, I'm sure they're cheap polyester. HR can play hardball right now. The latest class of medics just graduated. I get pissed and walk, they can hire a replacement from the bottom of the pay scale and keep the shifts filled.'

'This company sucks.'

'Yeah, but we all knew that,' I said. 'None of us are working for the glory of Flatline Ambulance. I'm spoiled for real work and where else can I get such a hot partner?'

'I didn't think Pete was your type.'

'Eh,' I shrugged. 'In the right light he's not bad-looking. How're you doing?'

'Devastated by your absence,' she said, 'but soldiering on bravely.'

'I had suspected. Not shaken up by that fight?'

'You think that's all it'd take to scare me?'

'It was enough for me. How'd Joe feel when you told him about it?'

'He freaked.' Her eyes flashed. 'Said he didn't like me working the street. He actually tried to talk me into going to school for my RN.'

'What'd you say?'

'That I will wipe ass for no man.'

'Your tact is matched only by your beauty. How'd he take that?'

'He saw it my way,' she said, looking shocked that I might have thought otherwise. 'Besides, I think he's secretly turned on that I'm such a badass.' She smiled wickedly.

'I think he's openly turned on 'cause you've got such a good ass.' I replied.

'You think?' She pirouetted, pausing to look back over her shoulder at me as she displayed the derriere in question. 'You don't think I've lost it?'

'My dear, if Helen of Troy could launch a thousand ships with her face, your ass could empty every port in the world.'

'You sweet talker,' she said. 'It's good to have you back.'

'Good to be back,' I replied. 'For a given value of "good". Let's grab some coffee.'

'Sure. By the way, we need to steal some supplies from the hospital, since Flatline doesn't believe in stocking the truck.'

'I figured they gave us pants with big cargo pockets so we could swipe stuff from the ER. What are we short on?'

'O2 supplies, IV drip sets and EKG electrodes.'

'Is that all?' I asked. 'Have you turned into a prima donna in my absence? You actually want to be able to treat patients?'

'I want it all.' She smiled.

'But you have me back.'

'And in return for keeping an eye on you, I think the company can at least give me a truck with some supplies on it.'

As we pulled the truck out, she turned to me. 'So, how'd you spend your mini vacation?'

'I met someone.'

'You did?' She studied me closely. 'Oh my God, you did. You're glowing. 'Bout time you got some action.'

'What's that supposed to mean?'

'Oh, don't take it like that, you were just getting really tense. You needed a roll in the hay.' She cupped her chin in her hand, regarding me as I drove. 'Come on, let's hear it. What's she like?'

'Her name is Sarah. She teaches at the college. She's funny and smart and way too pretty to be hanging with me.'

'Oh,' she cooed, 'you really *like* her.'

'What do you mean?'

'You put pretty third. And she isn't a waitress, bartender or nurse, which means you were talking to someone outside your regular circle, so you must really care to bother. I think that's sweet.'

'That I care about a woman I'm sleeping with?'

'That she isn't just some convenient piece of ass.'

'You think I'm like that?'

'Sean, you know I love you dearly, in a completely platonic way, but you are a paramedic.'

'Says the medic who's engaged to a medic.'

She waved a hand in airy dismissal. 'He's one in a million. It goes without saying. I'm just proud of you that you aren't a pig like most of the rest of the profession.'

I wasn't sure what to say to that, but I was spared the need as we were dispatched to an unresponsive male in an alley.

He turned out to be just very, very drunk. He was confused, incoherent, and spoke only Spanish, and not very clear Spanish at that, but he was breathing fine, his vitals were OK, and since he was homeless and wearing all the clothes he owned, he wasn't soaked through to the skin yet even though we found him lying in the snow.

We got him out of his wet stuff, examined him the best we could, covered him in dry blankets, and started an IV to dilute the blood in his alcohol stream. He objected incoherently to pretty much all our treatment, but he wasn't lucid enough for us to leave him, so we tied his hands, wrapped the rest of him in blankets and brought him to the ER. It was a bit like veterinary medicine.

Out Of Nowhere

We dropped our patient off, putting him in a room where he babbled at the ER staff and peed on their cot. We were making bets on what his blood alcohol would come back at when Brenda, the world's angriest charge nurse, walked over. She was a tall woman, maybe just a bit too thin, her hair dyed an aggressive blonde. She might have been attractive, in a cold, domineering, she-wolf-of-the-SS kind of way, but her eyes were too dead, her expression too hard and her heart too flinty. One good look through those frosty grey eyes into her even frostier soul could kill the libido of better men than me.

'Why didn't you do a blood sugar on that guy?' she demanded, her mouth compressed in frustration at having to accept a report from mere ambulance drivers.

'We did,' Nique replied. 'It was 106.'

'You could have let us know that,' she said, speaking slowly, as if to a wayward two-year-old.

'We did,' said Nique, all sweetness. 'I saw Trish write it down with the vitals. Maybe you didn't hear it,' she added in her most calming voice, 'what with all the confusion in there.'

Brenda maintained her stony expression, nodded curtly, forced out 'Oh. OK,' in a tone conciliatory enough to cut glass, and walked off.

'She's sexy when she scowls like that,' I said.

Nique faced me, her placid expression still in place. 'You know,' she observed sweetly, 'I think she really should just have the word "cunt" tattooed on her forehead.'

Not having anything to say to that, I just finished making up the cot.

On our way out to the truck, a disheveled man on a stretcher in the hallway hailed me. 'Hey, *Paramedico*.'

I recognized him immediately. '*Jose! Que pasa?*' I shook his grubby hand. 'What're you doing here? Racking up the frequent flyer miles?'

'My asthma,' he replied. 'It make my heart attack worse.'

'Sleeping in the parked buses at the station is making your asthma worse, *amigo*. You need to find a place. And get your own prescription for an inhaler. Stop using the ones you find in the trash.'

'What's you name?' he asked, ignoring the indispensable medical wisdom I was giving him free of charge.

'What? You know me, Jose.' I tapped the company-mandated name tag, the one which ensured every psych patient, drunk and heroin addict in Philips Mills knew me on a first-name basis. 'It's Sean.'

'What's you las' name?'

'Why you want to know that?' I smiled. 'I'm pretty sure we aren't family, unless there are Montreal Gutierezes. Even if there are, I don't plan on coming over for Thanksgiving dinner.'

'Just tell me you name.'

'It's Sean. My last name is The Medic, and my phone number is 911. I never let it go to voice mail,' I said in my all-business, no-longer-fucking-around tone. 'Now, why the interest in my name?'

Jose shrugged, smiling sheepishly. 'This guy, he say he pay if anybody know you. He ask for the gringo *Paramedico* who work with the partner *mas bonita*.'

'What did this guy look like?'

Jose's look morphed from sheepish to calculating. 'He the one pay for information.'

'Jose.' I tried to look hurt. 'How many times have I come out to find you grey and barely breathing and helped you out? That's not payment?'

'That's you job.' He crossed his arms.

I sighed. 'You're breaking my heart, *hermano*.' I pulled a five out of my wallet and put it in the pocket of his filthy flannel jacket. 'I'd tell you not to spend it on booze, but I'm a realist.'

'He was some big gringo,' said Jose, narrowing it down quite a bit in Philips Mills. 'He wear a long black coat. He speak English funny.'

'Not good like us, eh?' I replied. '*Gracias*, Jose.' I patted his shoulder. 'If he asks, tell him my name is Niemand.'

'OK.' He smiled. '*Gracias*.'

I walked back to Nique, who looked at me with a raised eyebrow. 'What was that about?'

'Our friend with the ankle is still asking about me. He's canvassing the homeless now.'

'Seriously?'

'He offered Jose there money for any info.'

'What'd you tell him?'

'That my name is Niemand.'

She shook her head blankly.

'That's "nobody" in German. Either our buddy will know I'm on to him, or he'll spend time chasing nobody, quite literally.'

'So what do we do now?'

'We violate the shit out of some patient confidentiality laws,' I replied. 'We need a hazelnut latte and my most charming smile.'

'Why?'

'Tiffany is working in medical records today, and she has a weakness for both.'

'Which one is Tiffany?'

'Not the old bat with the funny eye. Although it would be hilarious if *her* name was Tiffany. More like an Agnes, really. Tiffany's the little brunette with the nose ring and the rack.'

'Oh. Her,' she said, her voice thick with Gallic disdain. 'The one who thinks a neckline that ends at her navel is appropriate for the office.'

'Yep, that's the one.'

'I thought you had a new girlfriend.'

'You wound me,' I said as we walked to the truck. 'I'd never let it go anywhere. I'm just going to flirt and schmooze some info out of her. I'll play the clueless medic who needs to get info for the billing department.'

'Well, you do a good clueless medic.'

'That's why I need you to watch my back.'

A smile fought its way onto her face and she sighed. 'OK, let's go. I have to admit, I wonder why this guy wants to know so much about you.'

Chapter 11

HALF AN HOUR LATER, ARMED with a hazelnut latte, half skim, extra foam, we entered the patient records department of Philips Mills General. A vital skill to getting people to help you in emergency services is to learn and remember how they take their coffee. Forget birthdays and anniversaries if you must, but retain your coffee knowledge at all costs.

'Hi, Sean.' Tiffany rose from her seat, leaning over the counter as though she had no idea the effect it would have on any heterosexual male between the ages of puberty and death. 'Oh, is that for me?' She took the latte, sipped decorously, then wiped the foam from her lip and giggled. I swear I could hear Nique's eyes roll. 'Did you need something, or did you just come to say hi?'

In fairness, Nique was a bit cruel. Tiffany's neckline ended around the bottom of her sternum. She was a short girl with a friendly smile, big dark eyes and an exaggerated hourglass of a figure that made men drool and women seethe. Her dark curls were piled high on her head like a Greek goddess and a tiny diamond sparkled on her left nostril.

'Actually, I do need a favor,' I said. 'I lost a patient demographic sheet and billing is all over me about it. Do you think you could pull it up for me?'

'I'm not supposed to give that out,' she demurred.

'I know,' I sighed, 'but you'd be saving me, really.' I turned my smile on her. 'You can't just bend the rules a bit? Just this once?'

'Oh, all right.' She feigned reluctant surrender. 'You're gonna ruin my good-girl reputation. When did you bring the patient in?' She turned to her computer and brought up a menu, her long, graceful fingers flying over the keys with a speed and efficiency that few noticed beneath her bubbly exterior.

'Last Sunday, around two in the afternoon. He had an ankle sprain.'

'OK,' she replied, 'got it.' She punched some keys and a printer hummed and spat out a page. As she turned and walked over to it, I noticed that in addition to the low cut, midriff-baring, sleeveless blouse, she was actually wearing leather pants, slung just low enough to reveal a tiny tattoo on the small of her back.

She swept up the sheet and handed it to me, leaning forward just a bit farther than necessary.

'You're the best.' I smiled again, accepting the paper.

'Don't tell anybody I gave you that,' she reminded me in a stage whisper.

'I was never here,' I replied. 'Take care.'

I walked out, right into the beaten zone of Nique's reproachful gaze. 'You tawdry slut, you.'

I drew the cloak of my dignity around me. 'Your harsh words cut me to the bone, madame.'

'I never knew you could be such a shameless hussy. My image of you is forever tarnished.'

'I'll see if I can't find a scarlet letter to sew on my uniform. Let's roll, we've wasted enough time here. Got lives to save.'

She remained unmoved.

'Drunks to pick up. Addicts' misery to prolong. Insurance frauds to backboard.'

Still nothing.

I reached into my quiver again. 'Nurses to annoy.'

She smiled at that. She grinned despite herself and punched me in the arm so I wouldn't forget who was in charge. 'Let's get back to work.'

We climbed back into the ambulance. I scanned my ill-gotten demographic sheet on our curious European friend.

It wasn't very helpful. The name, Doors, had obviously been anglicized, the address was a post office box, and the phone number was a cell. The employer was listed as Doors Imports, with a number and address, so maybe I could run that down.

'She's really into you,' Nique observed as she pulled the ambulance out of the hospital lot. 'You two never hooked up?'

'Hmm?' I looked up from my reading. 'What? Tiffany? You're kidding, right?'

'Why not? I mean, yeah, you met someone, but why not a week ago?'

'It'd never work out,' I replied dismissively. 'I mean, have you seen the magazines on her desk? *Cosmo. Glamour.* God help us, *Us.* I couldn't fake an interest long enough to get through dinner.'

'Not even a fling, though?'

I shook my head. 'Still have to wake up next to her in the morning. I know it wouldn't work, and she works in admitting, so every time we needed to register a patient I'd have to see her. Not worth it. Besides, she's a sweet girl, even if she's not my type. It would just be sex and I'd feel bad using her.'

'That didn't stop you and that ER nurse at Holy Trinity.'

'That was different. Jenna knew the score and she was perfectly happy to be used.' Eager, even, but Nique didn't need that much detail. 'Tiffany actually kinda has a crush on me. Using that to get her into bed and then moving on would be a lousy thing to do.'

I *have* limits. Not strict or demanding ones, but limits nonetheless.

'If Pete hears that you could've slept with her and didn't, it'll just throw fuel on the fire of his gay theory.'

'Oh, God, please. Don't encourage him.'

'Half the EMTs and medics in the company want to bang her. I don't get what the deal is.'

'Of course you don't,' I said without looking up. 'You're not a guy.'

'I know who's attractive,' she replied defensively.

'OK.' I set my paper down. 'I shall try to explain the dark and sinister workings of the male brain. At first glance, Tiffany appears to be the perfect woman. Probably isn't, but she appears that way. Women don't think she's attractive because she doesn't have the body of a fashion model, but you need to realize that only women and gay men read fashion magazines, and they set the tone for movies, tabloids and so on. Real, meat-eating, sports-watching heterosexual men like a girl with big boobs, a small waist, nice hips and enough ass to get a good grip on. A million years of evolution has programmed that deeper than a mere half century of fashion and pop culture can touch. Plus, whenever we see her, she's always happy, smiling and, to the casual observer, uncomplicated. She looks low maintenance. She probably wouldn't be all that easy and uncomplicated in an actual relationship, and nobody's happy and giggly all the time, but that's how she appears.'

I shifted focus. 'You, on the other hand, are undeniably hot, and a better conversationalist, and probably much more fun to spend long periods of time with. But from a purely sexist, caveman view, you are less desirable because you look like more work.'

'More work?' She raised an eyebrow.

'Yes, my platonic soul mate, more work. This conversation, for example. For all your sterling qualities, I couldn't get you to drop your panties for a latte, and then distract you with a copy of *Us* magazine so I could just drift off to sleep after slaking my lust on your fabulous bod. You, my dear, are an investment. Well worth the effort, and a much better prospect when looked at long term, but more work nevertheless. Dating a pretty, low-maintenance, easily amused and uncomplicated girl is much less investment. Like buying a goldfish. Only a goldfish you can screw.'

'Lovely,' she responded. 'You men are disgusting.'

'That we are,' I agreed. 'But now, you tell me. Your fiancé Joe is a great guy, has a good job, and is, I can say as a confident heterosexual, not bad-looking.'

'All true.'

'So you wouldn't find an unemployed, arrogant guitarist really hot?'

I saw a brief, dreamy expression cross her features as she, no doubt, pictured an unshaven version of Joe with terminal bed head, dressed mostly in tattoos, guitar slung low across his hips. She made several attempts to speak, but finally shrugged. 'Fair enough. I can't explain that to a guy.'

'Exactly. Now, to reassure you as to the salvageable nature of mankind, it is a mark of maturity when a man realizes that complexity and dimension are good things in a woman and stops chasing bimbos. Much the same as when kids grow up and start preferring aged sirloin to a McDonald's hamburger.'

She shook her head, but her smile remained. 'So you can compare women to pets and food? Any other insights?'

'I could do cars or sports teams right off the bat,' I offered. 'Or with some work I could hammer out a flower analogy.'

'I think I'll pass.' She gave me that combination of a little sigh, sad headshake and indulgent smile that meant she found me at least slightly more amusing than frustrating, like a kitten who playfully drags all the toilet paper off the roll.

Chapter 12

WE MADE IT BACK TO THE BASE and had a chance to warm up dinner. I took my Tupperware plate of leftover pasta and walked into the day room. As usual, the TV was on and the stylish faux leather couches were covered by recumbent paramedics.

Looking for a seat, I noticed Pete sprawled across the slashed upholstery, his FirstLine Ambulance cap over his eyes. I walked over and kicked the couch near his unzipped boots. 'Rise and shine, Sleeping Beauty. I need a spot to sit.'

He opened his eyes, gave a slow smile and swung his legs out of my way, leisurely sitting up. 'No problem, man. I'm getting bed sores here anyway.'

'You slacking off and letting us do all your calls?' I asked. 'Nique and I have been out all day saving lives and making a difference and you tell me you've been here checking your eyelids for pinholes?'

'Don't try to bullshit me. I work in the same town you do. You been pulling drunks out of snowbanks.' He smiled lazily. 'Besides, I got no partner. Big Juan is on his way in.'

'What happened to Spaz McGee?'

'He accidentally slammed his hand in the door of the medication closet,' Pete replied. 'That was shortly after, but in no way related to his insistence on running up the stairs to treat the suicidal male rather than wait for PD.'

'How did the guy plan to off himself?' I asked around a mouthful of pasta.

'Well, he didn't have a gun or a knife, which is too bad, really, since it might have helped us solve our partner issues on a long-term basis,' said Pete. 'I think he was threatening to jump from the Singing Bridge.'

'Into the Merrimack?' I asked. 'Was he planning to poison himself?'

He shrugged. 'Anyway, no cops in sight, the sister meets us at the truck, bawling in Spanglish about how he's gonna kill himself. So Sparky grabs the jump kit and makes for the stairs like he's Johnny Gage.' He shook his head.

'So the sister didn't even say whether or not he had a gun or knife and Spaz wants to charge in?' Custer or Lord Cardigan would have thought twice about partnering with Jim Burton. He was the kind of man best used to find landmines and snipers.

'I swear it wouldn't have mattered if she said the guy had a hand grenade,' Pete replied.

'It would just excite him,' Nique added. 'He doesn't have the brains to be scared.'

'You scare the shit out of him,' said Pete.

She shrugged in regal dismissal, as though it was obvious that even someone as clueless as Jim Burton would recognize that she was not to be trifled with.

'So what did you do?' I asked.

'I just advocated caution in my own polite way,' said Pete. 'You know how polite I am.'

He reached over and plucked a piece of chicken from my bowl, popped it into his mouth and smiled, then wiped his fingers on the couch. If I looked very closely, I could just make out the new stain. Nique sighed, shook her head and arranged her meal on the only table in the day room, setting her salad front and center, a grilled skinless chicken breast on the left flank, bottled water on the right, and a container of yogurt in tactical reserve.

'Mmm,' Pete said. 'That's good. Not buyin' your sauce in a jar. Make a trip to mom's?'

I shook my head, chewing. I didn't want to talk with my mouth full in front of Nique.

'He met somebody worth a nice dinner,' Nique informed him on my behalf.

'Holy crap,' he said. 'He's a good cook. What's his name?'

'I made this.' When dealing with Pete, I felt the need to assert my culinary skills more than my heterosexuality. There really was more point.

'Jesus, he's got you in the kitchen?' Pete shook his head sadly, 'Queer

I was gettin' used to, but I didn't know you'd be the bitch.'

'Hey, if you'd treat me special once in a while, I might be cooking for you, you sexy beast.'

'You start dressin' pretty, I may *let* you cook for me,' he responded.

'When you boys finish this very mature game of gay chicken,' said Nique, dipping a forkful of salad into the tiny Tupperware container of dressing she had brought, separate of course, to keep the lettuce from wilting in the vinegar, 'I will point out that I think a man who cooks is a turn on.'

I was spared further exposure to Pete's rapier wit by the arrival of his new partner. Juan Lopez entered the dayroom like a liner pulling up to a dock. Slow, oddly graceful and impossible to ignore.

'Hey, Homes!' he boomed. 'Give me some love.' He bent down and gave Nique a kiss on the cheek, then clasped my right hand with his and hugged me with his left arm. 'How you been, man? Long time no see.' He noticed Pete and groaned. 'Oh, man, I gotta work with this guy?'

'You know Nique and Sean have to stay together so they can do each other's hair and discuss their boyfriends.' Pete stood for his handshake-hug. 'Good to see you again, man.'

Juan shucked his backpack and sat on an unoccupied couch, pretty much filling it. Everything about Juan was big. He was six feet tall, and nearly as broad. He could still move when he had to haul gear up three flights then carry the patient down, even though he was breathing heavier afterward. He was also funny, boisterous, generous and knew everyone and everything about this city. I worked with him when I first took the job here, and he taught me to recognize gang colors, to read the nuanced symbolism in the graffiti, what streets were drawn wrong on the map, where to eat the best of any given type of food, and Puerto Rican street-Spanish.

'I'll work with you,' he advised Pete, 'but if we meet that bitch we ran into last time, I'mma take her out.'

'That delicate flower?' Pete smiled in return. 'You have no sense of chivalry.'

'This sounds like a good story,' I said, grinning.

'Oh, man.' Juan shook his head. 'You tell it. I get too wound up.'

'So, there I was,' began Pete, drawing laughter with the universal intro to all EMS war stories, 'working with *mi amigo* Juan, and we get a call in front of 248 Broadway.'

'Like you do,' Nique agreed.

'Exactly. Anyway we get there, and there's this skinny white-trash chick dressed in a filthy hospital bathrobe screaming at this dude. She's reading him the riot act, so we walk up, do the whole professional "what seems to be the trouble, ma'am?" thing and she starts unloading abuse on us, "you can't take me, fuck you, I don't need no fuckin' ambulance" and so on. So we try and calm her down, and the guy she's yelling at says how she's been sick, she's using again, she needs help, he's a friend.'

'He's Puerto Rican,' Juan clarified.

'Or Dominican, whatever. Never could tell you guys apart.' Pete smirked as Juan flashed him a middle finger like a kielbasa. 'Anyway, yeah, the guy's Puerto Rican. Nice guy, polite, helpful, obviously concerned about this broad. Why is beyond me. She's nasty. Dirty and skinny. Like, skeletal, deathcamp, Sally Struthers Save-the-Children-commercial skinny. Stringy, bleached blonde hair, cigarette between her two remaining yellow teeth, and this disgusting red, weeping sore on her arm. Like, horrific. So I ask her about it, and she says it's infected from a dirty needle.'

'Wow,' I said. 'She sounds hot. She got a sister?'

'So I explain how the infection is dangerous, she could die, and so on, and she gives me the "nobody cares anyway" self-pity crap that *makes* you not care about these pathetic fucks, and so I say, "Well your friend here cared enough to call."'

'What'd she say to that?'

'Oh, dude,' he said. 'She flips out. Goes on a racist rant like she's my drunk Uncle Bobby at a Pat Buchanan rally. Caps the whole thing by saying how this used to be a nice town until the spics ruined everything. So I figure, fuck her. We ask three times if she wants to go, then get a refusal.'

'So, we're walking away,' Juan jumped in, 'and this guy,' he jabbed an accusing finger at Pete, 'says to me, "Shame on you for ruining this town for that nice white girl."'

We howled with laughter.

'So, Juan,' I said when I'd finished laughing, 'what brings you back here? I thought you were working for Tri City.'

'Tragedy asked me to leave,' he said. 'So I came back to FlatLine.'

'That's too bad.'

'I was coming up on my last day anyway, man.' He shook his head. 'That place is nuts. Write-ups for not having your collar pins, for using a blue pen, for having two extra 20 gauge needles in the jump kit. All bullshit. Plus the Riverdale contract sucks. Give me good old Philips Mills any day.'

'We've been doing a lot of backup to Riverdale, just so you know,' I informed him.

'Oh, man, don't tell me that. I was all happy and shiny and now you gotta break my heart.'

'Don't sweat it, Juan,' said Nique, 'I've kept Sean here from getting fired, I'm sure I can keep you safe.'

'Well, so long as I have your protection.'

'We have a plan anyway,' said Pete. 'Any time we get dispatched mutual aid to Riverdale, we set fire to something en route to the call, and then they get distracted and leave us alone on the medical.'

'Hey guys.' Jerry, the shift supervisor, or Marty's number two, walked in. He was a typical lower management type. Bad at EMS, good at kissing ass and ratting on his comrades. 'Anybody want some OT this Saturday?'

'What's up?' I asked.

'Bunch of guys are taking the Civil Service exam. Trying to get on a fire department. Left some holes in the schedule.'

'I'm always willing to take the company's money,' said Pete. 'Put me in for twenty-four if you have it.'

'Good man. Anybody else?'

Silence greeted his question.

'What about you, Sean?'

'Sorry, not this Saturday. Things to see, people to do.'

'I'm surprised you aren't taking the test.'

'I'm more comfortable running *away* from burning buildings and leaking chemicals, thanks.'

'How about you, Pete?' he said. 'You don't want to be a firefighter?'

'I did at one time, but not anymore.'

'What changed?'

'I turned nine and decided I'd rather be either a cowboy or an astronaut.'

'You know,' Jerry bristled, 'that attitude is why you're such a senior medic and never got offered a management position.'

'I thought it was because he never had a back injury or DUI that forced him into a desk job and substance abuse counseling,' I offered.

'Now, be fair,' said Pete, 'I could have fucked up a call bad enough that I was a liability on the street.'

'True,' I nodded.

'Hey, you guys looking for a write-up?' Jerry glowered. 'You can be suspended for insubordination.'

'Who's gonna staff the truck then?' snapped Pete. 'Or work with Jim Nightmare Burton? You? Marty?'

Juan turned to Nique, 'You notice he ain't asked us if we gonna take the test?'

'Why's that, you think?' She smiled.

'Well, I'm sure in my case it's cause I got these big ol' titties,' he grinned, shaking his ample bulk.

'And me?'

'Pretty sure the same reason, *chica*.'

'You think so?' she asked, aghast.

'Well, I think Juan's are bigger, but yours are perkier,' Pete observed.

I grabbed Juan's chest and gave it a jiggle. 'Pete's probably right. I'd be happy to judge for you, though.'

'You're too kind,' said Nique.

'Just here to help.'

She smiled indulgently.

'I think Fearless Leader is implying that boobies have no place in turnout gear,' I observed.

'You think so?' she asked. 'Is that sexual harassment? Jerry, you're a supervisor. You must know where I can get a form to send to HR.'

'Get me one too,' said Juan. 'This gringo is violating the sanctity of my body. Hey, bro, I didn't say stop!' he added as I took my hand away.

'Sorry, man.' I grabbed him again.

'Just like that. Yeah, that's what I'm talking about.'

Jerry threw up his hands and retreated into the office. The good news was that Juan and Nique had worried him enough about a discrimination complaint that he wouldn't mention my and Pete's attitudes. The better news was that he left the room.

'Thanks, guys,' I said. 'I think you saved me from myself again.'

'You guys need to watch it,' said Juan. 'One day the schedule will be full, and they will shitcan you.'

'Fuck 'em,' said Pete. 'Plenty of private ambulance companies out there.'

'Yeah, and they all suck at least as bad as this one. You just wind up low on the seniority ladder, puttin' up with the same shit for less vacation days. I keep tellin' everybody, you white people are crazy.'

Chapter 13

It wasn't long before the radio blared again.

'Paramedic 20, respond to 5 Beacon St. From the police, a woman says her upstairs neighbors are injecting her with a secret chemical that's making her swell up.'

'Rockin',' I replied.

'Be advised, she called the police to arrest the neighbors, but they figure this is an ambulance call.'

'Sure. The police obviously don't have any training or equipment for dealing with crazy people and transporting them against their will. I'll just swing over, unarmed, in my highly protective polyester uniform shirt and hope she's not a violent nutcase.' Jesus.

'Good for you,' came the reply. 'Strength and honor. By the way, she says she's gained twenty pounds since yesterday.'

'Well,' said Nique, 'we'd better hurry while we can still carry her.'

The address was a typical garden-style apartment building. We stopped in the entryway, near the bank of buzzers and shared a look.

'Anything even a little bit off, we beat feet, agreed?' I said.

'Absolutely. Meeting of the Live Happy Cowards Club at the Harp for drinks later?'

'I'm a charter member.' I smiled, pressing the buzzer.

'Hello?'

'Hi. This is the ambulance. You called 911?'

'Oh yes. Come right up.'

The door buzzed. I tugged it open, looking at Nique. She shrugged. I sighed and walked in warily. Nothing seemed amiss.

We walked up the first flight of stairs, senses straining for signs of danger. I hadn't climbed stairs this nervously since Seoul in 1950.

The thought reassured me a bit. I'd come through that OK. I didn't even have Nique at my back then. Just a PFC from West Virginia with a Tommy gun.

Reaching the second floor, we found a woman standing at her apartment door, lifting her shirt to display the alleged swelling.

The woman was short, about 5'2", more or less average build, with a bit of a belly. Not a distinct, firm bulge like she would have if she were pregnant, just a bit of a pudge. Nothing new, nothing to really be concerned about, unless she was looking to become a runway model.

Apparently, she felt differently. 'Look! Look at this. This isn't me. And look! Here!' She pointed to a mosquito bite on her lower back, 'That's where they injected me.'

'OK, miss. Why don't we start at the beginning. Are you having any other physical problems? Any pain? Shortness of breath?'

'Are you listening?' she demanded. 'They injected me! And,' she added, 'they stole two of my vertebrae.'

'I'm sorry,' Nique interrupted. 'They did what?'

'They stole two of my vertebrae. I used to be five foot ten.'

'Maybe that's your problem,' Nique whispered to me.

'I'm taller on my back.'

The patient was ignoring us. Probably for the best. 'Here,' she offered, 'look. Here's the scar.' She began to pull her shirt over her head.

'OK, why don't we step inside and hear your story.' We quickly herded the increasingly naked woman out of the high traffic hallway.

At this point, I was convinced that she truly and deeply believed what she was saying. To try to argue the point would be futile and inflammatory. Official policy tells us not to play along or encourage a patient in his or her delusions, but to convince the patient that they need treatment and to come along quietly. Whoever wrote those policies never had to spend a long time in a confined, uncontrolled environment with an unstable person.

'Ok,' I said, 'why don't you grab a coat, and we'll head over to the hospital. They can... look at your back. Maybe they can replace those vertebrae for you.'

In practice, I'd always prefer to tell a psych patient that the ambulance was a shuttle craft waiting to take them to the MIR space station if it would get them to the ER peacefully and save me the necessity of wrestling with the crazy, both metaphorically and more importantly, physically.

'You think so?' she asked, hope clear on her face.

'Can't hurt to try,' I replied in my most convincing tone. 'They transplant body parts all the time.'

'I guess that makes sense,' she conceded. 'I'll get my coat.'

As she turned away, I sighed in relief, hoping that we might manage this transport with a minimum of conflict. Nique, who had been checking cabinets for medications, handed me a list of half a dozen psych meds. Some of the bottles weren't as empty as they should be, which told us that she probably wasn't medicated right now. Not really a surprise, but a nice confirmation of what we suspected.

Our patient was soon ready, smartly dressed in a long wool coat. She stopped at a mirror to give her hair a final brush, make sure she looked good for the ER. 'Oh, my God!' She suddenly froze, the color drained from her face, and she leaned forward, searching the glass with a frightening intensity.

'What's wrong, miss?' I asked, trying to keep my tone light and breezy, despite my growing dread of the answer.

She turned to me and with absolute sincerity and conviction said, 'These aren't my eyes.'

I'm forced to admit, that stumped me. I looked to Nique, but she didn't seem to have any insight either.

'How do you know?' Nique asked, after a pause of about a year.

'These are brown,' said the patient.

Well, they were. I checked. 'Ooooookaaaaaaaaaay. And yours were...?'

'Blue.'

'Ah.'

The uncomfortable silence settled once again.

'Well.' Nique stepped in smoothly. 'While they're checking for your vertebrae, maybe they can call the eye bank at Mass Eye and Ear.'

'Really?' asked the patient. 'They can do that?'

Nique's elbow in my ribs shocked me into action. 'Hm? Ah! Oh, absolutely. Do it all the time.'

'Oh,' she sighed in relief, 'that's great. OK, let's go.'

I held the door open, slightly bemused, and she walked down to the ambulance.

Sometimes it really is that easy. Provided you have decent people skills, a solid partner and are willing to ignore the holy bejeesus out of official policy.

We got to the hospital, dropped our patient off, and smiled at the thought of her and Brenda discussing the intricacies of eyeball replacement.

I noticed Juan and Pete wheeling in a stretcher. A young Hispanic man lay back on it, pale beneath his olive complexion, a sheen of sweat on his forehead and a massive bandage swathing his right hand. He had a Pittsburgh Steelers hat on, and there was a Bruins jacket over his knees.

On top of that, in a plastic bag, was a finger.

As they passed, Juan gave me a fist bump and Pete shook his head.

It seemed like there was a good story behind this one, so we camped out at the EMS desk while they took the patient into a room and gave report.

When they returned, I asked 'So what's up with this guy? He think that the hole in the middle of the bagel was to put his finger in while he cut it?'

'He didn't say,' smiled Juan, 'but I believe he bein' made an example.'

'Example?' asked Nique.

'You notice he all in black and gold?'

'Latin Kings,' I responded.

'Well done, Grasshopper.'

'You sure he ain't just a big hockey fan?' asked Pete.

'I tol' you, man,' said Juan. 'Only white boys watch hockey. And that's just because the only way you get to see white guys fighting on ESPN is they got skates on.'

'So, what finger?'

'Right index,' Juan replied. 'What does that suggest?'

'Trigger finger?'

'Yep. This boy a shooter for the gang. Somebody want to send a message to the Latin Kings that it may not be a very secure profession.'

'Yeah, but how much difference is that gonna make?' asked Pete. 'It's not like you Latinos hit anything you aim at anyway.'

'That's 'cause we all exhausted from those long nights at your mom's.'

'He say who did it?' interrupted Nique.

'Some dude he never saw before,' Juan replied. 'Same as always. Just minding his business, feeding the homeless or whatever and some dude comes up out of nowhere like a ghost and carves on him for no reason. Then he vanishes.'

'That Sumdood guy is a real prick,' added Pete. 'But this time we got a description. Turns out Sumdood is a white guy.'

'That's a switch.'

'Don't know what this town is coming to.' Juan shook his head sadly. 'Used to be safe out there dealing smack and stealing cars without worrying about those white guys.'

Chapter 14

ONCE I GOT HOME, I FED THE CAT, then turned on my computer. I dug out the demographic sheet that Tiffany had given me and ran searches on the name and birth date, the phone number, the social security number; all quickly led to dead ends. I got further on the company. Doors Imports had a website, the usual corporate boilerplate: a Mission Statement, testimonials. Nothing about hunting down rogue healers hiding out in EMS. There was an address in town, on South Canal St, a little spur of a road that ran along a tiny island between the canal and the Merrimack. There were a few businesses in the old mill buildings there, but none of them were very busy or remarkable. The road was a dead end, accessed off a narrow right of way near the Central Bridge. In years of working the city, I'd only been down there a handful of times. A nice, inconspicuous place for a front.

In theory, with a name, date of birth, employer and so forth, I should be able to find out a lot about my adversary. In practice, I just wasn't very good with technology. I'd done all my reconnaissance work back before computers. I knew people who could dig this stuff up, but I'd have to come up with a reason to explain why I wanted the info. Leave that until later.

What could he want from me? So far as I could remember, I hadn't crossed anyone in a long time. I hadn't knowingly slept with anyone's wife in years, and I hadn't killed anyone since Korea. The man I'd healed looked around thirty. For his entire life I'd been laying low, working as a medic. Had I healed someone he didn't want healed? Had the firefighters' union gotten sick of my wise-ass remarks and put out a hit on me?

I stopped, reviewed my thoughts.

Mr Doors looked about thirty.

But so did I.

There was no reason to believe I was unique. Well, beyond the usual. Just because I'd never met anyone like me didn't mean others didn't exist. And if they hid, if they didn't advertise, how would I recognize them?

Could I have wronged this man *a long way back*? It was after I'd healed him that he noticed something. Who had seen me do that? Well, lots of people, but generally they just thought the injury hadn't been all that bad, and I'd gotten to them quickly.

He maybe looked a bit like that Prussian Baron whose fiancée had run off with me. I'd really done them both a favor. They'd never have been happy together.

Or that Hussar lieutenant whose horse I'd stolen at Borodino. To be fair, I'd stopped him bleeding to death as well, but cavalrymen get touchy about their horses. If you think about it, I'd done the only reasonable thing. He was an officer and a man of means. The kind of man who gets taken prisoner and exchanged or ransomed. The Czarist cavalry would have treated another horse soldier like a brother. It's not like I left him to the Cossacks. I, on the other hand, was in the uniform of a *voltigeur* corporal at the time, and the Russian lancers would have spitted me.

I shook my head. If Doors was more or less immortal, like me, he could have any number of reasons for disliking me. No way to know.

Bad form in an immortal, holding a grudge.

I took the knife out of my desk drawer and looked at it. What did those symbols mean? Writing on weapons always has some deep meaning. This wasn't a presentation blade to hang on a wall. This was a well used utilitarian weapon. The balance, the shape, the spring of the steel. This was to cut people.

Warriors are a superstitious lot. Anything written on a weapon they planned to use in combat would be important. I'd carried a lot of weapons, and marched beside a lot of soldiers. Why didn't I recognize this inscription? If I'd wronged Doors, I should at least be able to identify his alphabet.

I was sitting on the couch when the phone rang. I let it go to machine, since I was in no mood to work an overtime shift, but picked up as soon as I heard Sarah's voice. 'Hi, I'm here.'

'Screening again?'

'Ever since my secretary quit on me,' I replied.

'Well, if you can find your social calendar without her, see if you're free tonight.'

'I'm sure I can find some time. I'll just cancel with the Prime Minister.'

'You're too good to me,' she laughed. 'Just get over as soon as you can.'

'Anything the matter?' I asked.

'Nothing terrible. Tough day at work. I was hoping to relax with some takeout and a movie. A little company wouldn't be unwelcome.'

'Sounds great. Anything I can bring?'

'Something alcoholic.'

'Can do,' I replied, avoiding the obvious joke about how I was bringing myself anyway. 'See you in an hour.'

'I'll be waiting.'

I hung up and jumped in the shower, shaved, dug through my wardrobe for a shirt without an ambulance company logo on it and ran a comb through my hair. There would be time enough to worry about angry foreigners with knives. Tonight a beautiful woman was requesting my company.

'How do I look, buddy?' I asked the cat. He raised his head, squinted at me for a moment then lay back down. 'So, the green shirt is OK, then?' He ignored me. I did throw a change of clothes and a toothbrush in a bag, just in case. Being male, the polite thing to do would be to leave it in the car. Showing up at the door with a gym bag in one hand was a bit presumptuous. A woman could always pack the essential in her purse, thus remaining subtle. And even if a woman walked into a man's apartment at the beginning of a date and bluntly asked if there were someplace she could put her toothbrush, spare panties and diaphragm, chances are there'd be few complaints.

I drove over, stopping on the way for a six-pack of a winter warmer: a heavy, very alcoholic beer, almost a barley wine. A good choice for relaxing after a hard day in the middle of winter. It was a bold choice, maybe, but I knew she drank good beer, and it wasn't bitter. I also picked up a bunch of flowers. I don't understand the power flowers have on women, but I know not to underestimate it.

I arrived at her building, a nondescript apartment block in the middle-class town of North Andover. I walked to the elevator, noting that the lobby was clean, well maintained but decorated with a nod to 1974. I pressed the button for the third floor, found my way to the door and knocked.

She answered the door dressed in a t-shirt, oversized flannel shirt and blue jeans. She looked a little tired, but still treated me to a kiss and a warm smile that broadened into delight when I presented the bouquet.

'Flowers,' she said, 'you shouldn't have. Thank you. Come in, come in.' She gave me a quick tour of the apartment, a simple two bedrooms, one of which had been converted into an office, a comfortable living room and a small but efficiently set up kitchen. Decoration was mostly books, including some old and rare examples, a few photos and some prints of landscapes hung on the walls. A cabinet of curios and knickknacks stood near the front door.

She took the flowers and went in search of a vase. 'Have a seat on the couch. I'll be right there.'

I sat and opened two bottles and she returned with a bowl of popcorn and a phone. She set the bowl on the coffee table. '*Bon appétit,*' she said. 'After we get comfortable I'll call for delivery. You feel like Italian or Chinese?'

'I'm easy,' I replied. 'You're the one who had the tough day. Whatever you'd prefer, unless choosing is too much effort.'

'No, but thanks for thinking that way. I'm leaning toward Italian.' She rolled her head, stretching her neck. 'Too long at the computer today.'

'Here.' I dragged an ottoman in front of me. 'Have a seat and let me take a look at that neck.'

She sat in front of me, and I swept her hair aside and gently kneaded her neck and shoulders. I sensed the tense, knotted muscles deep under the skin, and sent a little energy to relax them. Again, cheating, but nobody's ever complained.

'Oh, God,' she moaned, 'where did you learn that? If you dated a masseuse, I swear I won't get angry, so long as you keep doing that.'

'Nothing so exciting,' I replied. 'I just have a knack. So, what's on your mind?'

'Eh. Students,' she sighed. 'Just when I think I might actually be reaching some of them, they relieve me of that illusion. Nobody's in class to learn things. It's about checking a box for a course requirement, or an easy boost to the GPA or that they're stalking a fellow student. I'm almost no longer horrified when one of them asks if I could please not write in cursive on the board, because they can't read it. I've come to terms with that kind of thing.'

I kept working on her neck, slow and gentle.

'And, you know,' she continued, 'I'm just starting to get cynical enough that it doesn't bother me anymore. I just tell myself that they're young, they're mostly from well off families, they don't know much about life yet. It's extended high school.'

'So what happened today?' I asked, kneading her shoulders.

'Clueless entitled nineteen year olds, them I'm used to. I didn't expect that level of delusion from parents.' She shook her head. 'I got a call from an irate father today. Says he's not paying forty grand a year so his unique special snowflake of a son can get a C.'

I laughed. 'You point out he may want to let Junior know he's not paying forty grand a year for the kid to get a C?'

'I know. It's like he bought a defective cell phone. Or like the transmission in his Audi is slipping and he expects me to make it right.'

'Well, I'm sure he's not the first important man to expect things to be handed to his sons,' I said.

'He's an entitled yuppie douchebag,' she agreed.

'A species that thrives in temperate suburban climates.'

'How do you do it?' She turned her head to look at me. 'You must see stupidity and repeat customers all the time.'

'Yep. I don't want to brag, but I'm on a first-name basis with half the drunks and addicts in the Greater Philips Mills area.'

'Doesn't it ever frustrate you?'

I shrugged. 'Not really. You need to want to do it. The pay's lousy. It has to be its own reward.'

'The tragedy and stupidity don't wear you down? How do you keep from smacking them or cutting your wrists?'

'A lot of medics burn out,' I admitted. 'I don't feel that coming any time soon. I mean, you can't focus on the bad outcomes. People die, people get hurt. You can't save everybody, and you certainly can't help people who won't be saved. Once in a great while a call does bother me. If it's kids or when you watch a patient you've gotten to know slowly fall apart. Mostly I look at it like dinner theater.'

'Dinner theater?'

'Seriously. Where else can you get called out by the cops to evaluate the injuries of the John and the she-male hooker who got into a broken bottle fight over the quality of the crack tendered as payment? And get paid for it!'

She laughed. 'OK, but what about the drunks and addicts? You don't think it's futile, when they're just going to overdose again?'

'You can't think of it that way. We can enjoy a great meal right? But we're going to be hungry again in the morning. That doesn't make the meal futile, or diminish it in any way. It's never futile to alleviate suffering, even temporarily.'

'You make it sound noble.'

'Only by accident. I think of it as being in the moment. Life is fleeting. Enjoy what you have while you have it. Don't just eat, suck the marrow and lick your fingers.'

I rubbed a bit harder with my thumbs, loosening a cramped muscle. She groaned and hung her head. I ran my fingertips up her neck, through her hair, massaging her scalp. I leaned in and kissed the back of her neck, still flushed and warm from the massage. She sighed and leaned back against me.

'I'll give you no more than an hour to knock that off,' she threatened.

'Or what?' I breathed between kisses.

'I shall have to ravish you, kidnap you and force you to spend your days slaving in my kitchen and bedroom.' She twisted around, wrapping her arms and legs around me and kissing me. 'Now, your first order is to carry me to my bed. I wish to learn more of this marrow sucking, finger-licking approach to life.'

'As you wish,' I replied. I was always capable of following orders. Provided they were what I wanted to do anyway.

I was gentler and slower this time. I could tell she was still tired and wanted to relax, not try and wake the neighbors. I took my time, paid attention to her cues, prolonging and luxuriating in the moment. The first night, we'd both been like people stumbling onto an oasis after starving in the wilderness. This time I savored her like dessert.

Hunger of a more mundane sort eventually got us out of bed and dressed. We ordered food from Giovanni's, a better-than-average Italian takeout joint, and settled on the couch. I got us two new beers to replace the ones that had gone warm and flat while we were in the bedroom.

'I never seem to finish my beer around you.' She smiled.

'I know,' I said. 'I try to do the gentlemanly thing and get you drunk before taking advantage of you, but you keep dragging me into the sack before I can.'

'Yeah,' she said, 'I'm too slutty to be a good tramp. It's really embarrassing.'

After our food arrived, we settled down and she turned on the TV.

'So, what are we watching?'

'A romantic comedy,' she replied, hitting a button on the remote.

I resigned myself to sit through whatever was coming. Anything would be bearable so long as I had this beautiful woman beside me and a good dinner in front of me. I sat up suddenly once the film started.

'*The Three Musketeers!*' I exclaimed. 'The good version!'

'Of course it's the good version. My degree is in literature, you know,' she replied. 'Plus, Richard Chamberlain was gorgeous back then.'

I put my arm around her and smiled. 'I think I could adjust to the life of your kitchen and bedroom slave.'

Chapter 15

I WALKED INTO THE AMBULANCE BASE, dropped my bag in the day room and headed out to the garage. On the way through the kitchen, I noticed the deep utility sink full of assorted debris. The whiteboard where the daily assignments were written had been taken off the wall and put there, as had one of the old, unreliable portable radios. I shrugged and continued out to the truck.

Pete was standing by the open side door, going through the checklist, a styrofoam cup of coffee in his hand.

'Morning,' I said.

'Hey,' he muttered. 'How's it hangin'?'

'Listing to starboard. What's up with the slop sink?'

He chuckled. 'Oh, that. Marty got a hair across his ass about people leaving dishes in the sink. I guess he wants us to wash up before running out the door when we get a call or something. He posted a memo saying "Anything found in the sink after five PM will be thrown out". I threw the chore board in, Nique got fed up when P20's portable wouldn't hold a charge and tossed that in. We tried to wrestle Burton in, but he's a scrappy little fucker.'

I laughed. 'Think I can drive Ambulance 18 into the sink?'

'Good idea,' he said. 'If the tranny doesn't drop out halfway there.' He took a sip of his coffee, made a face. 'Jesus, is Dunk's trying to hire the dumbest employees they can find or does it just happen? No fucking sugar.' He opened the drug box, rummaged around and came out with a prefilled syringe of dextrose solution. He popped the cap off, injected about ten cc into his coffee cup, then tossed the syringe into the trash. 'Thank God D50 isn't a controlled substance.'

'That'd stop you?'

'Nah, but I'd need you to perjure yourself as a witness in the drug log.'

'Let's get this checksheet done and get out of here before the boss gets in,' I said. 'Then I'm gonna go get a decent cup of coffee.'

'Where you gonna do that in this town? Half the employees at Dunkin Donuts don't speak enough English to understand "cream and sugar".'

'*Yo quiero un café medio con crema y dos azucares,*' I replied. 'If they still don't get it, just talk really loud.'

'See, I knew that worked.'

'Anyway, let's hit the Korean doughnut shop.'

'What the hell do gooks know about doughnuts?'

I shrugged. 'Dunno where they picked it up, but the coffee is good and they put Dunk's pastry to shame. I'm sure they still use lard in the dough.'

'Whatever you say.'

'And it's convenient to Park Street, for all your heroin and crack cocaine needs.'

'One-stop shopping for the discriminating addict?' asked Pete.

'Pretty much.'

We drove over and I bought a coffee and a raspberry turnover with a flaky, dense, buttery crust that would harden an artery at ten paces. I pulled out of the parking lot of the doughnut shop and raised my coffee to my lips when the radio squawked.

'P20, respond to 135 Overlook Heights for the possible sudden. PD is responding.'

'Possible sudden,' mused Pete. 'That mean it might be a gradual?'

For reasons beyond my humble understanding, a patient found in cardiac arrest was often dispatched to us as a "sudden death" or "sudden".

'20. Responding.' I flipped the lights on and set off toward the address. Overlook Heights was a wooded hill sitting above a curve of the Merrimack River. It was where the mill owners built their homes back when the city was planned. As promised, it had offered a sweeping vista of the bustling, thriving immigrant city that the textile industry built. Now it offered a sweeping vista of the abandoned brick mill buildings, leaning three deckers, hourly-rate rooming houses, low-income housing projects and the shiny, tricked-out sports cars that the heroin industry built.

We pulled up in front of a nicely renovated old Victorian house, two SUVs in the driveway, and even under a foot of snow I could see more than six months of my rent's worth of money sunk into landscaping.

The engine crew was leaning on the truck, laughing with the two cops. Even with my too-often-justified dim view of their clinical skills, I figured that meant the patient was beyond any urgency.

'Hey, guys,' Pete said as he ambled up. 'What've we got?'

The assembled crew traded winks and snickers. One of the police officers beckoned us aside. I knew him from doing some calls together. Tony Angelo, promoted to detective as far as I remembered.

'Hi guys,' he said quietly when we were away from the group. 'OK, this guy basically hung himself. Accidentally. While… well… you know. The wife is horrified and in denial. I kept the Bad News Bears out here. You guys just need to go in, confirm he's dead and bang out a quick report for the ME.'

'I think we can handle that.'

'And, please, when you see him, keep it professional. For the wife, OK?'

'You know, Tony,' Pete said, 'you're insulting me. When have I ever been anything but professional?'

Tony shook his head. 'Just do your thing, man.'

The interior of the house was gorgeous. *Better Homes and Gardens* cover story gorgeous. Hardwood floors, refinished molding around all the doors and windows, a kitchen I'd stab a guy for, set up with all new stainless steel appliances, pans better than what they use at your favorite restaurant hanging from a rack over the island. The whole place was a story of new hedge-fund money moving in to take advantage of low property prices. The comparative bargain of the most expensive neighborhood in a cheap town. The robber barons of the twenty-first century squatting in the palaces of the robber barons of the nineteenth.

The grieving widow could have been on a magazine herself. Probably early forties, but holding age back with a bulwark of cosmetics, surgery and personal training routines. She was dressed impeccably. I don't follow fashion, but looking at her, I didn't have to.

The detective led us up the stairs, through a tastefully decorated bedroom, through a small doorway into a crawlspace to the attic. There we found our patient.

He was in his mid-forties, in good shape, well groomed, stark naked, and may have been considered handsome if not for the fact that he'd been hanging from a rafter for the past few hours. A leather collar was around his neck, attached to a line which ran over a pulley fastened to a rafter. The loose end of the rope lay slack near his right hand. A pillow was on the floor in front of him; beside him was a glass of wine and a bottle of lotion.

This didn't look much like a suicide to me. He hadn't stepped off a chair or anything so dramatic. He was on his knees, sagged against the cinched rope. A close look at the set-up showed that the rope had slipped off the pulley and snagged. It looked as though he'd indulged in a little autoerotic asphyxiation, blacked out, let go of the rope, expecting to slump harmlessly onto the pillow—and the safety mechanism failed him.

'The wife says she was out of town last night,' said the detective. 'Her story checks out. Looks like he took advantage of having the house to himself. Glass of wine, head to the secret love dungeon for some relaxation…'

'I guess Whitney Houston was wrong,' said Pete quietly.

'What do you mean?' I asked.

'Clearly, learning to love yourself isn't the greatest love of all.'

While Pete finished his paperwork, I chatted with the cop. 'How'd you get pulled into this one? I thought you were on Graffiti Patrol.'

He shook his head. 'The guy's wife's in total denial. Called it in as an execution, so dispatch kicked it to the Gang Task Force. There's a theory that the Russian Mob is trying to move into town.'

'Really?' I asked. 'Why does anybody think they're moving in here?'

He shrugged. 'Plenty of heroin comes through here. Plenty of cars get stolen and chopped. There's money to be made. It may be nothing, but somebody's been muscling a few dealers. White guys, which is rare enough. Sounds like Russians, from the descriptions, but how a Puerto Rican tells a Russian from a Swede I don't know. Like when the Korean doughnut shop opened and I was getting tips about Cambodian gangs moving in. Shit, racism's bad enough without getting your minorities wrong.'

A group of Russian sounding thugs moving in was the last thing I wanted to hear.

'So,' I angled, 'any solid evidence?'

'Nah,' he replied. 'Nothing I'd call definitive. Like I said, some Caucasian hoods have been moving on the small dealers. And there was a home invasion. Description from the neighbors was white guys speaking "probably Russian", but who knows?'

'Home invasion? I didn't hear anything about it? Anybody hurt?'

'Not really. I think the guys busted into the wrong apartment. Kicked in the door, tossed the place, tried to scare some info out of the tenants, but looks like they figured they didn't know anything pretty quick. Family was just some Vietnamese immigrants, barely spoke English, these white guys break in and start screaming "Where is he?" kinda thing. Even a dumb thug must've realized his info was bad when Mama-san can't understand his question, let alone answer it.'

I felt a sinking sensation in the pit of my stomach. 'Where was this?'

'That's the thing. The apartment building on the corner of Hawley Street. The big drug trade is on Holly Street. Guys must've gone to the wrong side of town.'

'Sounds like,' I agreed. 'Nice to know we're not the only ones who drive to the wrong street all the time.'

The feeling in my stomach got worse. I used to live in that building. In fact, that was still the address on my paychecks because, regardless of the fact that I'd submitted the paperwork three times, the glorious HR department at FirstLine persisted in keeping the old one on file. Since my money was directly deposited and I picked up the stub at work every week, I gave up caring that they had the wrong address.

For the first time ever, I felt relief that I worked for a company that couldn't tie its own metaphorical shoes.

On the other hand, my secret admirers had graduated from surveying the homeless to kicking in doors, and somehow gotten into my records, even if they were out-of-date records. I didn't like the chances that I'd be as lucky next time. They were smart enough to get into the records, and they must have gotten my name right somehow.

My less admirable voice pointed out that this might be a good time to disappear. I tried to think of a good counterargument, because I really didn't want to leave, but that voice is usually right, as well as craven. My history of grievous bodily injury is pretty much directly related to how often I ignore that voice. Right at that moment, the voice was pointing out a lesson I learned repeatedly during my many years in uniform: when the incoming rounds start landing too close, it's a good idea to find someplace else to be.

Leaving wouldn't be that difficult, physically at least. I'd made preparations against the need for a quick exit. A locker at the train station two towns over held a small stash of emergency cash and a set of documents that would let me establish a new life and get a job under a new name. I could be gone tomorrow, said the little voice, and start fresh anywhere. Seattle, the voice offered, was supposed to be a nice town.

As we drove away from the house, leaving the deceased for the Medical Examiner, Pete kept up the expected chatter about the situation—which, I had to admit, was one for the books.

'So,' he wondered aloud, 'do you think you can sue the hardware store if your home masturbation equipment fails and kills a loved one? How do you think they test that kind of thing for safety?'

'Why?' I forced myself to join in. 'You looking for a second job?'

He chuckled at that. It was rare that I got him with a one-liner. He leaned back in the seat, pulled his cap over his eyes and drifted off. Within two blocks he was snoring. I envied him. I never could get to sleep in the seat of a truck.

I sipped at my coffee as I drove and tried to think. Did I want to run? Well, no. Was it really that dangerous? I mean, I had survived worse. Although *worse* included crawling back to the perimeter on Guadalcanal with half a dozen bayonet wounds, and did I really want to go through that kind of thing again?

What was worth sticking around for? Well, I liked my job, I had some good friends here, I had a guilty affection for this town, and I'd just met a girl.

Was that it? Was this real love?

I enjoyed her company, we laughed, the sex was great. That was half of any relationship, as far as I was concerned. And when I held her or looked in her eyes, I felt safe and warm and happy, and that had to be the other half.

Alright, so maybe it wouldn't last, but nothing ever does, and what point is staying alive if you don't get to enjoy life?

My survival instinct tried to argue that there would be other cities and friends and jobs and women, the world was full of all those things, but it was only half-hearted. Being cynical, my survival instinct knows when to give up a hopeless fight.

'Hey, man,' Pete said suddenly, blinking the sleep from his eyes, 'you doing anything tomorrow?'

'I didn't think you swung that way.'

'A bunch of us are going to the Harp...' He ignored me. 'Drink some beers, shoot some pool. Bring the new boyfriend,' he smirked. 'Or don't, if you're looking to play the field.'

I thought for a moment. I could use some relaxation. I should be working on figuring out who my stalkers were, but since I couldn't think of my next step, I may as well clear my head. 'Sounds like a plan. Who's coming?'

'Nique and the ball and chain, Tina, and Katie the multiply pierced.'

'Is Katie bringing the boyfriend of the moment? And if so, is he a cop or a fireman?' Katie was a good EMT, if you could keep her from flirting too much on scene. She had a somewhat deserved reputation for sleeping with anybody in uniform. Not that it made her a bad person.

'As far as I know, she's single at the moment.'

'Does Katie shoot pool?' I wondered.

'Who gives a shit? I just invited her so I can see her bend over the table. You think she's got any piercings below the neck?'

That was a subject of speculation and debate among many of the medics we worked with. Besides her ears, she had a ring in her nose, her lip, her tongue and two in her left eyebrow for all to see. Rumors of others circulated.

'Couldn't say,' I replied. 'The answer's probably written in a stall in the bathroom of the police station.'

'Like cops are literate enough to write on walls,' he sneered. 'It'd be like looking at pornographic cave paintings.'

'The fire station?' I offered.

'You've seen them do a physical exam. They probably can't name half the places she's pierced.'

'Good point.'

'Maybe I'll just bring some refrigerator magnets along and throw them at her. See where they stick.'

'So much respect for a colleague.' I smiled.

'I respect her plenty,' he replied. 'I just want to respectfully put my cock in her mouth.'

'Fair enough,' I observed.

'I want to see what that pierced tongue is worth,' he clarified. 'You ever get a blow job from somebody with a tongue stud?'

I grinned. 'No, but I dated a girl who used to call me Tongue Stud.'

'Say goodnight, Gracie,' he laughed. 'Seriously, you do that?'

'Live for it. I'll admit the first people to try it must have been the world's bravest couple, but yeah. Best idea since the wheel. You mean you don't?'

'Strictly quid pro quo,' he replied. 'I feel it just perpetuates the myth of the female orgasm.'

'Ya know,' I said, 'sometimes I wish I had a sister just so I could not let her date you.'

Chapter 16

I CALLED SARAH'S NUMBER.
'Hello?'
'Hi. Can Sarah come out and play tonight?'
'Who's asking?' she inquired.
'Her sexy new boyfriend.'
'Could you be more specific?'
'Ouch,' I said, as she laughed on the other end of the line. 'Well, I was hoping I could see you tonight, but now I'm not sure.'
'Tonight's not good anyway,' she replied. 'I have a lesson plan to work out, and an early class tomorrow. Don't you know it's a school night?'
'It's been a while since I paid attention to school days,' I admitted. 'Sure you can't ditch and play hooky?'
'Sorry,' she said. 'I'm a good girl.'
'Hmm. I may have a wrong number. I'm looking for Sarah Deyermond.'
She laughed. 'If you're free tomorrow, I'm off work after one. You can try to corrupt me then.'
'It's a date.'
'Oh, by the way, I may have something for you.'
'Yeah?' I asked.
'Well, that, obviously, but I may have a lead on your inscription.'
'Great,' I replied, surprised. 'How'd you find anything?'
'The wonder of the Internet. One of the linguist forums.'
'Sounds too wild for me. You try to save some of that energy for tomorrow.'
'I'll do my best,' she laughed. 'Have fun tonight. I'll call you tomorrow.'
'I shall count the minutes,' I replied. 'Take care.'
'You too.'

Out Of Nowhere

* * * *

The small EMS group descended on the Harp at about seven o'clock that evening. There was myself, Pete, Monique and her fiancé Joe, who was as unrealistically attractive as she was, tall, dark, and laconic with a slow, easy smile. He was also secure enough that he could be engaged to a woman as hot as Nique without becoming a jealous asshole. The aforementioned Katie was there, low slung jeans and a short top displaying yet another piercing, no doubt enabling Pete to check off a mental box labeled "navel". Rounding out the group was Tina Ferrel, a short, bubbly EMT who was just starting Paramedic school. Her ready laugh hid a sharp mind, solid street smarts and intuitive rapport with patients. She would make a good medic.

We staked out a table, Pete racked the balls and we selected cues. I'd brought my own. I took it out and assembled it, enduring ribbing, hoots and accusations of being a hustler.

'Hey,' I said, 'I like pool. You can drink while you play, and it's usually played in bars filled with men who don't stand on ceremony and women of questionable virtue.'

'So what are you saying?' asked Tina.

'That virtue is overrated,' I replied, lining up a shot.

A waitress arrived and took our drink order. I ordered a Guinness. Pete ordered a Bud, since he claims it's easier to order smashed, and nothing makes a bartender shut you off faster than slurring the name of your drink. Katie ordered a Miller Lite, which told me her questionable taste wasn't limited to dating. Nique and Joe each ordered a Long Trail Ale, because they had impeccable taste and were disgustingly in synch, and Tina ordered a Margarita.

'No salt,' she added.

'A Margarita with no salt?' asked Pete, scandalized.

'I'm watching my blood pressure,' she shrugged.

That made me laugh just as I shot, sending the cue ball wide of my mark.

'Nice shot,' Tina remarked, stepping up to the table. 'I thought you were a hustler.'

'Watching your blood pressure?' I grinned.

'It's a silent killer,' she said, lining up her shot, 'often under-diagnosed in women.'

'And that wasn't an attempt to distract me?'

'I thought you were a paramedic with nerves of steel. Sink a tube though an airway full of blood and broken teeth in a speeding ambulance bouncing over a street full of potholes.' She sank a ball, walked around the table and picked her next shot. 'At least that's how we humble EMTs look up to you. Maybe I was wrong.'

'I thought you were pretty smart, but now I find out you look up to paramedics.'

The waitress returned with our drinks. I paid for this round, adding a generous tip and a smile.

As I turned back to the table, reverently taking my first sip, I noticed Nique looking at me.

'What?'

'What is it with you and waitresses?'

'Pretty girls who bring you booze? What's not to like?'

She replied with an elegantly arched eyebrow.

'I'm on my best behavior,' I assured her. 'I'm just friendly out of instinct. It's pure reflex.'

The eyebrow remained where it was, but her lips twisted into her indulgent smile.

'My conduct will be unimpeachable.' I raised my hand. 'Honest.'

At that moment, Pete's phone rang.

'Yo!' he answered it. Suddenly his expression turned to shock. 'What? When?... She alright? Yeah, there's a bunch of us here...We'll head over.'

'What's up?' asked Nique. 'You look terrible.'

'That was Juan. They just picked up an assault victim. Chick got the shit beat out of her. Turns out it's that hot girl from admitting at the General. He says her face was so bruised and swollen he didn't recognize her right away.'

The assembled group uttered variations on 'Oh my God!' and 'That's terrible'. I just froze. This had to be connected to Doors.

Which meant it was my fault.

I sank half my pint in one long swallow. I needed it. Needed it more than my next breath, though my stomach wondered what it had done to deserve that.

'Tiffany,' I said. 'She's in the ER now?'

'Yeah,' Pete replied, grabbing his jacket. 'We should swing on by.'

She wasn't an EMT, but she was one of our own, in a way. We saw her almost every day in the course of getting patients registered. We saw pain and injuries and death routinely, and we got used to it. It just wasn't the same when it was somebody you knew.

We arrived at the ER, barging in through the ambulance entrance like usual. Juan was waiting, sitting by the EMS desk. 'She's in Special Care Four,' he said. 'Jane's her nurse. Just check before you go in.'

'How is she?' Nique asked with deep concern, her earlier disdain for Tiffany banished.

'She's in and out. Got hit on the head bad. They're just waiting for CT. Got a bunch of bruises on her face. Not much below the neck.'

'They see who did it?' asked Pete.

'Not really. She was walking to her car when this dude jumps her. Brian from security chased him off. Said the guy just vanished into thin air. He called 911 on his cell, since he didn't want to move her and carry her into the ER.'

'Vanished into thin air?' said Pete. 'Yeah, right, happens all the time. You mean Brian couldn't catch him 'cause he wasn't dressed like a doughnut.'

I walked toward the room. I caught Jane's eye on the way, gave a quick concerned look and pointed at the door. She nodded.

I pushed open the door and walked in. There was a tech checking the monitor but she recognized me and looked away quickly. I looked down at the form on the hospital stretcher. She was still on a backboard, the cervical collar on her neck. She was breathing on her own. Small, sobbing breaths through split lips crusted with blood. Her face was a swollen mass of bruises. There was an IV line in her left hand, and another up high in her forearm. Her right hand was hastily splinted, the once deft, graceful fingers reduced to purple sausages sticking out from the wrapping.

'Hey, you,' I said quietly, brushing a long curl, now stiff with dried blood, from her forehead. As I did, I felt her injuries, down to the small bleed in her brain that the CT scan would show whenever they got it, if the machine was up tonight and the tech was on the ball and the radiologist answered his pager. He probably would, and since she was a hospital employee, they'd go the extra mile; but I wasn't going to leave it to fate.

I rested my hand against her forehead, in a way that would look normal enough for a distraught friend if somebody walked in, and let the energy flow. I sealed the bleed, and sent some energy to quiet the nerves, easing her pain a bit. I gave the tissues a nudge in the direction of healing, willing the swelling to go down, the damage to start to reverse. I couldn't do much more without being obvious, and it pained me to hold back.

Still, I stopped the life-threatening issue and eased the rest. That was as much as I could do in safety. Maybe I could visit her later and keep an eye on her, make sure she recovered properly.

It was a hollow comfort. I felt like a coward because I was being one, withholding healing to keep myself safe.

Withholding healing for injuries she got because she did me a favour.

I shook with frustration. I could fix all of this. But if she got up from the cot, walked out to the desk with a smile and signed herself out, Bad Things would happen. A dozen people knew she was hurt. There were x-rays. Indisputable evidence. There could be no explaining a miraculous recovery, and people would talk and wonder and start looking around. And I would have to leave.

For good.

I took a deep breath. I'd done what I could, I forced myself to believe, and I'd do more when it was safe to. But first, I had to eliminate a threat.

How the hell had they tracked this back to Tiffany, anyway? I wondered. *The demographic sheet she gave me had very little info and that had run me to a dead end...*

It had *trapped* info. Not just bad info, trapped info.

I saw it all now. The info he gave out would be just a bit wrong, so he couldn't be tracked, but uniquely wrong, so all he had to do was watch the false address or phone for a hit, and if it wasn't from the hospital billing department or an insurance company, he'd know somebody was after him, and where they'd gotten the lead. We used to leave trapped info all the time when I was doing recon. It helped us find out which locals were in bed with the enemy. You tell each suspected leak a slightly different thing, and see what the enemy act on, then you know your informant.

And we all knew what happened to informants in the Old Country.

So, when I went online to check out his info, he'd found out about it and tracked it back and...

Out Of Nowhere

Online?
Sarah was surfing linguistics sites looking for a language.
A language used by brutal men.
And she said she'd found a lead.
I turned and ran from the room.

Chapter 17

I THREW MY CAR INTO GEAR and fumbled my cell phone out of my jacket pocket, tearing out of the parking lot as I punched in Sarah's number.

Come on, come on, I pleaded as it rang twice. Then it went to machine.

'Fuck!' I yelled and hung up before the beep. Sarah didn't screen. She was brighter than I was, and knew how to use the caller ID. She was out, or somebody was there. If somebody was there, the last thing that would help would be my voice on the machine.

I stomped on the gas.

In a few minutes, I pulled into the apartment complex, threw the shifter into park and reached into the back seat. I had no time to go get a real weapon, but I had my cue. I opened the case and took the heavy half of the disassembled cue, sliding it up my right sleeve, then ran to the door.

I stopped, looking at the row of doorbells in between the sets of big glass doors. I didn't want to ring Sarah's, in case they were there now, but I had to get in. I could use my cue as an Irish lockpick, which would have the added bonus of sounding an alarm and bringing the police, but it might also make anyone there panic and do something drastic. I'd just seen their version of drastic.

And if I was wrong and smashed my way in, I might wind up explaining things to the boys in blue myself.

I calmed down, chose a button other than hers and pressed.

'Hello?' came the voice.

'Ambulance,' I replied.

'I didn't call for the ambulance,' the voice said.

'No ma'am, but your neighbor did, and she's fallen and can't get to the buzzer. Could you buzz us in?'

'Oh, yes, right away.' The door buzzed and I was through it in a heartbeat.

'Thank you,' I said into the intercom, just to maintain my ruse.

'Who are you here for?' asked the voice. 'Is it Mrs O'Leary?'

'Sorry, ma'am, patient confidentiality.' I bolted away, leaving the intercom babbling questions.

I pushed the elevator button, waited impatiently for a three second eternity, then sprinted to the stairs. I sprang up two at a time and grabbed the handle of the door on the third floor when some ancient instinct made me stop.

It was a cold, calm voice cutting through my rage and fear like a knife. While most of my brain screamed to hurry, to think what might be happening in that apartment, the clear, rational, cynical voice that had saved me before, preserved me through too many campaigns to ignore, told me to wait, to slow down and do some recon.

It's not a very noble part of my mind, but it's hard to argue with.

I slowly pushed the door open a crack and peered down the hallway.

A burly guy in a black trench and a crew cut stood at parade rest in front of Sarah's door, one hand inside his coat, keeping watch.

His attention was on the elevator doors because, really, who takes the stairs anymore?

I slipped my shoes off, stuffed them inside my jacket and quietly stalked down the hall, thanking the landlord for the ugly but functional industrial carpeting. Now that the enemy was in sight, I felt the surge of adrenaline. I let the pool cue slide into my hand as I accelerated over the last few yards, just like before we crashed into Cope's line at Prestonpans.

He must have heard something, because he began to turn at the last minute, pulling something from his coat, but I was already on him. Driven by the energy of my charge as well as all the anger and panic boiling inside me, the cue cracked across his temple and he fell to the floor, arms and legs twitching.

I reached down to his nerveless fingers, expecting a gun. What I found was another knife, twin to the one I took from the man back outside Dugan's. I shifted the cue to my left hand and took the knife in my right.

The door was slightly ajar, closed on a rumpled welcome mat.

Hearing sounds of violence within, I pushed it open.

The apartment was a wreck. The curio cabinet lay on the floor, crockery scattered in shards, pictures knocked off the walls. I took a second to slip my shoes back on before crossing.

Maybe a hero wouldn't have wasted time on that, but then a hero wouldn't mind fighting on lacerated soles.

I heard raised voices in the back. I moved in as fast and quietly as I could, the knife in my fist and murder in my heart. I rounded a corner and saw the broad back of another muscle blocking the bedroom doorway. He had his fist balled up and barked an order in that same guttural, almost-Slavic dialect to someone I couldn't see. I heard pained, frightened sobs beyond.

'I will not ask you this again,' he said with more accuracy than he realized.

Dropping the cue, I stepped behind him, yanked his head back and rammed the point of the knife into the side of his neck, then ripped it out the front in a slashing sweep that severed windpipe and blood vessels and turned him into a Hired Thug Pez Dispenser.

That, kiddies, is how you cut a throat. Brutal, perhaps, but if you have an issue with brutal, you have no business cutting throats.

I shoved his body aside. As it fell, jerking and kicking and leaking, I looked into the room and saw Sarah slumped to her knees on the floor, bruised and battered, one eye wide in shock above her tear-streaked cheeks, the other a slit in a bulging purple bruise. Another heavy held her up by the arms.

The thug looked at me, his eyes widened and the color drained from his face. He looked as though he were peering into the abyss, staring into the eyes of the Grim Reaper.

Again, totally accurate.

The man pushed Sarah towards me, drew his own dagger and lunged at me, staking his hopes for survival on a single vicious thrust. I dodged sideways, deflecting his attack with a swipe that cut open the inside of his right forearm. I grabbed his injured knife hand and thrust my own blade at him. He caught my wrist and we lurched into the dining room, spinning around one another. He tried to twist my wrist, but I snapped my head forward, butting him in the face. He staggered back into the table. I drove forward, my legs churning as the table slid scraping along the floor and smashed into the wall. I brought a knee up between his legs, wrenched my hand free of his grasp and then slammed the knife into his body again and again. No finesse, no technique, just white-hot rage. I stabbed until his struggles stopped and he went limp. I released his body and let it fall, first to the table in a crash of plates, then to the floor with a dull thump.

I was on my haunches beside Sarah by the time he hit the floor.

She looked bad.

One eye was already swollen shut, her lips split and bleeding. She breathed in short, painful gasps and held an arm across her side.

'Oh, God,' she sobbed.

'Shh.' I held her gently, letting my senses sink in, looking for the source of the pain. 'It's OK. They're gone.' I winced as I catalogued her injuries. Orbital fracture, damage to the globe of the eye, loosened teeth, cracked ribs, lacerated liver, broken wrist. What kind of sick fuck could do this to a woman?

A dead one, I reminded myself. *That's what kind.*

'It's OK,' I repeated. 'You're gonna be fine.'

'Don't lie to me,' she whispered. 'I know it's bad. I feel things broken inside. I might not make it, that's true, isn't it?'

'No,' I said simply. 'It's not.'

I sent messages to the nerves first, to quiet the pain, then I focused on the liver, the most immediately life-threatening injury. I coaxed the tissues to knit, the vessels to stop leaking. I repaired the cheekbone and eye next, then the teeth, lips and wrist. I felt her stiffen as she realized something was happening far beyond her understanding, but I held her close, whispering the nonsense sounds you make when comforting a spooked horse or a crying infant, and kept pouring healing energy in.

I kept on until she was as good as new, physically at least. Better, even. She'd been brutally beaten because of me; if she decided to look for a pitchfork when I finished, so be it. I was through hiding.

She pulled back a bit, but didn't break away.

'My God,' she said. 'Who are you?'

'Just a man. With a talent, but a man just the same.'

'No.' She shook her head, looked around at the carnage, touched the soft, whole flesh below her eye. 'I don't know what you are, but you just healed me. Instantly healed horrible, probably permanent injuries. After you brutally killed two men.'

'Three. There was a lookout in the hallway. And they deserved it. Believe me.'

'Who are they? Why are they looking for you?'

'I swear to you, I don't know,' I said earnestly. 'I have no idea what they want. I had no idea you were in danger, really.'

She nodded. 'But how do you... do...?'

'I don't know. Well, I know *how*, I don't know why I can do it. Just that I can. I couldn't tell anyone; people wouldn't understand.'

'You could do so much!'

I shook my head. 'Been there, tried that. People fear what they don't understand. Then they lash out at what they fear. I've seen it.' I gestured at the room. 'Now you've seen it.'

I gently took her shoulders, looked into her eyes. 'We need to go. Now. I completely understand if you don't feel safe with me, if you don't feel right being around me, but let me get you away from here. I'll get you to the airport, the train station, wherever. You aren't safe here, and I couldn't bear the thought of these filth finding you again.'

She nodded. 'I'll throw some things in a bag. I can be ready in five minutes.'

'Good girl. Where can I take you?'

'Your place.'

While that's what I most hoped to hear, I shook my head. 'That's probably not a good idea. They'll be looking.'

'They don't know where you live,' she said, grabbing a gym bag and transferring clothes from her dresser.

'How do you know that?'

She stopped packing. The biggest, prettiest, greenest eyes I'd seen in a thousand years peered into mine, just a suggestion of tears welling up.

'Because I wouldn't tell them, no matter how much they hit me.'

Chapter 18

A QUICK SEARCH OF THE BODIES while she was packing didn't yield much. I dragged the first man out of the hallway, because one simply doesn't leave corpses in a hallway in North Andover. I pocketed drivers' licenses and what looked like company IDs—badges with a photo and a magnetic strip—from each man. The one whose throat I'd cut had a folded piece of notepaper in his pocket with Sarah's address on it. The handwriting looked European; they write some numbers very differently across the Atlantic. Ones and sevens are the big giveaways.

Which all qualified as interesting, but not terribly helpful. I wiped down the handle of the knife I'd used but left it on scene. If somebody found it on me later and tied traces of blood to the victims, that would be hard to explain.

I knew my prints were all over the apartment; nothing I could do about that. And, oh God, when had she last changed her sheets?

So, I could be placed in the apartment. Not too much trouble there; enough people knew we were dating. I just had to make sure I couldn't be tied to the dead bodies.

I had blood on my shirt and jacket. A quick look in the mirror showed a splash of it on my cheek. That would be a real conversation starter if I got pulled over for a burned out tail light on the way back to my apartment.

Leaving my bloody clothes here would be like signing a confession. I went into the kitchen, washed the blood from my hands and face and found a trash bag. I took off my bloodstained jacket and shirt and stuffed them inside. I'd get rid of them once I was far enough from the scene of the crime. How much could the police tell if you washed your clothes? I hadn't needed to cover up a crime in a long time, and technology had changed. Shouldn't let myself get rusty like that. Sloppy.

Out Of Nowhere

I borrowed an oversized sweatshirt from Sarah, which fit, more or less, and would draw less attention than walking out in January in my t-shirt. Well, sober in January wearing just a t-shirt.

We drove to my apartment in silence. I took a roundabout route, keeping an eye on the rearview mirror, trying to see if anyone was following. It's hard to follow someone who's looking for a tail. Every turn you take, the pursuer has to either take it, or risk losing sight of you. If the same car follows you through enough random turns, heading nowhere, then you're being followed. It could be done if they had enough cars and good communications, but I doubted that was happening here. One car waiting for the hit team, seeing the two of us leave could follow us and call for help, though.

My thoughts were a chaotic whirl. I still didn't know what I was going to do. I'd never shown myself to someone like this. Not on purpose, at least. I was wrestling with guilt for putting Tiffany and, especially, Sarah at risk, anger at those who'd hurt them and fear of what they would try next.

Sarah was quiet. I couldn't speak to what was going through her mind, but I didn't imagine she was used to days like this. I was grateful that she seemed to be holding up at all.

After "how can I survive this mess?" the big question was whether I could salvage any relationship even if I could keep her safe. I hadn't been completely forthright with her, and even if my reasons had been very good, I'd not known many women to tolerate that, even when what I held back didn't get them beaten up.

We took the stairs, just as a paranoid precaution, and I went up three steps ahead of her. Nobody was standing outside my door, and the lock didn't seem to have been tampered with. So far, my adversaries had worked with all the subtlety of a bat with a nail in it, but I didn't want to bet our lives that they couldn't learn.

Plus, who knew, I might just have killed all the dumb ones.

We walked into my apartment. Sarah dropped her bag on the couch and blew out a deep breath. 'I need a drink,' she said.

I wordlessly took a bottle from the cabinet and sloshed a few fingers into two glasses. She drained hers in one long swallow and handed the glass back. I refilled it and took a healthy sip of my own.

I could feel the pounding of hooves, see the sabre points getting more distinct. Worse than a squadron of Cuirassiers, the Talk was bearing down on me.

And, to stretch a metaphor, I would have only one chance to defend myself, and if I flinched or mistimed my shot, it was over.

'Alright,' she said. 'I know we haven't known one another very long, and I can see why this isn't a first date kind of secret, but I need to know some more about you. And about this situation.'

I bought time with a sip of whisky. 'It's hard to know where to start. I can heal people. I've been able to as long as I can remember. But people get nervous about things they don't understand, so I keep it quiet. I took a medic job because it lets me do what I do without drawing attention. I don't know who these guys are, or why they're after me. As far as I know, this is a very recent development.'

'That's not gonna do it,' she said. 'Who are you? Who the fuck are you?'

I heard a catch in her voice and I saw tears in her eyes.

'I'm just a paramedic—' I began.

'Bullshit!' she said, then sniffed and turned away angrily, wiping her eyes. 'This isn't normal, Sean. I've dated guys and found out about ex-girlfriends and criminal records and cheating, but not fucking supernatural powers. I'm not naïve; I know you have a past. Hell, everyone has a past, but your past clearly has more knives in it than I'm comfortable with. Jesus! I can't even believe I'm having this conversation.'

'I know this is hard to wrap your head around,' I said. 'It's complicated. Please hear me out.'

'You've got one shot. God knows why the hell I'm giving you that.' She paused, fighting back tears, and shook her head violently. 'No, that's not fair. I'm really falling for you. I want this to work so much. You'd think this would be a deal breaker, but I need to give you a chance. Or I wouldn't forgive myself.'

'Sarah, I want to explain.'

'And I want to believe you. God, how I want to believe you. But… Jesus Christ. I mean, I just got *beaten*. And then you killed people. Like it was something you'd done before. Done enough to get good at. And how the hell did you… fix… everything?'

'It's hard to explain.'

'Try,' she said, her eyes cold now and deadly serious. 'Try really, really hard.'

I took a drink to buy time, to fight down my urge to babble. To focus my thoughts. This wasn't a conversation I'd had with... well, anyone.

'Well?'

'I'm trying to think where to begin.'

'How about at the beginning?'

'That's the part I don't know,' I replied. 'For starters, I'm a lot older than I look.'

'How old?'

'Old enough to know better. I really don't know. I can remember back over centuries. When I said I liked Alexandre Dumas and Mark Twain, I meant it. They were both worth knowing, and always willing to buy their round. But I can't remember all the answers you deserve.'

She looked incredulous. 'Shall I start with what you've just said, or what you're not saying? How can you not remember? Did you hit your head? Wake up shipwrecked? What?'

'I don't think it's anything that romantic,' I replied. 'I just think there's a limit to how much you can stuff into long-term memory. Wait, listen.' I quickly pushed on as I saw suspicion creeping over her face. 'What do you remember about first grade? Probably your teacher's name, maybe your best friend, maybe who you sat next to. But what color was your bedroom when you were five? Did you have a favorite stuffed animal? Memories fade. The big events fade slower, but they do get fuzzy with time, right?'

'I guess.'

'Now, instead of twenty years, think about ten times that. I remember battles, lovers, beauty, joy and trauma. I can't remember my parents, or a childhood of any kind. I know I tried to do the village healer thing. I remember being happy at it, but needing to travel before anyone did the math on my age. I know I was driven out of a few places as a witch. I served as a soldier in a lot of places, since there's always hurts to heal and men come and go. I did that for ages, until I found EMS. The good parts of soldiering—without sleeping in muddy holes or hand-to-hand combat. Usually.'

'Have there been a lot of lovers?'

'Depends on what you consider a lot. By the standards of a rock star or professional athlete, hardly any. And I would ask the court to take the time into consideration. I'm human. Probably. I need companionship like anybody else. For obvious reasons, long-term relationships can be problematic.'

'So where do I fit on this list?'

There was no right answer. I've known enough women to know that. She was too smart to accept something like "none of them compare to you". I decided to take a shot at her sense of humor.

'Just ahead of Madame Dubarry. In a three-way tie with Lola Montez and Lady Emma Hamilton.' I smiled.

She laughed. A sound that made me happier than the skirl of approaching bagpipes drifting over the walls of Lucknow, or the roar of Corsairs flying in to strafe the Korean hillsides. 'Lord Nelson's mistress?'

'Yeah, but I used to sneak out on his blind side if he came in unexpectedly. He never caught on.'

'Good thinking,' she smiled, sniffing and wiping away a tear.

'One way you're different from all the others,' I said seriously. 'You are the only person I've told the whole truth.'

'You don't give this speech to all the girls?' she asked. A definite thaw. The bantering tone was back in her voice. 'Why only me?'

'You're smart, you're funny, you're beautiful. I haven't felt this way about anyone in as long as I can remember. I can talk to you. Plus, there's that thing you do with your tongue.'

'So,' she asked, the smile still there, but also a glint of steel in her expression. 'What happens from here? You vanish on me? Or string me along until I get wrinkly?'

'My hope, if you'll still have me, is to stay with you. To keep you by my side as long as you'll let me. I'd never have told you what I did if I didn't trust you and care about you. And unless I find a way to outsmart these guys, a long lifespan may stop being a problem.'

'And what about them? The ones with big knives and definite views on getting an answer?'

'All I know is I fixed a guy's ankle a while back. On the ambulance. He had a bad break, I repaired it so when he got to the ER it was just a bad sprain. He had the same accent as these guys. I thought it was strange because I couldn't place it, even though it was a bit familiar. He seemed suspicious, which is odd. Usually I get away with a lot pre-hospital, since nobody knows how bad an injury really is before the x-rays. That's one reason I like to work as a medic, not a doctor. Anyway, this guy started asking about me, and shortly after that, there was an attempt on me. That's how I picked up that knife and got the cut on my hand that you saw the day you met me. Since then it's been a competition to see which of us can learn about the other guy first.'

'How's that working out?'

'I think we're both pretty bad at it.' I shrugged. 'I'm just hitting dead ends, and the best they've managed is to kick in the door of a place I used to live, and beat up you and a girl from the hospital who gave me some info...' I froze. 'You said you had some leads on that inscription. Did you find something? Talk to somebody who knew something?'

'I got a reply on one of the ancient language forums online. I uploaded a scan of the copy you gave me, and some professor in Chicago replied and asked about it. Said he's seen similar stuff in old eastern European burial sites.'

'So he asked about where you found this inscription, what it was about, and so on.' I sighed. 'It was a trap. They must monitor any searches on their languages, or the info they give out, and then trace the leads back. They're looking for me, they know that the inscription you posted is from the knife I took in that first attack. Every time I look for them, I give away my position.'

Like a muzzle flash in the dark.

I turned to her, guilt twisting a dagger in my belly. 'I am so sorry. I had no idea this could put you in danger. I just thought you might recognize an alphabet, I never expected they'd come for you.'

She shrugged. 'It's OK. How could you guess? Traditionally, a bunch of ancient-language nerds sitting around in their carpet slippers sipping Earl Grey aren't known for sending teams of thugs with knives to torture people for information. The Tweed Ninjas are a closely guarded secret.'

'The best thing to do,' I thought aloud, pacing, 'is go to ground. I have some money and fake papers stashed. I can get you some IDs, we can be off the radar in a day. Then, we pick a new city—'

'I'm not running,' she said. Not defiantly. Just with absolute conviction.

'Sarah,' I pleaded, 'think about what these people are willing to do. I've seen how people react when they begin to think what I can do is a threat.'

'So have I,' she pointed out.

'And that is what I can't risk. No. I'm not going to have them work their way through my friends. I'm not putting people I care about at risk.'

'I'm staying here. I have a life.'

'I've had to pull up stakes before. It's not that bad. It's starting fresh. We can go anywhere. I've never gotten to Australia. You want to see Australia?'

'Sean, I'm not leaving. I like my job. My family is here. My friends. I've known you for a week. Now, you're good company, a good cook and there's that thing *you* do with *your* tongue, but I'm not running away. You want to stay here and deal with this, I'll be right by your side. You run, you run alone.'

I opened my mouth to argue, but saw a look in her eyes and realized there was no point. I'd seen that look on some of history's famous faces, generally followed by fixed bayonets and a period of stark terror. Wellington had worn that look at Waterloo, and MacArthur at Inchon. Of course, so had Bonnie Prince Charlie at Culloden and Travis at the Alamo, so I won't say I viewed it without some trepidation.

I took a deep breath, that little voice screaming at me to run, get out, move across the country, grow a beard, go to bartending school. I wrestled it down. I was going to stand my ground, for once. These people had hurt a woman I loved, and one who'd helped me out, and they wouldn't stop coming after my friends just because I went away.

I blew out a long breath. 'If you stay, then I stay.'

She nodded. 'That'll do.'

I held her then, gently, protectively. She squeezed me tightly, then kissed me with a fierce intensity. It was desperate, possessive, almost violent, like she needed to assert herself after all that had happened to her tonight, all the helplessness and confusion and fear.

I felt a surge of relief, a loosening of the knot in my gut. The buoyant exhilaration of a bullet dodged, a skirmish survived. Whatever I still had to face, at least Sarah wasn't leaving me. I crushed her against me and returned her kiss. Too much emotion and adrenaline still flowed through both of us, demanding an outlet.

We made it to the bedroom, but only just.

* * * *

Afterwards, on the tangled sheets, her head on my shoulder, I lay still for a long moment, drinking in the warm, comforting exhaustion. The fact that she wanted to stay with me blunted the fear, softened the edges of danger and doubt.

I couldn't explain why she meant so much to me. I just accepted it.

That begged the question: why did I mean enough to her that she was willing to face knives and fists and whatever else might be waiting? And not just in the abstract; she had actually felt the effects of that danger. She hadn't even passed comment on my extraordinary age. It would come, I was sure, but her capacity to just accept me was extraordinary.

'Hate to break the mood,' I said, 'but I have to ask why you seem to be taking all this in stride. Not that I'm complaining. But I didn't expect it.'

She was quiet for a moment. 'Because I finally want to have my cake and eat it too.'

I waited, content to enjoy the feel of her body against me as she marshaled her thoughts.

'My family is working-class Irish,' she said. 'Dad was a successful contractor. My relatives, and everyone in the neighborhood, were roofers, carpenters, plumbers, one or two cops and firemen. The boys, anyway. The girls worked until they got pregnant, then raised kids and volunteered at school. Nobody I grew up with had any vision or goal beyond the house in the burbs and seeing little Timmy play baseball. They lived for the beer after work and opening day at Fenway.'

She paused. 'I hate to sound so condescending, I really do. But I was the first one in my family to graduate college. I put myself through grad school, since none of them could see why anyone would waste money on more education when I should be finding a nice boy while I still had my looks. I got my PhD in 2004. You mention that year in my dad's house and he'll cry tears of joy because that's the year the Sox finally beat the Curse of the Bambino and won the World Series. I wanted to get out of that world so badly, to meet boys who had read something deeper than the sports pages of the *Herald* or the pledge on the back of a Rolling Rock bottle.'

I laughed at that.

'So I went to college. I met boys who could play the guitar and quote Byron. I was excited until I saw that their intellectualism was just a different kind of parochialism. They were only halfway men. Sure, the boys I knew from the old neighborhood spent too much time out drinking with Sully and Fitzy, punching each other in the arm and calling one another a "buncha quee-ahs", but even if they got hammered on a Thursday, they dragged themselves to work on Friday. They were never too sick or too hurt to do anything, and if they said they'd help you move a piano on Saturday, they showed up, hungover or not. The grad students could quote Marx and Engels and talk about the plight of the worker, but they had no idea who the worker was. They couldn't change out a light switch or check their oil or work a sixty-hour week. They were all for women's equality and empowerment, but they still wanted a relationship on their terms, not mine. They wanted to think and talk and profess theories about how the world should be, how people should be, but they didn't want to be those people. They were unreliable, unable to stand on their feet.'

'So then,' she kissed my neck, 'you walked into my office, swaggering like Douglas Fairbanks with a bag of swords over your shoulder, and swept me off my feet. And you were educated and well read, you could cook, you *listened* instead of just waiting for a chance to talk. And then, when I needed rescuing, you showed up, and you were strong and terrifying and savage without hesitation. Intellectual, sensitive, but reliable and... well... masculine, I suppose. So now, at last, I want to have my cake and eat it too.'

I squeezed her shoulder. All that was flattering, but frightening in its own way. 'That means a lot.' I kissed her. 'Don't worry, I'll get us out of this mess.'

'You sure you want to stick around?' she asked. 'You're risking more life than I am.'

'Life's what you make of it,' I said, as much to my inner voice as to her, 'and I've been pretty tough to kill so far. You're in? Even seeing what could happen?'

'I have faith in you,' she said. 'I saw you fight back there. You're really terrifying when you want to be.'

I felt a tightness in my chest. I didn't feel comfortable with so much faith placed in me. For all my military service, and some of it fairly decent service, I'd tried to avoid as much responsibility as possible. In fact, one of my most carefully honed skills was knowing when to get out of Dodge.

Sure, I survived the Alamo, but that was luck, a decent command of Spanish, a knack for fast talking and the foresight to stab an enemy about my height and steal his uniform jacket. The fact that it was pretty dark out, everybody's face was covered in soot from firing black powder muskets, and the Mexican army's love of big, conspicuous hats with wide, concealing bills all helped.

'You look tense,' she said. 'Grab a shower, I'll give you a backrub and we'll figure out our next move.'

'Sounds good,' I admitted. 'How are you holding up?'

'Surprisingly well,' she replied. 'Better than ever. You do good work.'

I wondered at that as I walked into the bathroom. I turned on the shower, stepped inside, and let myself think as the steam rose around me. Was I sure I wanted to stay? Well, yes. OK, that was easy.

So what do I do now?

That one wasn't so simple.

I was sure I wanted to find these bastards and make them pay. For Sarah, and for Tiffany, and for threatening my current situation, with which I was very happy. It felt strange to be planning to take on such a challenge. I'd been running so long. Sarah shamed me with her unhesitating courage. Maybe I should have been chasing English professors instead of waitresses all these years.

I toweled off, pulled on a pair of flannel pajama bottoms and a robe and came out. I smelled fresh coffee. Sarah pushed a mug into my hand.

'I put a splash of whisky in it,' she said. 'I know you need your caffeine, and I think we both need another drink.'

'Thanks. You're too good to me.'

'I am,' she agreed. 'It's my curse. Now, sit on the edge of the bed and get that robe off. I'll see if I can't massage some tension out of those shoulders.'

I complied readily. The laced coffee burned its way down to my stomach, the warmth of the alcohol spreading out to my limbs. Sarah sat behind me, close against my back, her knees on either side of my hips, kneading my knotted shoulders with strong hands. I groaned as she worked the sore, tense muscles.

'Oh, that feels good.'

'You're very tense,' she replied, pausing to knock back the last of her coffee. She rolled the empty mug, still warm, across my shoulders, letting the heat sink into the tissues. 'How's that?'

'Oh, God, feel free to keep that up as long as you like.'

'You know,' she said, working away, 'this is the first time anyone ever came to my rescue. Of course, it is kind of your fault I was in danger, but it was exciting, nonetheless.' She leaned close and kissed my neck. 'It means a lot to me that you decided to stay. And that you opened up. That must be tough.'

'You believe me?'

'Why not? I mean, how many guys can heal with a touch? And you have a skill set that includes cooking, history, literature, medicine, and stabbing thugs to death. Your story explains all of that. You sounded sincere. And why would you make that up? There has to be a more plausible lie.'

'Fair enough,' I conceded. 'It feels good to talk to somebody. It's like a weight off.'

She leaned into me, her nails sending shivers down my spine as she ran her fingers through my hair.

'Lie down,' she breathed in my ear, 'I want to get your lower back.'

I did as directed, and she drove the heels of her hands deep into the muscles of my lower back and buttocks. She leaned over me as she did, I could feel her breath as she panted with the effort. Her hair hung down, brushing tantalizingly over my skin.

I rolled over and slipped an arm around her. 'I think you've worked out most of the stiffness.'

'Or not,' she smiled, her hand working its way south. 'It looks like you still have a little stiffness. Or maybe not so little.'

'Be careful,' I warned, 'too much flattery and I may become insufferable.'

'Fear not,' she said, swinging her legs to straddle my hips. 'I come to bury Caesar, not to praise him.'

Yes, I told myself, I had definitely been missing out by not dating English professors.

Chapter 19

Sarah sighed contentedly and whispered, 'I'm glad you decided to walk into my office that day, you know.'

I breathed in deep, inhaling the scent of her hair, the clean smell of her shampoo with an edge of sweat beneath. 'So am I,' I replied.

After a while we got out of bed. I made coffee and turned on the news, wondering how an apartment full of dead bodies would play on the local broadcast. To my surprise, there was no mention of it.

I flipped to another station, wondering how a triple murder wasn't a lead story. My struggle had to have gotten the downstairs neighbors nosy. In the projects of Philips Mills, neighbors turned up the TV and didn't get involved with the violence next door, but the solid citizens of North Andover generally didn't roll that way.

Sarah's phone rang. She looked at the number then at me. 'It's the police.'

'Better take it,' I replied. 'Act surprised. Say you're out of town.'

She nodded. 'Hello... This is she.'

I smiled. English professor.

'Oh my God! No, no, I'm fine. I had no idea... I'm... away. In Vermont. No, not business... Just a little Bed and Breakfast... Not that I can think of.'

I began to make the classic "cut it short" motion across my throat.

'No. No. Look.' She lowered her voice. 'Is there a number I can call you back at, officer? Sorry, Detective. Alright, thanks. Yes, yes, I'll be in touch.'

She hung up. I smiled and applauded. 'Encore.'

'Thank you, thank you.' She bowed. 'But I really want to direct.'

'So, what's the story?'

'Well, they said there was a break-in and my apartment was trashed.'

'That's all?'

'He asked about an angry ex. I'll bet he thinks I'm up in Vermont with some new flame, shaking the paintings off the walls. I could hear the leer through the phone.'

'You played it up nice. Let him go looking for the mythical jilted ex-boyfriend. Nothing about the dead guys?' I wondered.

She shook her head. 'Not a word. I can't imagine it slipped his mind, so what happened to the bodies?'

I had no idea. The most likely answer was that the organization did a quick cleanup when the team didn't report in, but how they moved three corpses and cleaned up the gore without leaving a trace or drawing stares, I couldn't say. Or maybe Doors and his buddies had bought a few cops, and were keeping things quiet that way. That was one reason I had her cut the conversation short. If the investigation was legitimate, her excuse made sense; but if the detective were somehow involved, I didn't want to give him time to trace her cell phone signal.

'I'm beginning to realize just how much I don't know,' I said.

'So what do we do about that?'

I shrugged. 'I've hit a bunch of dead ends, and even those brought down more heat than I wanted. I have an address for a business that's probably a front.'

'They have a website?'

'A typical one. Vague mission statement, in the finest corporate inspirational language, list of services that somehow omitted strong-arm tactics and body disposal. Nothing distinctive. I'm hesitant to go online again. I'm not the most tech-savvy person, and they tracked you down through the forums.'

'Well, I wasn't exactly being careful. I'm a professor of languages, I'm on there a lot. Anyone can trace the ISP of visitors to a site if they're paranoid enough to want to—'

'Which I think we can safely assume they are.'

She paused and thought, chewing her bottom lip. 'If we could get onto one of the computers at that address you've got…'

'You think they just have this stuff on a computer? It's probably pretty secret stuff.'

'Showing your age,' she smirked. 'People put everything on their computers. Trust me. The horror in the eyes of a freshman who just realized she left her cell phone in the classroom is a memorable sight.'

I chuckled. 'So, how could we get a look at that info?'

'It depends. Somebody who knows what he's doing could hack in to most companies through their website. These guys might be a bit security conscious for that. Maybe if we could actually get into the boss' office.'

'You think there won't be security on his machine?' I asked.

'Not as much. Think about it. The boss probably employs a computer guy; *he* isn't a computer guy.'

'How do you know he isn't?'

'Almost a statistical certainty. The kind of guy who gets promoted to boss is going to be a manager. That very seldom translates into a guy who's really good with computers.'

'You can say the same about EMS,' I observed, thinking of Marty.

'Whoever's their computer guy, he'd put the most security on the website, since anyone can stumble across that. He'd probably set up firewalls to keep someone from accessing sensitive info remotely. But chances are he'll compromise with the boss's machine, so he doesn't have to hold the guy's hand every time an email comes in. Plus, he'll figure anyone that gets into the boss's office is supposed to be there.'

'We're assuming these clowns operate like a regular company,' I said. Most companies didn't field heavies with knives.

'Every organization works the same way, more or less,' said Sarah with a shrug. 'University, corporate outfit or Thugs Inc.'

'That makes sense,' I replied. Another thought occurred to me. 'Even if we get to the boss's computer, won't there be a password?'

'That's easy enough to get by. You can just go online and download a recovery boot disk.'

'Whatever that means,' I said. 'So if I got into his office with this disk, I could just bypass his password and download his files?'

She nodded. 'You think you can get in, get a look at his computer?'

'Probably. I've done a lot of sneaking around in my long and checkered career.'

'Behind enemy lines or into bedrooms?' she asked with a curl of her lip.

'More of the first and not as much of the second as I'd like. Anyway, the building is a front. It's supposed to be an import company. It's not like they can have barbed wire, attack dogs and armed guards walking the perimeter. Even in Philips Mills that would cause talk. It's in an old converted mill, most of which is vacant. There'll be a way in.'

It may seem odd that I, as a self-confessed coward, spent so much time in the notoriously dangerous job of reconnaissance. The lone commando, the sniper, the Special Forces team member, operating behind enemy lines, performing feats of daring and courage.

The truth is that it's only statistically more dangerous than any other kind of fighting. And, to an individual, statistics mean nothing.

In any army, your fate hung on the decisions of the commander and the whims of chance. Every time you take enemy fire, there's a chance, however small, that you will be hit. Even a good battle plan exposes troops to some risk, and if you show up for enough battles, sooner or later, you're going to stop some nasty piece of metal.

Off on my own, I could gauge risks for myself and move when I thought it was a good idea, not when somebody gave an order. I had a lot of faith in my self-preservation instincts. Operating alone or in a small group had its perils, but the guys who got killed doing that were the ones who got careless and forgot the limitations, forgot they were outnumbered and started to believe that they were elite unstoppable supermen. Once you start thinking the enemy isn't good enough to beat you, you get reckless, and then you get killed.

You don't succeed at those kinds of missions by being a tough, macho, bloodthirsty superman. You succeed by being smarter and sneakier than the enemy.

Chapter 20

HUDDLING IN THE WEEDS AND BRUSH overlooking the canal in the cold of the wee hours, a flash drive, thumb drive, CD and floppy disk in my pockets (to cover all the bases), with enough code to hopefully get into the computer in question and enough space to copy what I needed, I felt sneakier, but I wasn't sure about smarter. I also had a name badge from one of the thugs at Sarah's—the one who had been asking the questions, who had the address on the note in his pocket. The one whose throat I'd cut. There was a magnetic strip on it; maybe it would open doors. Okay, so I might be walking into another of their info traps using the badge, but I had to start somewhere.

If I'd known for sure that they didn't know what I looked like, I'd have felt confident just bluffing my way in. Never underestimate the power of a pair of work boots, a shirt with a name stitched on it, a clipboard and a spiel about checking the sprinkler system or backflow device, delivered in a bored, working-class accent. It's effective, safe and, if you plan the visit for early afternoon when the important people are on lunch, you almost never get questioned. Even if you do, you just make noises about having your supervisor call later and you walk away.

Instead, I was hunched in the cold, dressed in dark, non-reflective clothes, everything metal taped or cushioned so as not to rattle, which would be hard to explain if I were caught.

Not as hard to explain as the .45 automatic tucked in my pocket, though. The last few times I'd met these guys, they'd been quick to get disagreeable, so I decided to reverse the old cliché and bring a gun to a knife fight.

Doors Imports occupied about a quarter of an old mill building on the island between the Merrimack and the canal. The building was too large to believably house a small company, but the rest of it was vacant, and the isolated location made it easy to guard. I ignored the roadway bridge and crept along the old, decrepit railway bridge. Nobody used it, so it was unlikely to be watched, plus the superstructure provided decent cover for a man moving in a crouch. The downside was that it was January, cold as hell, all the steel parts were slick with ice, and the wooden boards were rotten, creaking ominously as I shifted my weight. I could see the black water of the canal through the gaps between my feet.

I told myself this was all reassuring. It's the easy way that's most guarded. The lousy weather helped; guards would be huddled in doorways out of the wind, the collars of those stylish Eurotrash trenchcoats pulled up around their ears. I'd chosen the hour carefully: the time when a sentry's attention is at its lowest ebb, between three am and sunrise, when the body's reserves are used up, the cold seeps into your bones and sleep leers seductively and hikes up its skirt.

I reached the end of the bridge without plunging through, which was nice. Keeping to the shadows, I slunk across the patch of open ground to the mill. I crept along the wall, looking for a likely way in. I found a broken window near the ground not far from the section rented by Doors Imports. Peering through, I saw a large, mostly empty space, occupied by a few old, rusting machines and piles of old crates and pallets. The far wall sported large overhead doors. Most promising, in the far left corner near the door there was a stack of new cardboard boxes. It looked like Doors was using at least part of the area as a loading dock.

Perfect. The area was poorly lit, unlikely to be guarded all that well, and probably had access to the main offices.

I slipped the blade of my pocket knife between the peeling sash and rotted frame of the window, teased the latch aside, and pried it open. I pulled myself carefully through the opening, and dropped to the floor, crouching in the dark for a moment, listening.

The room was impressive in size, but little else. Once, it housed the busy looms that drove the textile industry, and the dangerous, crowded, tuberculosis-ridden conditions that sparked the Bread and Roses strike.

The years hadn't been kind.

After the New England textile industry collapsed, a series of small businesses had used bits and pieces of the old mill buildings. Short lived enterprises carried out in subdivided corners of the vast cathedrals of industry. The brick walls were blackened by soot and diesel dust, and abandoned machinery from a dozen failed startups sat rusting in the gloom. The beams and nooks in the high ceiling were home to legions of pigeons.

In the left-hand wall there was a new door. I could make out the faint red glow of an LED on the fancy new electronic lock.

I also made out an old fashioned flesh and blood sentry.

The ID in my pocket might get me past the one. I hoped my sneaky, underhanded nature would get me past the second.

After a moment to adjust to the feel of the space, I crept carefully toward the door. The sentry was sitting. That's never a good idea, especially at night. It's almost always against the rules. Standing your post or walking your post helps keep you alert. Generally, an employer who doesn't want the guards sleeping doesn't leave chairs around.

Which is probably why this sentry was sitting on a box dragged against a wall. His chin was on his chest, his collar pulled up around his ears just as I'd hoped. He wasn't snoring, because that was hard with his head forward, and because it would have been just too theatrical, but he was breathing slow and deep.

As I got closer, I made out a shotgun resting on his knees. It was a 12 gauge pump, just a pistol grip, no shoulder stock, with a riot grip on the forearm.

It seemed that they did have something besides knives, at least when at home base. At close range, which is pretty much a given indoors, the shotgun was a very effective weapon indeed, even if I did disapprove of the lack of shoulder stock.

While unwelcome, it was a good thing to know. My pistol was not quite the advantage I'd hoped. I wanted to avoid a fight if I could, but if one had to happen, I wanted it to be as unfair in my favor as possible.

I ghosted to the door, pulling out the ID with one hand, keeping the other on the hilt of the knife. If the lock made a noise, even a simple electronic bleep, or set off an alarm and the guard woke up, I wanted to take him out before he could recover his wits and ready that cannon of his. Without making too much noise, if possible.

I swiped the card and exhaled in relief when the light silently changed from red to green. The reinforced door with the high tech electronic lock was new, which meant it was strong, but it also meant it didn't squeak when it swung open. I slipped through, easing it closed.

Out Of Nowhere

I stood in a dimly lit hallway. There were doors on either wall, a few inspirational posters hung between them. Twenty feet ahead, the hallway opened into a reception area. I crept up until I saw an unoccupied desk facing the main entrance. Behind the desk were two elevator doors. A directory between the doors had the president's office on the third floor. On one wall was a mission statement that stressed Doors Imports' commitment to excellence, but neglected to mention beating up women for information.

Well, it's not like I don't leave some things off my resumé.

The hallway continued beyond the reception desk, ending in a door to the stairs. I took them up to the third floor. Elevators are not a good choice for sneaking. The doors chime, the light shows interested parties what floor you're on, and they tend to be high traffic. On stairs, you can hear someone coming and have a split second to hide. When an elevator door opens, whoever's on the other side sees you.

I paused at the third floor. I heard slow, regular footsteps beyond. I cursed. It sounded like the guard on the top floor was walking his post. That spoke for his professionalism, but at the moment it complicated my life and put his in danger.

I waited until the sounds started to fade, then risked a quick look through the small, wired glass pane in the door. The guard was walking away, letting his heavy boots clomp in that bored, ambling gait familiar to anybody who has ever guarded what they thought was a perfectly safe place in the wee hours of the morning.

He was a burly, squarely built specimen, his flat-topped crew cut making him look even squarer. Indoors, he chose to eschew the ubiquitous trenchcoat for a black, ribbed turtleneck. I saw a weapon sling on his right shoulder. The weapon was obscured by his broad back, but any weapon that needed a sling was probably more firepower than my .45.

Since he was bigger and better armed than I, I waited until he turned the corner at the end of the hallway before quietly pushing the door open and skulking along until I came to the door conveniently marked "President". It was locked, but my stolen ID card swiped me in.

If it hadn't, I could have jimmied the lock. It would have taken about thirty seconds, given that this was a simple, interior office door, but the card was quieter, and less likely to set off any alarms. There was a chance that a computer logged which cards were used to access which doors at what times but there'd been no sign anyone was expecting me. Perhaps tomorrow the head of security would have to make the march of shame up to this same door to explain how a dead man's badge had been used, but by then, it would be his head on the block, not mine.

Once inside, I shut the door. It swung quietly closed, which is to be expected of the door of the President.

The office was not what I expected. After the trenchcoats and accents I was prepared for steel and glass and abstract sculpture. Instead, it was all very old world. Finely carved wooden furniture, dark paneling, riding prints, fencing prints and a well used modern fencing foil hanging on the wall over a photo of the man himself.

The face in the photo was a few years younger than the man whose ankle I'd fixed, and less lined with pain, but it still radiated arrogance.

I turned my attention to the computer on the massive desk. It was on, in sleep mode. I moved the mouse and waited until the screen lightened. As expected, a password box popped up.

I reached into my pocket for the recovery disk.

I paused.

Could it be that easy?

The nameplate on the desk read "Joseph Doors". The photo of the young fencer was inscribed Josef Toren. Tor was German for *gate*, Tueren was *doors*.

I tapped the J key.

The username field populated itself with "jdoors", and the password field filled as well, with the bullets that hid the actual password from outsiders. It seemed that Sarah was right. My foes appeared to have placed an inordinate amount of faith in Sleeping Beauty and his shotgun to keep anyone from getting this far. I smiled and pressed "Enter".

The desktop loaded before my eyes. In keeping with the image of a corporate executive, the wallpaper was an artistically lit shot of a chessboard. I sat down, loaded a blank disk and opened up the main drive.

My run of good luck leveled off; there was no file named "secret identity", so I just opted to copy all of them.

I sat for a few moments and watched the blue bar on the bottom of the screen slowly grow. It looked like I'd be here a while. This is always the hardest part of any infiltration, sitting and waiting while in a dangerous position. As long as you can be doing something, it isn't so bad; but just waiting, trying to stay alert, puts a strain on your nerves.

I stood and paced in front of the desk, just to burn off nervous energy. I glanced at my watch, tried to slow my breathing and wondered if the way out would be as easy as the way in. I found myself toying with a paperweight, a heraldic beast in gold, suspended in a heavy glass globe.

The sound of the office door banging open shattered my reverie and the big, square individual I'd seen earlier burst into the room, a German submachine gun leveled at me.

Ah, part of my brain registered. *An MP5. Should have guessed.*

'Thank God you're here,' I said with relief, putting a touch of Hungarian in my accent. 'He went that way.' I pointed to a door in the back corner of the room.

Guards are generally ready for one of several predictable reactions. If I had started to duck behind some furniture or reach for the pistol in my jacket, he'd have emptied the clip into me. If I'd thrown up my hands and pleaded for mercy, he'd likely have thrown me down and held me for questioning. If I'd run, he'd probably have shot me and then thrown me down and held me for questioning.

He was utterly unprepared for me to be happy to see him.

The secret to bluffing is to project the impression that you really do belong where you are. It's not easy, particularly when you have an automatic weapon pointed at you, but I'd had a lot of practice.

That said, it was a bluff with a weak hand, and not one that would stand up for very long.

He paused for a moment, his steely glare took on an edge of uncertainty, and his eyes flicked to the door I indicated. Even better, the muzzle of his weapon drifted that way, just a bit to the left of me.

Short as the distraction was, it was enough time for me to bring the paperweight around to smash into the side of his head, raising my left hand to deflect the gun if it should swing back toward me.

The blow drove him to his knees, but he kept hold of his weapon. I was behind him in an instant, an arm locked around his neck. He tried to twist the gun around to point at me, then tried to grab my arm and pull it free, but he was already weakening.

'Take a nap. Take a nap,' I urged. 'Come on. Shhhhhhhh. That's it.'

His body went limp and heavy. I held the choke for a few more seconds, just in case he was faking it. Playing dead is a good way to get someone to release a hold, but it's hard to do, and hard to keep that fear down if the choke doesn't stop.

The computer chimed, indicating that the task was finished.

I lowered the insensate guard to the floor and checked the screen. Files copied successfully. I ejected the disk, returned it to its case and slipped it into my pocket.

I could have taken the guard's MP5, but I wanted to keep at least one hand free, and I have a long-standing reluctance to rely on a weapon I've never personally fired. I did take a moment to toss the submachine gun up on top of a high bookshelf. When he came to, he'd assume I'd taken it and, unarmed, he'd probably be less enthusiastic about chasing a guy with an automatic weapon.

I had no idea what had alerted the guard to my presence, but it seemed a good time to be somewhere else. I snuck a quick look into the hallway. Still deserted. I stepped out and made for the stairway, my .45 now clutched in my fist.

I had gone about five feet when the door to the stairs burst open and a man with a carbine surged through. I snapped off a quick shot and made for a side hall off the main passageway.

The man flinched as I fired, but I doubt I hit him. He was only about twenty feet away. If I'd taken a second to aim, I couldn't have missed, but that would have given him a second to aim, and he had a bigger gun than I did.

As it was, my shot probably distracted him enough that I was around the bend before his reply blew holes in the sheetrock of the corner at the height of my chest. I dropped to a crouch, waited until I heard his steps approaching, then popped back out around the corner, low to the ground, my trusty Colt extended before me.

He was moving quickly toward me, his weapon still at the ready, but pointed too high. About where my head would be if I hadn't crouched down before leaning out.

This time I did take a second to aim and shot him deliberately, twice, center mass. He jerked as the rounds hit, then flopped back to the floor. He fired reflexively as he fell, but it went high. Behind him, the door banged open and I saw more men swarming up the stairs.

I was running now, looking for a way down.

At the end of the short hallway I saw another door with a narrow, wired glass panel in it. More stairs. I heard footsteps pounding down the main hallway. I backed toward the door, my pistol aimed at the corner. At that moment I did regret not taking the MP5. Running around a corner into a hail of submachine gun fire at a range of fifteen feet would have been a nice object lesson for them.

As my left hand touched the handle of the stairway door, I saw a group of thugs round the corner. Probably three or four of them, but at that moment I'd have sworn there were thirty. I fired into the oncoming horde, which very impressively reversed course and took cover around the corner. If I hit any of them, they didn't fall right away.

I tore open the door and barreled down two flights of stairs. On the landing, I paused for breath and to consider my next move. This should have me on the ground floor, but not in a place I knew. An older, rusted steel staircase continued down into the basement. Most of these old mills had some access to the canal. Maybe there was a way out below.

Yeah, maybe. Through freezing water filled with ice and rats and the hepatitis bug.

Beat getting shot, though.

If I was lucky, whatever guards there were in the building would still be swarming up to where I'd just come from. On the other hand, they might be smart enough to have already sealed the exits. Maybe the basement was the best idea. But what if the access to the water was sealed off? It could be one big dead end.

My indecision came to an abrupt end as the door burst open and yet another armed heavy rushed through. This one was a taller, leaner model, but otherwise pretty much like the rest. He obviously wasn't expecting anyone to be there, which I attribute to just how stealthily I was waffling over my next move. He plowed right into me, knocking me back against the wall.

The good thing was that while he was too close for me to bring my pistol to bear, he was too close to bring his automatic weapon to bear, and both of his hands were full of gun, to my one. I grabbed him with my left hand and tried to get a knee in. He might not have been able to shoot me, but he managed to slam the toe of his gunstock into my ribs. I grunted as pain blossomed in my side, forcing air from my lungs.

He hit me one more time, then I grabbed his weapon and slammed my forehead into his nose. I felt the crunch and took the opportunity to swing him around into the wall. I hit him with the .45, kicked his legs out from under him and shoved him toward the stairs.

Unfortunately, he grabbed a handful of my jacket as he stumbled back. Off balance from the cramp of my bruised ribs, I couldn't break his hold, and we fell down the stairs together.

On the positive side, I managed to stay on top, using the guard like a well armed toboggan. On the negative, it was still falling down stairs. I felt jarring impacts on my knees and elbows as we tumbled down. My left hand, still keeping the muzzle of his gun away from my body, slammed into a steel baluster, sending a searing bolt of agony up my arm. My right foot hung up somewhere and my ankle wrenched painfully.

We came to rest at the foot of the stairs, tangled together on a dusty cement floor. I lay for a moment in a haze of pain. I shook myself, found that the guard was down for the count, and looked around the space.

The room felt spacious, wide open. I couldn't see the full extent, unlit beyond the trickle of lights filtering through small, high windows at street level, but I did hear the gurgle of water.

I tried to stand, but as soon as I put weight on my right foot, I collapsed. Moving fast was out of the question. I considered his gun, but doubted I could control it one-handed, and the throbbing pain in my left wrist left me no illusions about my ability to use the hand. I crawled a short distance on knees and elbows, looking for refuge. There was a steel door maybe twenty feet away, maybe some shelves with what looked like paint cans on them back in the gloom, but beyond that, nothing I could easily identify.

The sound of a door opening above gave me the motivation I needed to get up. Gritting my teeth, I made for the door with a stumbling, hopping limp, mewling in agony every time my right foot came down.

Chapter 21

SO THAT'S HOW FIXING A BROKEN ANKLE led to lying holed up, injured and low on ammunition in a janitor's office. The wages of virtue, to steal a phrase from P C Wren.

But that's OK. He owed me one from Algiers.

I watched the door over the sights of the pistol, trying to control my breathing to reduce the rise and fall of the muzzle. Soft footsteps approached the door.

I concentrated on my sight picture, pushing all the pain and worry to the back of my mind. Wait for the target. Nothing exists but my target and I.

A shape appeared in the dim shadow in the corner of the room near the file cabinet. It took me aback. The door was still closed—no way anyone could have gotten through. I shook my head and refocused, half convinced it was a hallucination.

It wasn't.

A man stood in the corner, flesh and blood, scanning the room. A naked blade shone in his right hand. I must have moved when I saw him, because he suddenly focused on me, his eyes locking on mine.

Well, his being there was impossible, but the knife looked real enough. As he started toward me, I swung my weapon to bear on him and fired.

He vanished.

Absolutely vanished. My mind jolted to a stunned halt.

Fortunately, a deep, subconscious instinct stepped in for the absent higher brain function. I twisted and flopped down on my back, looking frantically around the room. Not two feet away, a form was coalescing into being, an arm thrusting out above me. I pointed the .45 at the center of the rapidly resolving shape and pulled the trigger. The swirling darkness solidified into a human body twisting and falling to the floor.

Juan's words about the guy that jumped Tiffany came back to me. *He said the guy just vanished into thin air.*

The sound of the steel door banging open yanked my attention from the man writhing on the floor next to me.

A man stuck his head and shoulders around the jamb, pointing a pistol into the room. I snapped off a shot and he replied in kind, shrinking back behind the cover of the wall, firing blind.

After a few rounds, I realized that trying to hit the disembodied gun hand was beyond me in my current injured and agitated state, so I switched my aim to the wall that the rest of him had to be behind. I fired twice and the hand dropped the gun and jerked back.

I released a shaky breath, waiting for more movement from the door, thinking that any more foes out there might digest the lesson that sheetrock is no defense against bullets.

I heard urgent whispers, but no advance.

Beside me, my first victim moaned. I twisted painfully around to get a look at him. As I did, my elbow knocked something sliding away. I looked over and saw one of the ubiquitous daggers on the floor a few feet from me.

Shaking with adrenaline and my injuries, I had an urge to put another round in the man, but I restrained myself. There were too many questions.

Most important was: how do I get out of this mess? Most intriguing was: how did this guy do that? It was impossible, but I didn't get hung up on that for several reasons. One was that I could do the impossible myself, so who was I to judge? And a second was that, impossible or not, I'd seen it happen and lacked the all-too-common ability to ignore concrete fact.

Slowly, or slower than I'd have liked, anyway, I realized that the second question might contain the answer to the first.

'You want to live?' I addressed the man.

He groaned in reply. I dragged myself over to him, put a hand on him and sensed his wound. He had a hole in his liver, which bled like mad and hurt like hell. Out of pragmatism, and against my inclination, I sent a little energy through to dull the pain and slow the bleeding.

'I asked if you want to live,' I repeated.

'I swear blood oath,' he grunted.

'You want to die, that's your choice. But if you want a pass on this one, I'm willing to deal.' I saw uncertainty through the agony etched on his face. 'Say the word and the pain can go away.'

He nodded.

'OK, can you get me out of here?'

'You can't escape,' he said. 'Save me and it will go easy for you.'

I had no idea what he was offering, but it sounded like a very bad deal. 'Look,' I said, 'without your help, those thugs eventually get me. Without my help, you bleed out.' I shrugged. 'Your call.'

If he kept arguing, I could tell I was going to shoot him again fairly soon. Obstinacy strains my patience on a good day, and I was not at my best.

'If I get you out, you fix my wound?'

'That's still the offer.'

'And then?'

'We walk away. I don't shoot you, you don't stab me, and we live to fight another day.'

'I agree.'

'How far can we go?'

'A kilometer, perhaps,' he replied. 'I'm not pureblood.'

That was supposed to mean something to me. I nodded like it did. 'Outside this building, across the river and away from the lights will do.'

'Heal me and I get you out,' he grunted.

I didn't waste more breath on speech. I gave a quick glance at the doorway to make sure the guys outside weren't making a rush, then reached out and touched the wounded man, doing my thing. The bullet had torn a good sized hole through his liver. A .45 is a big, heavy round, so it took some effort to plug it, to stop all the little vessels from leaking and convince the tissues to knit. Fortunately, the liver is more predisposed to heal than many organs, which helps. I kept my word and repaired the worst damage, got him out of danger; but remembering how they treated Sarah, and Tiffany still lying in that hospital bed, I left him some tattered abdominal muscles. Petty, maybe, but I wanted him to have something to remember me by.

Maybe I was being a bit trusting, patching him up first, but I didn't know if he could work his magic with a half-inch hole in his gut, and he wasn't all that keen on helping me anyway, so I figured a little gesture might be called for. Besides, if he tried anything, I still had one more pistol than he did.

So I guess the moral is trust your fellow man, so long as you're better armed than he is.

'OK,' I told him, 'Let's get going.'

He looked in awe at the knitted flesh, touched the new scar over the wound, and registered that the pain was mostly gone. He gave me a long, conflicted look. I'd seen it before, the look of an uneasy truce. He had some grudge, some reason he felt he should hate me, but he was feeling reluctant gratitude for the man who took his pain away and gave him a stay of execution.

He shut his eyes, made that face people do when they concentrate hard, and suddenly the world twisted. My stomach lurched and my senses reeled as the dry, musty, dusty warmth of the custodian's office was replaced by the cold, misty, almost-clean air of Philips Mills in winter. We were at the bus station, but this late, it was deserted.

We looked at one another uncertainly. He wasn't the same man whose ankle I'd healed, but he could have been his younger brother. Tall and muscular, his blonde hair cut short, his face all sharp angles, strong chin, no fat to speak of. The eyes were blue and cold. Hard eyes. Eyes that had seen terrible things without blinking. But now, they held a flicker of doubt, of hesitation.

I felt the same conflicted emotions, the wave of unwelcome gratitude. Without his help, I don't think I'd have made it out of there, any more than he'd have survived that wound without me.

Of course, he wouldn't have gotten it without me, and I wouldn't have been in danger in the first place without...

But, there we go. Try to trace blame far enough back and you start sounding like an idiot.

And who knew? With any luck, we might still wind up having to kill one another.

'OK,' I said, 'get out of here.' I tried not to let the pain from my ankle or my wrist or my ribs show on my face or in my voice. I didn't know how much he knew about me or my power, whether he expected me to heal myself or not. If he didn't know my limits, there was no way I was going to enlighten him.

'This is not over,' he said. 'I cannot thank you.'

'We're even,' I replied. 'We both get to live for now. Worry about later when it comes.'

He made a few attempts to say something, then nodded curtly and set off, leaving by the South entrance. When I was sure he was gone, I limped out the North entrance, ducked down the first alley I could find, leaned back against some Latin Kings graffiti and spent some quality time being sweaty and shaky and nauseous until the screaming agony in my wrist and ankle ebbed. I thumbed the safety on my pistol, slipped it into my waistband and hauled out my cell phone.

I called a taxi to meet me in front of a nearby Spanish nightclub. Doors and his gang might know my car by sight, and maybe Sarah's, but a guy stumbling into a taxi in front of a club was nothing anyone would notice.

I set to wait, feeling secure in the dark, gang-tagged alley in the middle of the night. I knew the city, I knew the gangs. I had my command of Spanish, my natural charm and, if all that failed, a large caliber handgun. Plus, there were no white guys in expensive trenchcoats anywhere to be seen.

I'd gotten some info from Doors' computer, I hoped, and I'd discovered a disturbing capability of the enemy. How many of them could just teleport around? The guy I'd just met seemed to feel insecure about only jumping a half mile or so. How far could a "pureblood" teleport?

I thought back to what Juan had said of Tiffany's attacker.

He said the guy just vanished.

And the young gang banger Juan and Pete brought in.

Said some dude just come out of nowhere and cut him.

Crap. Should I have picked up on that? I didn't see how. I assumed that it was just a figure of speech. I'm sure everyone else, even the guys who said it, did as well.

I hobbled out as a taxi pulled up, and more fell than climbed into the seat. I gave the driver the address of a bar on Tower Hill, nowhere near my apartment. When he let me out, I started to the door until he was well out of sight, then limped two streets over and called a different cab company to take me home. Maybe I was being overly cautious, but if my Eurotrash buddies somehow did discover the cab I took, let them come to the wrong side of town looking for me.

Chapter 22

By the time I got to my apartment, I had just enough energy to stagger to the elevator and call ahead for Sarah to unbolt the door. She managed to get me into the apartment and into bed. For once, it was a struggle.

Once the lightheadedness passed and the sweating abated, I was able to talk her through some treatment. Like anyone with a physical job, I'd acquired an assortment of braces, splints and ACE bandages. Once they were on, limiting movement of the injured joints, the pain was much less. Coupled with a handful of ibuprofen, a mug of tea with whisky in it, and the tender concerns of an attractive blonde, I started to feel pretty good.

'You're sure you'll be OK?' she asked.

'Should be,' I replied. 'Nothing too bad. Nothing that won't heal. You should see the other guy.'

She was quiet for a moment. 'Did you kill anybody?'

I started to shrug, but winced and abandoned the idea. 'Probably. I choked a guy out. Shot at least one guy. Shot at a few others. Probably hit some of them. Dragged a guy down the stairs. That could have worked out better. He was at least unconscious. Wounded another guy, but I patched him up in exchange for getting me out. So I may have killed as many as four or five.'

'Plus the three at my apartment.'

'Not much choice.'

She rested her head on my shoulder. 'Does it bother you? I mean, you spend so much time trying to save lives, does it get to you when you end one?'

'Not all that much, as far as these guys go,' I answered. 'It's not something I do lightly, and I'd be thrilled if I never have to again, but to protect you, or my friends or myself, I won't lose sleep over it. Like the Bard said, it ain't no sin to be glad you're alive.'

'Shakespeare said that?' She frowned.

'Springsteen,' I corrected.

'You might actually be too old for me.' She kissed me gently. 'Try to get some rest and I'll see what I can dig up in these files.'

'Bolt the door,' I said.

'OK. Get some sleep.'

'And put my gun on the table. No. Other side.'

'Here?'

I checked that I could reach it. 'Perfect.'

'Now, get some sleep.'

'Check the windows.'

'Sure. Get some sleep.'

'Don't open the door to anybody unless you get me up.'

'Get some sleep.' She walked out of the bedroom and closed the door.

Of course, they could just teleport into the room. But if they knew where I lived, they'd have already done that, so I had a few hours to rest before worrying too much.

Feeling somewhat secure and very exhausted, I slipped into a deep, heavy slumber.

I woke some time later to a chorus of aches and pains. Probably the painkillers had worn off. I lay still for a few moments, debating whether or not I should move. My body was pretty unanimously against it, except for my bladder, which made a persuasive case for getting up. Stifling a groan, I heaved myself up into a sitting position and swung my feet over the side of the bed.

A wave of agony washed over me. I took some deep breaths and after a few seconds it settled down to just a background hum of pain with the occasional jarring stab if I moved wrong.

Or much. Or at all.

All things considered, it could have been worse. The ribs had settled down to where they barely hurt if I took shallow breaths and didn't move. With the brace on my ankle, I could rest my foot flat on the floor with just a twinge. The wrist hurt. I'm sure if I tried to do anything with the hand, it would hurt much, much more, but at least it was my left.

I grit my teeth and stood.

The ankle wasn't as bad as I'd feared. Oh, it was bad, but it held me up, which is, after all, what one asks of an ankle.

I made my way to the bathroom, stopped in front of the toilet and leaned forward, supporting myself against the wall with my right hand until the shaking stopped. When I felt I could, I released my hold on the wall and began the complex and undignified process of manipulating my zipper, and then my anatomy, one-handed.

Note to self: next time you break a wrist, wear elastic waistbands.

The bladder's bidding done, I shuffled back out toward the kitchen to appease the stomach, only now making its displeasure known. I must have shown weakness by giving in to the bladder.

Sarah met me in the hallway.

'Hey, you,' she hugged me gingerly. 'You sure you should be up?'

'Hard to keep a good man down,' I grinned.

'That's relevant how, exactly?' she asked. 'You got pretty banged up, you should be in bed.'

'I need to eat something.'

'You can call me,' she chided. 'I can bring you something. You have me here, use me.'

'Alright,' I said, leaning in for a kiss, 'but you'll have to be gentle. I'm not in peak condition.'

'I will take that as a sign that you're getting better.'

'I'm on the mend, but I could break every bone in my body and still lust after you.'

She blushed.

'I want to limp right up to you, fling you clumsily onto the bed, tear your clothes off one-handed over an embarrassingly long time, and then make cautious, hesitant, painful love to you.'

'Well, how can a girl refuse that?' She laughed. 'For now, why don't we just get something to eat? You're probably not up to cooking, and you should have your strength back before you try anything I cook. How's pizza sound?'

'Sounds perfect. By the way, did you find anything useful on that disk?'

'Oh, did I ever.' Her eyes widened with excitement. 'That thing is the fucking Rosetta Stone! There's some documents in this other language that have been translated, and some stuff they were translating from English. Once I work out the syntax, it'll be easy to cobble together a quick translation patch and unlock the rest of the stuff.'

OUT OF NOWHERE

'Glad that makes sense to somebody.'

'You stick to cooking, medicine and fighting. Leave the technology to me. All the electronics in your place still flash midnight on the timer, do you realize that? I checked.' Her eyes widened. 'Is that the secret to your longevity? Do you have the DVD player of Dorian Grey?'

I laughed, which brought a fresh stab of pain from my ribs.

'Sorry,' she said.

'Don't be. Blame the guy who hit me. But, speaking slowly for the old man in the room, can you translate the language on that computer?'

'I should be able to. There's enough documentation in both English and whatever this language is that I should be able to work it out, then run the untranslated stuff through the decryption program. *Et voila!*'

'*Tres bien,*' I replied, lowering myself carefully into a chair. 'Could you go get my gun from the nightstand? I'd like to be packing when the pizza guy shows up.'

'Paranoid?'

'Paranoid and breathing,' I answered.

She placed the order, and when she paid the teenage driver, I held my pistol down out of sight beside the chair, just in case he decided to pull a knife or teleport into the room. He did neither, but he did look her up and down with no subtlety.

I still didn't shoot him.

After eating, I limped back to bed. Drained, sweating and shaking. Not as badly as before the cab ride home, though.

I was healing.

Would I recover fast enough? Would Sarah find anything on that disk that I could use? Before they found me?

I shoved my fear back down. Worrying wasn't going to accomplish anything. I'd already decided not to run, so that was settled. Whatever grievance these people had with me originally, there had been enough blood spilled in the past week that a peaceful resolution wasn't very likely.

So, running was out, negotiation was out, that left fighting. And if I had to do that, I had to get back on my feet, which meant resting.

See? Eliminate enough options and life becomes very simple.

Chapter 23

SOME TIME LATER I WOKE to a gentle kiss on my forehead. I blinked and stifled an urge to sit up, knowing my ribs would make me pay if I did.

'Hey, you,' I smiled.

'What do you remember about your childhood?'

'Nothing, really.' I shrugged. Winced. 'Vague images. I'm not sure from how far back, or if they're even real or just a mess of dreams and wishful thinking.'

'Humor me.' She lay down beside me, slowly and carefully, so as not to jolt my battered body. 'What's your earliest memory?'

I wracked my brain, searching for that memory. It's harder than you think. Try it sometime.

Kneeling behind the low stone wall on the banks of the Mystic River, the sun hot on my back, holding my musket in hands slick with sweat as I watched the Fusiliers advance, waiting for them to pass the stake Colonel Stark had driven into the sand thirty paces away. Thinking how clearly you can see a man's face at thirty yards, before the command and the volley and the smoke and the screams.

Watching *Henry V* at the Globe because Kate wanted to see the new play, and thinking that finally some bugger had gotten soldiers right.

That night in that old hill fort in Wales, when Gwen came to my chamber disguised as a servant. She was too young and pretty and had too much of an appetite to tolerate her husband's neglect. To be fair, he was trying to unite the squabbling tribes of Britons to repel a Saxon invasion, but moderation in all things. He never learned that. A man ignored Gwen at his peril. Being respected as swordsman, scholar and chirurgeon at the time, I had my own private chamber. I knew it was a bad idea but, Gwen being Gwen, if it wasn't me, it would have been someone else, and she was so young and curvy and enthusiastic...

Well, I certainly wasn't telling that story.

I shook my head. 'I can't remember anything that you'd call childhood. Some stuff from way back, but I was already jaded and cynical.'

'Nothing about a mother or father?'

'Absolutely drawing a blank.'

'Well,' she said, 'it seems that you're the heir to a noble line. So are your buddies with the knives. In something that reads like Lewis Carroll meets Machiavelli, with a dash of Stan Lee, the various noble houses all had some supernatural talent. Marriages and alliances were built around honing and combining those talents. You hit the jackpot with healing and longevity. Both of those are recessive traits. Rare ones.'

None of that sounded the least bit familiar. It must have shown on my face, because she leaned in and began to rhythmically stroke my brow.

'You upset some people during a military expedition. The kingdom put together a group of nobles to lead their army. A guy who could teleport, a guy who could 'slow time', if my translation is right, a guy who could make fire, and so on.'

'So how did I disappoint the Dream Team?'

'Treason, desertion, or just being a decent human being. Depends on how you want to read it.'

'Let's read it the way where I'm just a decent human being,' I suggested.

'Well, you were recruited to go along, since you could patch up anyone who got hurt, and you could handle yourself as a swordsman, which was unusual for a healer. I guess healing generally manifests in females, and they didn't let girls play with swords back then.'

'The more fools them.'

'Anyway, there was an invasion, and your countrymen captured some of the home team. You were called to assist in the interrogations. To assist the royal torturers. Like: talk or we'll break your fingers, then he'll fix your fingers, then we'll ask you again and see how long you can keep being evasive.'

'Jesus!' I said. 'I've done a few things I'm not proud of, but that's nasty.'

'You refused. One of the others got in a fight with you over it, words came to blows and you killed him. You were accused of treason, and sentenced to banishment with your memories erased.'

'They can do that?'

'Oh, yes. That and more.' She smiled at me. 'You know how to pick your enemies.'

'If it's worth doing,' I said, 'it's worth doing right.'

'One of the other nobles could manipulate memories. Which explains why you don't recall important events from back then. It could also explain why none of this stuff ever showed up in a history book. People who know too much can be eliminated or just have their memories erased or changed. Anyway, the invasion collapsed, since they were short two important members. The family that pushed for invasion, whose patriarch you ran through, lost prestige and took a big hit in the hierarchy of imperial politics. They thought you got off easy. They wanted you executed, but you were from a powerful family yourself, and that family had the healing bloodline. Lots of pull there. Plus, you killed the other guy in a straight-up fight, and witnesses couldn't agree on who started it. The other clan swore a blood oath against you. Now, it looks like their descendants still care enough to fulfill it.'

She paused. 'How are you doing?'

'OK I guess, for a guy who just heard that his past sounds like something Jules Verne couldn't sell to his publisher. How did you get all this stuff?'

'A lot of this is me piecing stuff together from old letters. Most of the stuff is pretty slanted against you, but there are a few official documents that they scanned into the records. Your official sentencing is there, and the complaint from the Doors clan and the defense from yours. Nobles think this stuff is important.'

I spent a long moment digesting this information. I didn't actually remember any specifics about this, and her info was the handed-down version of guys who wanted me dead, so who knew how accurate it was? I was happy at least that at one time I seemed to have some principles.

I found that comforting, considering how my standards seemed to have eroded down to "don't steal anything you can afford to pay for or don't really need" and "don't hurt anybody more than he deserves".

'So where are they—we, I guess—from?'

She shrugged 'Ruritania, as far as I can tell.'

I shook my head.

'You disappoint me,' she smiled. 'Anthony Hope. *The Prisoner of Zenda.* Never read it?'

'Saw the movie,' I replied.

'If you say the Stewart Granger version, you're sleeping on the couch.'

'Ronald Colman, Douglas Fairbanks, Aubrey Smith, David Niven.'

'OK, that lets you off for not doing the reading,' she said. 'Ruritania is a fictional kingdom somewhere in Eastern Europe. It shows up from time to time as shorthand for a backward country with remote castles, trackless forests, superstitious peasants and a powerful, mysterious nobility.'

'Is that where Boris and Natasha were from?'

'That's Potsylvania and you know it. Anyway, I'm just working from some hints, linguistic cues, no hard names in any language but theirs, which isn't exactly Slavic or German or Russian but has elements of all of them. It has to be east of Austria, maybe Hungary or former Yugoslavia. Maybe we can get some maps, plot some likely points, see if they make sense.'

'So, what are they doing here?' I asked. 'They can't have this whole organization just to find little old me, can they?'

She shook her head. 'It doesn't seem like anyone was looking for you at all. At least not in the recent past. There's no mention of any leads about you. I'm guessing Doors recognized the fact that you healed him, and started thinking.'

'So what do they do when they aren't looking to avenge ancient wrongs or brutalizing unarmed women?'

'They're in the smuggling business. The shipping company is a front. They bring in a lot of heroin. Easy to dodge customs when you can teleport.'

Well, that was true. And where better to smuggle than Philips Mills, famed distribution hub for drugs, and a town nobody much cared about? A good place to lay low, or so I'd thought.

Probably explained why they'd been so bad at finding me, and so sloppy at security. They weren't running a counterintelligence unit, just pushing drugs. I was a target of opportunity.

'Is this just Doors and his organization, or are all the gang of supermen after me?'

'Just Doors, as far as I can tell. His ancestors swore the oath. It looks like the family business is smuggling now. Actual blood relative would be able to teleport, the rest may be retainers or just hired muscle. The other families may or may not have wanted to see you punished, but nobody seems to have taken it quite as personally.'

'Doors is just a descendant of this guy I killed, right? No chance he remembers it himself?'

She shook her head. 'Iosef Toren is thirty-four. He's the direct male heir, but he's not like you.' She touched my hand. 'Not like you at all.'

I didn't know what to say, so I just took her hand and kissed it.

'One thing I don't understand,' she said. 'The guys at the warehouse had guns, but none of the guys who attacked you on the street, or the ones who came to my apartment, carried anything but knives.'

'Makes sense for what they've been doing. Knives are good for sending a message. They're scary, and you can mark somebody up pretty badly without risking killing him. That way, instead of a dead dealer, you have a very frightened dealer who'll probably be inclined to be more co-operative the next time you meet. And the cops don't really care so much about drugs, or about dealers getting nicked up. Guns raise the stakes too much. With a gun, you pretty much shoot somebody and that's final. The cops can't turn a blind eye to that. Plus, I don't think they felt they needed them to take out an unarmed paramedic, or a hospital admitting clerk or a professor.'

'You don't think they'll keep on making that mistake, do you?'

'Probably not.'

'Too bad.'

'Yep.'

'So,' she said, 'now I guess we plan our next move? I'm just winging it here, I've never been in this kind of situation before.'

'I wish I could say the same.'

'Well, sooner or later you have to own up to your checkered past,' she chided gently. 'Now, what do you normally do after such a daring adventure?'

'You mean after getting my ass kicked and narrowly escaping death while snooping around a secret smugglers' hideout?'

'Yeah, pretty much.'

'Well, there are really only two options. You still don't want to just run?'

'You're not talking about laying low for a few weeks. You're talking about starting a new life in exile. I'm not cutting ties with my friends and family and leaving my career. I worked hard for my degree; I'm not hiding out in flyover country waiting tables at some truckstop. I'd rather get cut up.'

'So that's your final answer?'

'Yup. Christmas at my mom's house up in North Conway. You play your cards right, treat me nice and don't get killed by drug dealers, you might get an invitation.'

'I'll look forward to it,' I said. 'Well, that rules out option one. Leaving us with option two.'

'Which is?'

'We attack.'

'There's no nice safe middle ground? Like tip the police off to the whole drug-dealing thing?'

'Using evidence that I stole, and that you translated from a language nobody speaks, so they can arrest a guy who will just Quantum Leap his way out of the cell the second the cop looks away?'

'Huh. You don't think that'll hold up?' she asked.

'It would just annoy him a bit, make him move his business, and add a grievance to his list. Plus he'd still be coming after me. At least now I know to expect him.'

'Alright, so that doesn't solve anything. Good thing you're experienced at this stuff.'

'I may have been around the block a time or two,' I said.

'So what's your plan?'

'I'm still working on that,' I admitted. 'Thing is, blood oaths are a bitch. This guy has inherited this need for vengeance. It's been handed down like a title, or the family silver. It's unlikely that he'll want to cut a deal.'

'I don't understand this. It's been centuries. And you were cut off, thrown out with no memory, lost a title, lands, power and all that. Isn't that enough?'

'That's not how revenge works,' I said. 'Your family's Irish, right? Think of your most fanatic uncle. Does he still bring up 1918? Still swear at the mention of Ian Paisley even though he's lived in America for three generations?'

'That does sound like uncle Mickey.'

'If he met Oliver Cromwell on the street, you think he'd buy him a beer and say all is forgiven?'

'Point taken.'

'Some grudges have deep roots. If Doors' family thinks my betrayal was the start of their fall from grace, the last heir has no choice but to avenge his ancestors. I can't see a peaceful way out of this.'

'You think you'll have to kill him?'

'That's what I keep coming back to, and I'd rather not. It's not that I'm squeamish about it. This guy is really pissing me off. No, it's the fact that if we eliminate the head of the family, somebody else just steps in. Dynastic politics are tough. I'd rather not do the whole traditional "wipe out all the heirs" thing. Not my style.'

'That's what drew me to you,' she smiled. 'Your unwillingness to slaughter whole families.'

'I have my good points.'

'So how do noble families usually settle their differences? Is there a protocol?'

I shrugged, then regretted it. 'Well, it's usually unpleasant. Wars, assassinations. Duels, if everyone's feeling really civilized.'

'Any chance this guy and you could do the pistols at ten paces thing?'

'I don't know. First, this guy seems to share my aversion to fair fights. And if, as you say, talent relates to breeding, if Doors is the direct heir, he's probably the best at teleporting, so his dying would be a big loss, the new heir would probably have even more of a score to settle.'

'His heir wouldn't be bound by some kind of honor? Wouldn't going after you after you won a duel break that code of honor?'

'Mr Doors would be bound by the terms of a duel. So long as he's alive and in charge, yes, he probably would honor the results. Dead though? His heirs would feel compelled to avenge him.'

'How the hell do these things end?' she asked in exasperation.

'Everybody dies. Come on, you've read Shakespeare. Either one side totally wipes out the other or, when they're too evenly matched, the two sides come to a realization that nobody wins and they negotiate. That's when you get partitions of nations or arranged marriages.'

'You don't see any negotiated settlement in the cards?'

'Nothing springs to mind.' I said. 'This is all a shock. I never really had to think of something like this. I've had differences with people, but those all went away with the next move and the next name change. Why haven't any of Doors ancestors found me in all this time?'

'You were banished,' she reminded me, 'with no memory. It's not like you were going to give anyone your name or your family name, since you didn't even remember it. And the other family was supposed to lay off, accept that judgment. I'm sure they looked for a while, but after a few generations, I just don't think they saw any point. Something just clicked for Doors when he ran into you and set him off researching the old records. If he hadn't slipped on the ice, or a different ambulance crew went to that call, none of this would have happened.'

'But then I might never have met you,' I pointed out.

She smiled at that. Leaned in and kissed me gently.

She was quiet for a few moments. I took the opportunity to caress her cheek with my good hand. As I did, I noticed she was chewing her lower lip. That seemed to indicate that she was deep in thought. It also kinda turned me on, but I thought it best not to distract her.

'I need to do some more picking around in those files and think,' she said. 'You get some more rest.'

'We really should find someplace else to lay low, at least for a little while. If they really apply themselves, and they have any connections who could run either of our license plates, they could find us. They're slick for drug dealers. Well financed. They tracked you down from a computer search, and got my old address from my employer. And how did they clean up three bodies from your place without the police getting suspicious? Maybe they have a connection somewhere. We should get out of Dodge while we plan.'

She thought for a moment. 'How do you feel about the woods?' she asked.

Chapter 24

A FEW HOURS LATER, I was trying to find a comfortable position in the passenger seat of a rented Jeep heading North on Route 93. We'd stopped at a locker I rented at the train station, picked up a fake ID and some cash. I didn't want to rent a car in either of our names, and I didn't want to get stopped by the police if they ran our plates.

Technology had made establishing a fake ID tougher, but you could still do it if you knew people. Working in EMS, I had access to billing info for patients, some of whom died. If you acted quickly, you could get a credit card with that info, and a decent fake license was just a question of finding the right person and paying enough. I kept a few ready, and changed them out every so often, just so I didn't try to vanish with nothing but expired IDs.

One of the first rules of survival in the Paranoid Handbook is to indulge your paranoia. If Doors was going to keep looking for me, it would be best to leave the apartment for a bit. Up until now, I'd been a footnote in the family history while their main focus had been drug smuggling and consolidating their position among the dealers and distributors. Drug dealers were easy to find. They had to be for their customers. There were signs, signals, graffiti. Even the cops can find the street dealers, but those guys are a dime a dozen, and usually don't know enough to be of any use in bagging the higher level operatives.

Doors and his merry band didn't have to find the higher level guys. They could squeeze the street dealers, chase off the clients, leave messages enough that the bosses would want to make contact. They weren't trying to halt the drug trade, just make sure that the dealers bought from them, and that the money wasn't skimmed.

That's why they hadn't needed to get good at finding people. It was pure fluke—pure fluke and plain bad luck on my part—that had put me in their path when they weren't even looking.

Having found me, I'd probably moved up the old "to do" list. How can you ignore it, when the object of a centuries-old grudge suddenly lands right slap-bang in the middle of your life? Hell, I'd even arrived with a siren blaring.

Now they'd start doing the legwork to track me down. It wouldn't be a good time for them to find me, injured as I was. I packed a bag, and left the World's Oldest Cat with my downstairs neighbor who owed me a favor.

There were plenty of places in Philips Mills we could have gone, paid cash and checked in with no ID. Rooming houses, flop houses, places where people didn't ask questions. The thing about those places was that Doors and his cronies were muscling drug dealers, interrogating the homeless, the addicted and the indigent, who made up a good portion of the clientele of the rooming houses. I had been to a lot of those establishments working as a paramedic, so people might recognize me, and thanks to the company nametag policy, some would know my name.

And while I had helped many of the pale and downtrodden, as Pink Floyd would say, these were fearful people easily intimidated by burly guys with knives. These were addicts, easily swayed by the offer of drugs or money for drugs. These were people who often couldn't afford the price of loyalty to me for saving their lives.

I'm not really bitter about that. I often felt I wasn't doing them much of a favor.

'Where are we going, exactly?' I asked, trying to find a position where the seatbelt didn't bother my ribs.

'My Uncle Bob's place,' she replied. 'Well, he's not my uncle by blood. He was dad's army buddy, and we saw him a lot growing up. He used to do magic tricks. He's a bit of a mountain man. Hunts, fishes, brews his own beer. I think he distills his own moonshine. He claims he can dowse for water. He was kind of a second father to my brothers and me. He has a place way out in the woods and we used to go snowshoeing and camping and canoeing. He bought a cheap camp when he got out of the army, fixed it all up, insulated it and made it livable year-round. He put in solar panels because he was so far from the grid and got sick of losing power for a week at a time. It's about as good a place to hide as you could ask for.'

'Perfect,' I grunted. I'd shifted to where my ribs didn't hurt, but that put my ankle in a strange position. I could tell that wouldn't last long. 'How long is this drive?'

'Probably three hours. Maybe longer, depending on the weather and the roads once we get up in the mountains.'

'Joy.' I shifted again, taking pressure off the ankle. I was rewarded by a stabbing pain in my side. 'Fuck this.' I unfastened my seatbelt. Much better. 'This thing is killing me. Try not to run into anything.'

'I know it's a long time crammed into a seat. You don't think we could hide out closer?'

'If I didn't suspect a police connection, we could rent a hotel room around here. I just don't want anybody running our descriptions past desk clerks. I can handle a little discomfort for the sake of safety.'

'We should be far enough away from Philips Mills, anyway.'

'So these are your old stomping grounds?' I asked.

She shrugged. 'Kind of. Dad loves the outdoors. Mom hates them. We compromised and took a lot of short trips. I like it in small doses. How about you?'

'I've spent my share of time out in the boondocks, but I prefer cities. I like being around people, I like being able to walk to a dozen different ethnic restaurants, or to see a band or a show or just not having to drive everywhere. I like hearing different languages. I also like the fact that you can have anonymity when you want it. City people mind their own business. Move to a town of a hundred people and ninety-nine will know your name in a week. Move to a city of eighty thousand and maybe five people will know you in a year.'

'I never looked at it that way.'

'The larger the city, the less chance a mob will try to burn you for witchcraft,' I replied.

'Realtors never mention that kind of thing.'

We drove north for about four hours, counting a stop at State Liquor Store for a bottle of good Scotch for Bob, and for dinner in Lincoln.

A snowstorm caught us halfway through Franconia Notch, reducing visibility to a few feet, so instead of a breathtaking view of the steep granite cliffs sloping down to the river, we got much too close a look at the dented and rusty guardrail. Since Sarah was driving, I just did what I usually did when my actions couldn't affect the outcome.

I closed my eyes.

We eventually arrived at the house. Off the beaten track was an understatement. Uncle Bob's place was down a dirt road, off a slightly less rutted dirt road off a barren stretch of Route 16. Only about twenty miles and a few hundred moose separated us from Canada. The driveway was unpaved and too steep to attempt in winter. It ran maybe fifty yards through the woods down toward the house, a frozen lake beyond that.

The house sat in a clearing in the trees. It had begun life as a simple cabin with a few bunks and a woodstove, a place to stay while hunting, fishing and canoeing, but it was newly sided with cedar shingles, the windows were modern and a mast of solar panels was aimed out over the lake through the gap in the trees.

The temperature was twenty degrees colder than it had been in Philips Mills, the snowbanks on the sides of the road were five feet high. The bite in the air, the chill seeping through my jacket, the snow falling through the evergreen branches all brought back memories. It felt a lot like the Ardennes had back in forty-four. Maybe expecting to get jumped at any moment by guys with central European accents highlighted the similarity.

We parked at the top of the drive and made our way down to the house. Uncle Bob met us at the front door.

He was a big man, probably around sixty, long hair and untrimmed beard gone to grey. He wore an old army jacket, a 3rd Infantry Division patch on the left sleeve. It stretched a bit over his midsection, but other than that, he seemed in fighting trim. He reminded me of a French Canadian fur trader I'd spent some time with on the St Lawrence. Hell, he might have been a direct descendant. God knows Jacques spent enough time producing them.

He had a smile and a hug for Sarah. I got an appraising look. Not unfriendly, but not warm either. One of my old sergeants had given out the advice "be polite, be respectful, but have a plan to kill everyone you meet". I think Bob had heard the same, and taken it to heart. There was a look in his eyes that I recognized. He'd been in real combat, killed men who were trying to return the favor. He looked even more like Jacques up close. I remembered that face, calm and concentrated in the firelight, sharpening his tomahawk the night before we rescued his Huron wife from the Iroquois. Uncle Bob looked like he'd be right at home sneaking into the enemy's longhouse.

'Uncle Bob, this is Sean.' Sarah nodded at me.

I stuck out a hand. He took it in a grip that would have put me on my knees had it been my injured one. 'Sarah says you're a good man but you got some trouble.'

'She's half right,' I replied.

That got a genuine smile.

'Come on in out of the cold. I have dinner in the oven. Should be about a half hour.'

We walked in to the house, through a mud room filled with coats and boots, skis and snowshoes on the walls, into a large kitchen. A big woodstove sat in the center of the room, along with a good sized table. The sitting room beyond was dominated by a gun rack. And I mean *dominated*. Uncle Bob had a .30-06 bolt action deer rifle, a pump action shotgun, an old side-by-side shotgun, a semi-automatic .22 rifle, a lever action rifle and a Soviet SKS assault rifle, although it was probably made in either Bulgaria or China depending which hemisphere he'd brought it home from. There were a few sidearms as well. A big Ruger revolver, probably a .44, and two semi-automatic handguns.

I'd led squads with less firepower.

'Something smells delicious,' Sarah said, shucking her bag. 'What's for dinner?'

'Moose tenderloin,' he replied. 'Buddy of mine shot one early in the season, wound up giving me quite a bit of meat. After you called last night I got some out of the freezer. Been marinating it all day.' He went to the refrigerator and handed us each a beer.

'You shouldn't have gone to the trouble for us,' she said.

'Company gives me an excuse to cook a roast. No point in doing that for one.'

'Sean's quite the cook,' she said. 'You guys can swap recipes.'

'You still useless in the kitchen?' he asked with a smile.

'I'm fabulous in the kitchen,' she said.

I covered my reaction to this shocking falsehood with a sip of beer.

'Still can't cook,' she added.

Bob's massive hand thumped on my back as I choked and coughed on my beer.

'Thanks,' I gasped.

'You OK, Sweetie?' asked Sarah, all innocence.

'I think I'll live,' I said, trying to ignore the new pain in my ribs.

'Never a dull moment with this one,' Bob told me.

We ate a leisurely dinner, accompanied by several beers, followed by coffee and finally the ceremonial opening of the bottle. After a drink, Sarah stood and excused herself.

'I want to dig around some more on that disk. You boys get to know each other.'

'I should try to call some people back home,' I said. 'Make sure these guys aren't leaning on my partners.'

'It's late,' said Sarah. 'Why don't you just call your voice mail?'

I looked blankly at her.

She sighed. 'You have no idea how to call your voice mail, do you? After I get my laptop out, I'll set it up so we can download your messages, see if anybody called.'

'You're too good to me.'

'I am,' she said. 'Remember that.'

As she walked out of the kitchen, Bob turned to me. 'She's quite a woman.'

'She is.'

'She really cares about you. I can see it. Known her a long time.'

I waited.

'You want to take that seriously.'

'I take it very seriously,' I replied.

'I'll spare you the speech. She's a big girl; she can make her own decisions. Just be careful.'

'I will.'

'So,' he refilled our glasses, 'where'd you serve?'

'I did a stint in the Marine Reserves,' I began.

'No,' he interrupted. 'The truth. You may have been a jarhead. Might even have stayed on in the weekend warriors for a while, training the newbies how not to get ambushed in Iraq and Afghanistan. But you've done some real fighting. And some black stuff. Let's not lie to one another.'

'How do you mean?'

'I saw the way your eyes moved when you walked in. You checked the approaches to the house; looked for cover, concealment, areas that are blind spots from the windows. You thought about which way would be the quietest to stalk the place. You gave the gun case a long look. I bet you could name every piece in it. Probably know that the SKS wasn't bought Stateside.'

'Fair enough,' I said. I wracked my brains for a story that would fit what he thought he knew and make him believe I'd served the government sometime since the Korean War.

Soldiers hadn't changed much, but equipment and lingo had. A missed detail would stick out to a guy like Bob.

'Did a hitch in the Seventh Marines. Got transferred to Force Recon. Went a lot of places. I was a decent shot, decent with languages, good with the locals and a ghost in the boonies.' I shrugged. 'I may have been temporarily assigned to a few government agencies.'

He nodded. 'Now, this trouble you're in,' he said, 'does it have anything to do with what you were doing for the government?'

'You could say that.'

'So, tell me about it. The broad strokes, no names, no places.'

I thought for a while. I could give him bare bones, let him understand the basic idea. He was offering us a place to hide, maybe he could help.

I was used to keeping secrets, hiding myself behind the things I didn't say. What I wasn't used to was the new secrets, the stuff about myself I'd hardly had time to assimilate. I decided to try it out on Bob.

'I refused to follow what was basically an unlawful order. An immoral order. They wanted me to help torture a prisoner. We were in an unconventional situation. We unconventionally resolved our differences with a little bit of violence. The higher-ups stepped in, I quietly went away and things got smoothed over. Now somebody wants to resume our disagreement.'

He nodded. 'I know the drill. I started out in 3ID. With Sarah's dad. He did his four and got out. I went to Ranger School, got into Special Forces.'

He paused, looking out the window over the frozen lake.

'Too much of what we were training for had too much scary potential for domestic spying, way I see it. That's why I moved out here, away from the watchful eyes. Off the grid.'

'You think somebody's keeping tabs?'

'I don't give 'em much reason, but I don't trust 'em. I've seen the evil that a government can do.'

I remained silent. Tried to keep my expression neutral.

'You look like you're not convinced,' he said. 'Didn't figure you for a guy who bought the bullshit about freedom and security. Figured you'd seen what makes a government scary.'

I'd hit a nerve by not agreeing. Probably a mistake, but too late to back off.

'Did you ever serve in Africa?' I asked.

He shook his head. 'Asia. Some time in the Middle East. What's special about Africa?'

'Let's just say I've seen what makes a lack of government so scary.'

I'd seen it in lots of places that weren't Africa, but in Uncle Bob's lifetime, most of those had been relatively well ordered. It didn't really make a difference. When the system breaks down, and there're no roads and no clean water and not enough peace to allow the construction of sewers or hospitals, or enough troops to keep order—well, you really don't care if it's Hutus or Vikings or Visigoths burning your hut and violating your women.

He grunted. Took another sip of whisky. 'I still don't trust them. Don't trust anyone who wants that much power.'

'There's plenty of happy middle ground between a horde of rebel child soldiers with AKs and machetes invading the village, and jackbooted secret police hauling off the undesirables. Ambitious men will always seek power, and when they get it, they'll seek more.' I shrugged. 'At least here, you can vote the sons of bitches out.'

He gave me a long look. It belatedly occurred to me that it was the kind of look he kept for men who enjoyed his hospitality, ate his food, sought sanctuary at his home, boned the daughter of his army buddy and then pointed out the holes in his deeply held worldview. It was also the kind of look that highlighted just how remote this house was, and how big he was.

That was a lot to get into a look.

After a long moment, the ice broke up and he gave a sour grin. 'You might have a point. Mostly I think you only think that way because you're still young and idealistic, but maybe you have a point. Maybe we're so used to being safe from the Mongol Hordes that we forget.'

I smiled, partly out of the novelty of being called young and idealistic, and partly because we weren't going to have a knock-down drag-out over the pros and cons of civilization.

He nodded. Finished his drink.

'Well, you're both welcome to stay here while you figure out what you want to do. If I think of anything, I'll let you know. It's about time I turned in. You two can take the guest room at the top of the stairs. If I'm not here when you get up, make yourselves at home. There's food in the fridge, Sarah says you know your way around a stove. Just so you know, there's a Browning 9mm in the drawer of the bedside table up in your room. Just in case trouble follows you.'

He heaved himself out of his chair and headed off to the ground floor bedroom. I looked at the narrow staircase, thought about my ankle and poured another drink before making the trek. At least there was a beautiful woman at the other end.

Chapter 25

I WOKE THE NEXT MORNING feeling merely awful, which was a step in the right direction. I dragged myself out of bed and shuffled slowly toward the kitchen. Through the window I noticed that Bob's truck was gone.

As I passed the living room, I saw Sarah sitting at the computer, chin cupped in her left hand, one leg tucked under her, the other curled beneath the seat, her foot hooked behind the back leg of the chair.

I smiled as I admired the curve of her body, from the attractively disheveled blonde curls, down her neck and back, over her hip and down her leg. It was a pose that Rubens would have spent hours on, and Degas would have suggested with a single brushstroke.

'So, who's Monique?' she asked in a flat, expressionless tone, not turning toward me.

My pleasant reverie shattered as alarm bells clanged behind my eyes. Survival instincts, honed by years of experience, called for a quick escape.

'My partner on the ambulance,' I replied, keeping my voice light and carefree. 'Why? Is something wrong?'

'I wouldn't know. Why don't you listen to the voice mail I downloaded and tell me.'

That sounded bad. I limped over to the machine and she clicked the mouse.

'Hi Sean, It's Monique.'

Crap. I'd never really paid enough attention to her voice, but now that I did, I realized she sounded like she should be charging me by the minute.

'I just wanted to make sure you're OK. You took off so suddenly the other night. Call me when you can. Hope everything's alright. Hugs.'

Thanks, Nique, I thought.

'She sounds pretty,' Sarah commented. 'Is she pretty?'

I knew there was no right answer. I gave the rightest one I could think of, with the added bonus that it was the truth. 'Not as pretty as you.'

She tossed her head and her eyes flashed dangerously. 'Dammit, Sean!' she said, throwing her hands up in frustration. 'How the hell am I supposed to know what to think? I like you. I really like you. You're funny and thoughtful and I'm ragingly attracted to you, but the surprises are coming a little too thick.'

'I'm sorry,' I said sincerely. 'I'm not trying to deceive you. I really like you. The last thing I want to do is screw this up.'

'I really want to believe that,' she shook her head. 'I do. It's just that I think to myself, finally, after all the jerks, all the posers, all the guys who just get theirs then roll over and fall asleep, I finally meet a guy who's actually *read books*. Who can have an intelligent conversation, and cook and make me laugh and make love to me so my legs don't stop shaking for two days, and I'm walking on air. Then I find out the great guy I'm so excited about is a fugitive with magical powers who's being chased by knife-wielding, teleporting drug dealers, and spends twenty four hours a week in a truck with a girl with a phone sex voice and a stripper name... so, yeah, I'm a little fucking upset.'

She paused for a moment, breathing heavily. 'Why did you have to run off so suddenly on Monique the other night?' she asked with a trace of venom.

'That was the night I invited you to go for drinks with some of the gang from work. I wanted to show you off. I took off early after we found out that a girl from admitting at the hospital got beat up. I realized that she had given me the info on Doors. The fact that you were digging for info for me on line made me worry that you might be in danger. I ran out suddenly and never explained leaving because I was so horrified at the thought of someone hurting you.'

She stood silent for a few heartbeats, then sniffed. 'Oh, shit.' Her lip began to tremble. 'I'm sorry.' Her body started to shake with sobs. 'I didn't know.'

I limped over to her, put my arms around her shaking shoulders and pulled her close.

'It's alright,' I said softly. 'It's all my fault. I had no idea how bad this would get.'

She shuddered with sobs for a while, muttering, 'It's just too much. I'm sorry, but it's too much.'

My own eyes welled with tears. I just held her and rocked her while my heart sank at the thought of losing her. The cynical part of my brain tried to make the point that this is what came of honesty, but that was only half of it. She had gotten beaten up before I'd opened up. 'I'm sorry I wasn't honest with you from the start. I'm sorry you were ever in danger. You mean the world to me, and I will move mountains to keep you safe and stay by you.'

'You mean that?' she asked at length, when she had cried it out.

'I do. I just want to be with you and keep you safe.'

'And you're not sleeping with any tramps from the ambulance?'

'Not a one. Nique is my partner, and a good friend. We depend on one another, and we're close, but I promise you, there is absolutely nothing sexual. And there never was.'

'You really want to be here with a boring old professor and not run off with the French paramedic with the bimbo voice?'

'You're hardly boring, my sweet. If I'd met more professors like you, I'd have stuck around and earned a few degrees. All I want is to hold you and cook for you and make you laugh and all the rest.'

'You're not forgetting the part about making my legs shake, right?' she mumbled into my shoulder.

'I'm not forgetting that part.'

'Because that's a very important part.'

'It's one of my favorites,' I assured her.

'So you want to spend your life with me?' She pulled her head back to look up at me.

'I do.'

'Your freakish, unnatural, immortal life?' She smiled. It was a small smile, but just then it was like the sun breaking through the clouds.

'Every bit of it. I just want to not grow old with you.'

'I'm gonna hold you to that,' she warned.

'So long as you hold me to this,' I replied, giving her a squeeze.

'Oh, double entendres,' she said. 'Be still my heart.'

She kissed me then, lightly at first, then with an increasing intensity, a passion with an underlying desperation. She clearly didn't want to let go, and in view of her earlier concerns, she probably needed reassurance that she turned me on.

There are times, I reflected, when you need to man up and prove a point, injured or not.

I returned her kiss, running my good hand through her hair, and wrapped my other arm around her waist, squeezing her with my forearm and stroking the small of her back with just my fingertips. Fortunately, I still had the brace on my wrist.

I maintained the embrace as I steered her toward the bedroom, which allowed me to lean on her a bit to spare my ankle, and to pass off my wincing and gasps of pain as animal passion.

Only slightly distracted by my injuries, I did my best to reassure her that she held the prized position of object of my lust. That was one thing I didn't have to fake, at least.

Afterwards, I held her close for a long time, and not just for her. With the warmth of her soft curves tight against me, I could forget the pain, the gnawing fear, the bafflement of not knowing my next move. I was, if only for a moment, happy and safe and... home.

Chapter 26

SARAH FELL ASLEEP PRETTY QUICKLY, but the throbbing in my wrist and the cramping of my ribs with every breath, as well as the racing of my thoughts, kept me awake. I eventually gave up, slid out from the covers and made my way to the living room.

I lurched to the liquor cabinet, poured a stiff measure and sat for a while, trying to figure my current situation.

Fuck, I summed up. That seemed to do it.

I was outnumbered, outgunned, out-resourced in every meaningful way. Doors and his minions knew more about me than I did, and if they had done a lousy job of tracking me down so far, their luck had to change sooner or later. Even if they didn't know exactly which door to kick in to find me right at the moment, they knew enough about my job and my contacts that it was only a matter of time.

Hell, after my little visit, they might just start kicking in any door with the vaguest connection to me and work from there.

I was hiding out with a broken wrist, a sprained ankle, and no plan at all. They had an organization of heavily armed, if unimaginative, thugs, at least some of whom could walk through walls.

I had friends who were all I could hope for on an ambulance call, and a beautiful blonde who had, admittedly, helped me plan a moderately successful burglary. But they were hardly a team of killers, and just knowing me put them in danger. Doors and his thugs were willing to hurt people to find me. It was only a matter of time before they got around to my partners.

Maybe the best thing for everyone would be if I disappeared.

No. Doors and his men would still go after Sarah and Nique and Pete and all the rest, even if I didn't tell anything he could use. They were his best leads, and they'd suffer.

Shit, shit, *shit*.

Fighting was unrealistic, running was no good and I doubted I could talk my way out of this one. I felt paralyzed.

For one brief, frightening moment, I very uncharacteristically considered walking into Doors' office and going out in a blaze of glory, like a short-handed Butch and Sundance, just to spare my friends. I hope that was just the drink talking.

I heard Sarah walking around the bedroom. I decided if she needed me badly enough, she'd find me.

She did. She came up behind me and put her arms around my neck. 'Thinking?'

'Making an effort,' I replied. 'I've gotten as close as "drinking", which at least rhymes.'

'I may have an idea,' she breathed, kissing me on the side of my neck.

'While that seems like a good idea, I was hoping for a solution to our current life-threatening problem.'

'Conrad,' she muttered in my ear.

'It's Sean, my sweet,' I replied. 'I expected it to take longer for you to start calling me by the wrong name.'

'*Joseph* Conrad,' she elaborated. 'Ever read any of his stuff?'

'Just *Heart of Darkness*.'

'He wrote a short story you might like,' she smiled. 'About a duel between two of Napoleon's officers. It's called *The Duel*, originally enough. Take a look and see if it gives you any ideas.'

'I'll keep an eye out for it.'

'Or,' she handed me some pages, 'you could read this copy I just printed off the Net.'

OK, I reflected, *maybe we have an entry in the column against dating English professors.*

'Pirating intellectual property?' I asked with a grin. 'Shocking lapse in professional ethics.'

'Eh,' she shrugged. 'It's not like Conrad needs the dough. You look that over and see if you think that's something that might work. I'm going to do some more digging through our friends' files.'

As she left, I read through what she had printed. I didn't expect great things. I had served with a lot of Napoleon's officers and, as a group, they weren't known for subtlety. Brave and dumb got one further than clever in those days, which is one reason I tried to stay off on my own as much as possible.

It turned out I was wrong. Conrad came up with a solution that could just be twisted to my situation. I'd need some more leverage, but maybe there was more in the files Sarah had. I chuckled, heaved myself out of my chair and made my way to the other room. Sarah was still at the computer, sifting through the stolen files for details.

'So,' she said, turning at my approach, 'you think that might work?'

'In theory, it's brilliant,' I replied. 'In practice, I just have to beat this guy in a fair fight, crippled though I am.'

'You still have a few moves in you,' she smirked. 'And I've seen you fight. You're scary.'

'I just project the abject terror I'm feeling,' I explained. 'But you've probably come up with the solution we were looking for.'

'I do my best.'

I had a thought. 'Hey, is there anything in those files about his fencing? I saw a photo of him in his gear and some medals.'

She handed me another printed sheet, '*Voila.*'

'You even know I'd rather read hard copy than a screen,' I marvelled. 'How have I survived this long without you?'

'Well, most old guys like hard copy.' She grinned. 'But I'm surprised by how *much* I'm having to pick up the slack on the whole thinking half of the game.'

'That's because you have a PhD and I just have lots of low, animal cunning.' I replied. 'Honestly, I think I'm just starting to lean on you because you're that much smarter than I am.' I started to look over the pages, 'Too bad we didn't have you during the Russian campaign.' Not that Napoleon would have listened. Or even Ney. Travis? Not a chance. MacArthur? Unlikely. Vandegrift would have. It occurred to me that a defining trait of leaders who got us into an unwinnable mess was the inability to listen.

I spent the ensuing day reading and resting. Healing.

Bob came back late in the afternoon and we had a pleasant meal, unmarred by me saying anything stupid. I made the trip upstairs with only minor difficulty.

Things were looking brighter.

Chapter 27

A BRIGHT LIGHT IN THE DRIVEWAY woke me in the dead of the night. I looked out and didn't see Bob's truck. I shook Sarah awake.

'Get dressed and ready to move,' I whispered. 'Somebody's here.'

She nodded and reached for her clothes without question.

That gave me a warm, fuzzy feeling that I might have chosen well. I winced as I laced up my ankle brace and my wrist splint, then dragged on some pants, a thick, dark green sweater and my shoes. I dug out my .45 and tucked it in my waistband, then fumbled in the drawer and found Bob's Browning. I quickly loaded a magazine and chambered a round.

We eased downstairs and out into the kitchen. Like most people who live in the woods, Bob seldom locked his doors, but the bright motion activated security lights were on outside, spilling a pool of illumination through the windows onto the pine planks of the kitchen floor.

Maybe it was just a bear or raccoon rooting through the trash.

Someone barked an order in that guttural language I was growing to hate. Probably 'Stay out of the light and watch that door!'

Or not.

Keeping in the shadows, I stretched to look out the window. I could make out the dark shape of an SUV parked on the road at the top of the long driveway, and the shadowy form of a man about ten yards from the house.

I didn't bother wondering who they were. How they tracked us I wasn't sure.

'Sarah,' I said, pitching my voice low. 'Keep your back to a wall.'

A bulky winter coat and hat hung near the door made a vaguely anthropomorphic shadow. I looked around and found a canoe paddle, reached it out and moved the coat, hoping to draw fire.

I saw a swirl of deeper darkness in the shadow behind it. A shape taking on substance.

I aimed my pistol at the biggest piece I could see and fired. The shape became a man, clutching his right shoulder and staggering back against the kitchen wall. I fired two more rounds into the center of his chest and he gave a grunt and slid to the floor.

Outside, there was a rattle of automatic gunfire. Rounds splintered wood from the walls and shattered windows. The security lights popped and flashed and went out. Urgent shouts in the strange language I'd come to hate followed.

I took Sarah's hand, pulled her close and breathed in her ear, 'We need to make for the back door. Onto the deck and then down to the woods. Stay right behind me, move when I move and keep in the shadows. Got that?'

She nodded.

I pressed the Browning into her hand. 'You know how to use this?'

Again a nod.

'It's loaded and cocked. Round in the chamber. The safety's right here. It's on. Don't take it off until you're ready to shoot, and don't shoot until I tell you.'

'OK,' she whispered.

I crept to the back door, staying out of the light. Outside, I heard a debate in hissing whispers. I assumed the guy who phased in was in charge, and the lackeys weren't sure how to proceed.

If they were well trained and dedicated, they'd have surrounded the house.

My hope was that the snow and brush and slope of the yard would make moving around the sides of the house look like too much work, and that they'd be overconfident with machine guns and the ability to teleport. They had been playing the game like a street gang and not a rifle squad so far. Maybe my luck would hold.

If they were doing this right, we were screwed either way. They had the numbers and firepower to come in and get us eventually, or even just set the house on fire and pick us off as we tried to get out. Sitting and waiting to be wiped out was pointless. We had to move.

I opened the back door, gave a quick look around and moved out onto the deck. On one side it was only a five foot drop to the snow. I motioned Sarah over the side. I used my good hand, holding her arm and letting her down until she could drop the last foot or so. I tucked my pistol in my waistband, rolled over the edge and dropped, landing on my good foot, bending my knees and falling onto my side like they taught us in Jump School. Spared my bad ankle. Hurt my ribs, but what can you do?

I paused, listening. The conversation had stopped. I heard a few crunching footsteps as someone moved across the packed snow on the drive, then the sound of snapping branches.

Beneath the deck was an alcove, just a space between a corner of the foundation and a wooden bin housing the batteries for the solar electricity system. I pointed to the space.

'Get in there,' I said. 'Get your back to the wall. You'll be invisible unless somebody sticks his head in and whoever does that will be silhouetted against all this bright snow. Anybody does that who isn't me, shoot him. I'll be back.'

'Where are you going?'

'To kill the rest of these bastards,' I replied. 'It may take a while. Don't worry. I'm good at this.' I kissed her once, then moved away. I got out of the open snow as quickly as I could, into the rocks under the cedars, where there wasn't much snow to show tracks. It's harder to move quietly under the trees, but you can do it if you don't hurry. Since we had a lifetime, for some of us at least, I was content to move slowly.

They had me outnumbered and outgunned, but they were leaderless, hesitant and out of their element. The darkness leveled the playing field; better guns still need a target. I liked the darkness. I'd made friends with it a long time ago. Learned to trust my hearing, my sense of smell, of touch.

They would waste some time approaching and searching the house. When they didn't find us there, they'd figure we were trying to get to the cars, so they'd move back that way. If they were even a little smart, they'd have left one man back at the road to watch the vehicles. I made my way toward the shapes of the cars, taking it slow.

Footsteps on the front porch. Doors banging open. Curses and hissed replies. Must have found their buddy with three new holes in him. A light went on in the house. Could they be that stupid? Now they had no night vision. I sat still, looking at the ground in front of the house, keeping both doors in my peripheral vision.

A man came out the back door onto the deck. Must have seen the marks in the snow below. I thought about taking a shot, but it was a long shot for a pistol, and that would tell everyone where I was. He moved back inside. I heard a cellphone up the hill near the car. Probably the guys in the house telling the guy up top to watch for us. Just keep giving it away, boys.

Sloppy. But they'd been facing street gangs before this, not soldiers. And they'd had the huge advantage of a few men who could teleport. That was a big ace in the hole. A guy who could appear behind a lookout and take him out, unlock a door for the brute squad. That was enough of an edge for what they'd been doing.

But having an edge can make people careless. Make them feel invincible. They think they have a trump card, like a breech-loading rifle or modern artillery against some primitive tribesmen and they forget the basics.

That's how we get Little Bighorn or Isandlwana or Dien Bien Phu.

One man moved back out onto the deck and the other came out the front door, moving quickly into the brush on the far side of the drive. The man on the deck dropped down and began following my tracks. Sarah wouldn't have left any on the bare, frozen earth under the deck.

They were working toward the road, assuming I was as well. Reaching down, my hand closed on a large pine cone. I tossed it up the hill. They didn't shoot at it, but I heard the closer man stop, then change direction, stalking the sound.

He moved along the edge of the woods. The virgin snow muffled his footsteps, but his long coat snagged branches and dry thorns. He might as well have worn a bell.

I sat on my haunches, concealed in the shadows of the cedars, my pistol gripped lightly in my right hand, and waited. The cold seeped into my body, but I suppressed the urge to move. Graves aren't any warmer, as Sergeant Daly used to say.

The man's path took him right past me. I slowed my breathing, willed myself invisible and let him walk on by. He moved in a crouch, an MP5 with a collapsible shoulder stock held at the ready, his big stupid trenchcoat dragging behind him, the collar turned up and a balaclava pulled over his ears—ruining the best sense he had out here.

I let him pass within about five feet of me. Then I stood, extended my arm until the muzzle of my pistol was almost touching the back of the upturned collar, and pulled the trigger.

He pitched forward into the snow. I sank back down, shifting behind a thick tree trunk. It would be hard for them to pinpoint a single shot by sound, and my victim's head, while it hadn't served him very well, hid the muzzle flash.

There were a few more shouts, probably the remaining men calling out for their comrade. I heard a hushed conference. I almost felt bad. They were better armed, healthy and had started out with a huge numerical advantage, but they were flailing.

I, on the other hand, had been playing this game with armed men in the deep, dark woods since long before their grandfathers were just a glint in the mailman's eye.

Footsteps in the woods indicated that the man across the drive was moving toward the cars. He was smart enough to keep to the shadow of the trees, even if he moved too quickly to avoid making noise. I was fairly sure where he was, from the snapping of branches and the squeaking crunch of boots in the snow, but I didn't shoot. You never shoot without a target, especially at night. It shows exactly where you are; plus you'd have a better chance just praying for lightning to strike your enemy.

Boots on the gravel at the top of the drive told me he'd reached the vehicle. Maybe they were hoping to get away, or call for more help, or get the bazooka out of the trunk. Whatever the plan, I decided to throw a wrench into it.

I picked up the dead man's submachine gun. The road was pretty far away to start plinking with my pistol, and if I did give them something to shoot at—me with a .45 against two men with automatic weapons—I could still lose this fight. I took a moment to get my sights aligned, which is harder than it sounds at night, lining up a black front sight in a black rear sight against darkness. I had to aim at a snowbank to do it but, once I had it, I was good. I knelt, my left elbow on my knee, leaning into the tree trunk, aiming at the dark bulk of the car.

The car door opened, and the dome light came on. A black-clad man stood by the passenger door watching the forest, an MP5 in his hands. Another tossed his weapon into the back seat and began to slide behind the wheel.

The driver was on the far side of the car from me, so I shot him first. One round, in the head. Before he had time to drop, I switched my aim to center mass on the near thug, and squeezed the trigger until he fell over.

I waited in the quiet darkness. No shots, no cries, no phones. I crept up to the road and checked the enemy. Both men were dead, sprawled in the harsh illumination of the car's dome light.

Once the adrenaline of the fight drained away, I felt the cold in my limbs, the pain in my ankle and my ribs and my wrist. I hobbled back down to the house, stopped out of sight of Sarah's hiding spot.

'It's me,' I called. 'It's over, you can come out.'

She came out, shivering. 'You're OK?'

'Frozen and sore, but otherwise I'm fine.'

'And them?'

'Four. All dead.'

She nodded in silence.

'We should get in out of the cold,' I said. 'Then we need to get out of here.'

Chapter 28

WE QUICKLY GOT OUR THINGS TOGETHER. I limped into the bathroom and found a handful of ibuprofen to help ease the throbbing in my limbs. I wondered where Bob was, why he wasn't here when a hit team showed up. Had he talked to anybody? Asked someone he trusted to check on me and tipped somebody off? I still wasn't sure how Doors' people found me two hundred miles away, in a car rented with a fake name, in a house this far off the beaten track. While Sarah packed, I stole the address book from beside the phone. Maybe there was something there. I held on to the Browning and also took a .22 target pistol from the gun cabinet.

Sarah helped me drag the body of the teleporter off into the woods, where a snowfall would cover our tracks and he wouldn't be noticed until the late spring, when he started to smell.

I stole his cell phone, figuring I could go through the call record and see what was there. OK, I was going to have Sarah go through the call record, but it was my idea so it counts. I also found a pair of hotel key cards, the protective sleeves helpfully marked with the room numbers, and slipped them into my wallet, along with his cash.

We dragged the other bodies off the road and left them in the snow of the yard. There wasn't much traffic out here, but two dead men lying in the road wouldn't take long to be spotted.

I kept one of the MP5s and two spare magazines. I'd learned my lesson about leaving heavy firepower behind. Besides, in New Hampshire I probably didn't even need a permit for it. I think they make you fill out a card and show two forms of ID for crew served weapons, but that might be out of date.

'I'll drive their car up to the first nice pull-off and ditch it,' I told Sarah. 'Follow me in the Jeep.'

'Why are we doing all this?'

'If one hitter and the car are missing, maybe somebody will think he's gone freelance, or maybe that we captured him, made him talk,' I replied. 'Maybe not, but let's give 'em something else to worry about.'

Sarah got in the Jeep without a word. I started the other car, wondering how she would hold up through this latest crisis. So far, she was coping, but I'd seen men take a lot without cracking before they collapse from one more tiny setback. Her composure couldn't be that supreme; I couldn't see the cracks, but they had to be there, and that scared the hell out of me.

I drove until the first pull-off at the head of a hiking trail. I parked the car far back under the trees, the side with the bullet holes against a snowbank. It would be invisible from the road, and even if it was found, it wasn't uncommon for people to park at the trails and go snowshoeing or snowmobiling.

I threw the keys into the snow and got into the Jeep.

'Where?' Sarah asked without inflection.

'Head south,' I replied. 'We'll stop at the first hotel and figure out our next move.'

I pulled out the phone I'd stolen from the man I'd shot. I managed to access the recent calls, and scrolled through until I found something that stuck out: most of the calls came from area codes in Massachusetts, but there were a few odd ones, including a 202 number, which was Washington DC.

My stomach dropped. I had a hunch but I really didn't want to be right.

I pulled out Uncle Bob's address book, and thumbed through it, looking for DC numbers. Unfortunately, I found a match.

'What are you looking at?' asked Sarah.

'One of our friends' phones,' I replied. 'Trying to see who he's been talking to.'

'You're staring and chewing your lip,' she said. 'The red button usually turns it on.'

'Har, har.'

'Then I guess the look of concentration means you found something.'

'Maybe,' I replied. The entry in Bob's book next to the same number just had a first name: Dan. No address, no last name, nothing. But, given that it was a Washington number, and who Bob had known in his days with the government, I really wasn't happy to see this Dan in contact with Doors and his crew.

'What is it? Does it have anything to do with how they tracked us to Uncle Bob's?'

'Maybe.'

'Well?'

I sighed. 'I think Bob may have tipped them off himself. By accident,' I added quickly. 'I think he reached out to a guy he knew, maybe an old army buddy or a guy in the intelligence community, and they passed it on to Doors.'

'What?'

'I think there may be a connection between Doors and a secret government intelligence program.'

'And Uncle Bob?' she said. 'That's insane.'

'Well, Bob did do some work with the Special Forces. You've heard rumors of secret government programs? Mind control, psychic warfare, intelligence gathering?'

'But those are just...' she trailed off.

'Crazy rumors,' I finished. 'I know. Like the aliens at Roswell or the black helicopters. Or guys who can teleport or immortal healers.'

'Just like that, yeah.'

'You said he used to do dowsing. Finding water or something like that?'

She nodded. 'He always said he could do it. A few people did pay him to tell them where to dig wells. I never paid much attention. I saw him do a few tricks, but I thought they were just... well, tricks.'

'Like what?'

'Like he'd find people's lost keys, or he'd have somebody hide something and he'd find it. I never thought anything of it. I was a kid. It was like card tricks. I mean, everyone has an uncle who does card tricks or pulls coins out of your ear, right?'

I nodded. 'I wouldn't have thought anything of it either. Anyway, if Bob had this talent, maybe he did some work on one of these projects. Maybe the CIA wants some guys who can teleport and one of Doors' clan gets recruited. Anyway, I think Bob reached out to an old contact, to see what he could learn about Doors, or to help us, or maybe even check on me and see if I was good enough for his niece, and this guy passed the info on. I'm sure Bob didn't try to sell us out, he just misjudged an old friend.'

'You think they might have grabbed Uncle Bob?'

I cursed. Yeah, that made sense. I was thinking they just knew his address. But he might be paranoid enough not to let even his old special ops cronies know that. If they grabbed him, it would explain why he didn't come home last night. I didn't think he'd sell Sarah out. Me maybe, but not Sarah. He didn't strike me as a guy who'd do that even to me, but I hadn't known him long. If he was the kind of guy who'd sell out his army buddy's daughter, I had seriously misjudged him.

'If they did, they might be holding him,' I said. 'Keeping him secure until they see how the info panned out. We have some hotel keys with room numbers.'

'You think we can do anything about that?' she asked. 'You're hurt, and I'm a professor, not a Navy SEAL.'

'You're smart, I'm sneaky and underhanded. Plus, if they do have him, we can't just leave him.'

We could. We really could, and it would be the smart thing, but it wouldn't be the right thing. He meant a lot to Sarah, and he'd extended hospitality to me when I was in danger. I owed him.

'You have an idea?'

I thought for a moment. 'Maybe,' I did a quick search on the hotel using the stolen cellphone. 'The hotel is in Berlin. It's a good hour away. Just stay on route 16. I'll come up with something.'

The stolen cell phone rang. I looked at the display.

'Let it go to voice mail,' she said.

'Why?'

'Because it's easier to listen to his message than it is to impersonate the guy you shot.'

'Good point.'

The ringing stopped and soon afterwards the message alert beeped.

'That guy's ringtone was the Skorpions,' I said.

'So?'

'Makes me want to go back and shoot him again.'

'Give me the phone,' she said. 'I'll check his voice mail.'

She took the phone, punched a few buttons and listened.

'I think he says he's not getting any cell reception at the hotel. Says to call the room phone when they get back.'

'He left a message in English?' I asked.

'No, but the words *phone* and *hotel* are pretty much the same in every European language. It sounds like a German dialect, but with a different accent. Like he grew up speaking Hungarian and learned Austrian German.'

'Wow.'

'PhD in languages,' she reminded me. 'This is the first time I've heard it conversationally. Not orders barked at guys who were shooting at you.'

Chapter 29

WE WALKED INTO THE DESERTED HOTEL LOBBY, arms around one another, her head on my shoulder, looking for all the world like a honeymoon couple. The desk clerk barely looked up, didn't challenge us as we made our way to the elevator.

We reached the third floor and followed it along until we found room 367, the last door on a long corridor. They probably had Bob in there, with 366 as a buffer for any sounds from the interrogation. I didn't like to think about that, and I didn't mention it to Sarah. She probably had an idea, having been through it herself.

We stopped in front of 366. No light trickled out under the door, there was no sound of television or voices. A faint sound of the TV came through the door of 367.

I took out my pistol and nodded to Sarah, who swept the key card into the lock of room 366. Then I pushed down on the handle and, ignoring the twinge in my ankle, I moved through quickly, putting my back to the wall and sweeping my weapon across the room.

The room was vacant, but some bags sat on the floor and one of the beds was unmade. The bathroom door stood open. Nobody in there.

I waved Sarah into the room, pointed to the phone. 'Just like we talked about.'

She took a deep breath, blew it out and nodded, then picked up the receiver and dialed room number 367. While she did that, I took out a pair of athletic socks, folded them over the barrel of Bob's .22 and taped them in place.

'Hello, sir,' she said into the phone. 'This is Carol at reception. Your friends are back. They say they ran into an old school friend and need a hand getting him out of the car. I guess he's had a little too much to drink... Not at all... Thank you, sir.' She hung up.

'Damn, you're good at that,' I said with a smile.

I moved to the door, the pistol ready, and waited until I heard the next door open and close and footsteps pass by. I eased the door open just enough to see a tall, lean man walking briskly toward the elevator. Like all the others I'd seen, he wore a black turtleneck, tailored jeans and black jump boots. His blond hair was cut high and tight.

I raised the pistol and shot him in the back of the head. He jerked and fell on his face, twitching for a few seconds.

It was quiet for a gunshot, being only a .22 and with a hillbilly silencer on it, but it was still a gunshot. I hoped the rest of the guests were heavy sleepers.

After a quick look to make sure he didn't have any friends coming out of 367, I tucked the pistol in my waistband and hobbled out.

Sarah stood in the doorway, a look of shock on her face.

'Help me with this,' I said, grabbing one of the man's ankles. 'He's heavy and I only have one good hand.'

She shook herself, then took his other leg and we dragged the body into the room. Luckily, being only a .22, the bullet had gone in the back of his skull, but not out the front, so he didn't leave a trail of blood and brains.

'Did you have to kill him?' she asked.

'Yep.' I said. 'Wasn't gonna step out and say "freeze" then have him teleport behind me and put a knife in my kidney.'

She absorbed that in silence.

'I'm injured,' I continued. 'Our bluff would only have held until he got to the lobby. Maybe he's not one of the guys who can teleport, but I'm not betting your life or mine on that. These guys play hardball.'

'I guess,' she said.

'OK, he was probably alone,' I said, 'but let's go in next door assuming he wasn't.'

I was actually very happy about this so far. If Bob wasn't in the room, why would they have left a man behind? And why leave two behind to babysit a prisoner and weaken your assault team if they only planned to be gone a few hours? Still, no reason to stop being cautious now.

I put the .22 away and took out my trusty .45. The .22 is a fine gun for shooting unsuspecting people in the back of the head, and it's nice and quiet, but if Bob had another guard, and he was up and moving and shooting back, I didn't trust a .22 to put him down quickly.

I stood to one side of the door of 367 while Sarah slid the card key into the lock. I went through quick and low, wishing my ankle hurt less.

The lights were on, the TV flickering pay-per-view porn. The room was free of gunmen. Bob sat, his wrists and ankles secured to a chair with plastic zip ties, his...

'Stay out there,' I told Sarah.

'What is it?'

'Everything will be OK, I promise, but please, stay out there and give me a minute.'

I crossed the room. 'Bob? It's Sean.'

He raised his head and turned toward me.

'Just relax. It's OK. The guard's gone. Sarah is fine. I'm gonna take care of this.'

He was gagged, which was a mercy. They'd worked him over pretty badly. He must have been tough to crack, if they ever did. Maybe he never told them anything and they just checked his address from his license. His eyes were ruined, crusted blood trails down his cheeks, and his hands were a mess, fingers twisted at terrible angles.

I put a hand on his forehead. He flinched at the touch.

'Shhhhh,' I soothed. 'It's OK. I'm gonna do a little something for the pain.'

I let the energy seep in, calming the nerves. First ease the pain, then fix the damage. I grimaced as I explored his injuries. Nothing was life-threatening, and most of it was superficial, calculated to hurt, but to deny the prisoner the refuge of death. I'm sure if they hadn't found us at his place they'd have come back and asked more questions.

I did the eyes first. There was a lot of damage to the right, but everything was still there, so I was able to get it back. The left was... mostly missing. I could only stop the pain, quiet the nerves, and close the wounds to keep out infection. Then the fingers. I rotated each joint back into place and urged the bones to knit, the torn tendons and ligaments to come together, the broken skin to heal over.

Sarah came in as I finished. I sighed and sagged down by the chair. 'Cut him loose, could you?' I asked, handing her my pocketknife. 'I'm out of steam.'

She quickly cut the plastic ties and hugged Bob tightly. He held her for a moment, then looked at his fingers, turning his hands over as he examined the repaired flesh. He touched the scar tissue over his left eye.

After a long pause, he turned to me. 'OK, what the fuck just happened?'

I shrugged. 'It's a long story. I can heal people. Only other people, though, which is why I had to limp to the rescue. I can't fix your left eye, but your right should be fine.'

'Who are these guys?' he asked, looking again at his hands. 'They're not CIA. Not special forces or anything.'

I shrugged again. 'I don't know. The boss wants me dead for something personal a long time ago. The organization is just running drugs, as far as I know.'

'Ah,' he said. 'That makes sense.'

'It does?' I sat up. 'You know something I don't?'

He was quiet for a long time.

'I did some checking on you,' he said. 'First off, I couldn't find any Sean Danet who served in the 7th Marines.'

'That's because my name wasn't Sean Danet when I was in the Seventh,' I said. 'But go on.'

'Like I said, I went into the Special Forces. Around that time, the CIA was doing a lot of experiments in paranormal abilities. Remote viewing. Translocation. I used to mess around with dowsing, back a long time ago. I talked about it to one of the officers, he recommended me to somebody, and I worked in the remote viewing project for a while. They were intelligence gathering. Experimenting with a lot of psychic warrior stuff. My ability was finding water. I located some interesting mineral veins, too. But they wanted a guy who could find rebel hideouts. I wasn't there long. Saw some odd stuff, though.'

He fixed me with a penetrating look. 'I'm guessing you have, too.'

I thought about that. I'd heard rumors of government experiments; that was as old as governments. But I hadn't taken any of it seriously. Outside of the shaving mirror, I'd never seen anyone who could do anything that couldn't be explained.

Maybe that was a bit shortsighted of me.

'Let's say maybe I have.'

'I had a feeling.' He looked away again. Everywhere but my eyes. 'So I reached out to a friend in the intelligence community. He said he'd do some checking. An hour later, he called back. Said he had some info. He'd have someone deliver it, meet me at a restaurant tonight. Instead, these thugs cornered me outside. They weren't very professional, I saw they were up to something, had my Ruger out and pointed at the first one before he could say a word.' He stopped, looked directly at me for the first time since I'd fixed his eye. 'Then he vanished. And then he was behind me, with a knife under my chin. How the fuck did he do that?'

I took a deep breath before answering. 'Like you said, I've seen some strange things. I figure your buddy has worked with these guys before, tipped 'em off. Figured you could tell them where to find me.'

'I didn't tell 'em shit.'

'I believe you. But you probably didn't have to. They got your address, came to check it out.'

'What happened?'

'I had to leave some dead bodies up at your place. And I borrowed a couple of your guns.' I handed him the .22. 'You might want to get rid of this one. The guy who was guarding you is in the next room with a slug from this in his head.'

He took the gun, checked the chamber and pocketed it. 'Thanks.' He looked at me for a moment. 'You killed four men who came to my house?'

'They drew first.'

'Then you planned a rescue and killed another one here, all with a bad wrist and a bad ankle?'

'And the ribs,' I said.

'Maybe you were a jarhead,' he said. 'You're crazy enough.'

'Hey, I had backup. They never expected a college professor. Seriously, you said it yourself, these guys aren't exactly Green Berets. And I knew what they could do. I was ready for it.'

'Never seen anything like that,' he said. 'Or anyone do what you just did. You can't fix you own injuries?'

'Nope.'

'Why not?'

'I really don't know. Why can't you tickle yourself? There's probably a reason, but I didn't want to sign up for more medical exams.'

He nodded. 'I can see why the government would want a guy who could do what they can. Or what you can. They let you walk?'

I shook my head. 'Not many people know what I can do. I never exactly put it on my resumé. Most of the time, people don't even know I've done it. They just think they got lucky.'

'Maybe you aren't the young idealist I thought you were.'

'You said something when I mentioned the drug dealing?'

He nodded. 'There's a lot of black ops guys in Afghanistan right now. CIA, special forces, private contractors. You know, Afghanistan, where they grow the poppies? I'll bet there's a nice little pile of money to be made. This guy who's pissed at you already has a relationship with the military thanks to this superpower thing. Let's say he gets the chance to extend that relationship, with someone operating out of Afghanistan. What with superpowers and uniforms, it wouldn't be too hard to get the drugs past customs and into the US.'

'Well, shit,' I said.

'You're still ahead on dead bodies,' said Sarah.

'Yeah, I guess that's something.'

'The Spartans were ahead on dead bodies at Thermopylae,' said Bob. 'They still all got killed.'

I conceded the point. 'We should get out of here. Sooner or later housekeeping is going to find our friend or some boss is going to check in on the hit team.'

'I put the Do Not Disturb sign on the other room,' said Sarah. 'That should keep the maid out until checkout time, anyway.'

'You're getting good at this,' I said.

She smiled weakly and looked away. I realized that I might have been a bit insensitive. Being under fire like this put me back in warrior mode, and the fact that Sarah had been holding up so well made me forget she was a civilian. I had to be more careful about that.

'What you need is something on these people,' said Bob as he got to his feet. 'I have a few names and interesting facts that some people might not want to see the light of day, especially if I can connect them to heroin. I'll get them to you.'

'Thanks,' I said. 'You sure you want to get involved in this?'

He gave me a grim smile. 'You couldn't keep me out now. They leaned on the wrong guy.'

'I appreciate it,' I said. 'But I've already gotten you in enough trouble. And you've lost enough.'

'It's not my aiming eye. And you came for me when the sane thing would be to run. Even hurt, even when it looked like I might have sold you out.'

'Didn't seem like you'd do that,' I replied. 'And I was sure you wouldn't put Sarah in danger.'

He looked at me for a long moment and nodded.

'Be careful, please.' Sarah gave him a hug.

'Girl, you been laughing at my backups for my backups for a long time,' he said, grinning, 'but now I'll be so far off the radar it'll make my off-grid house look like downtown. I have hideouts and stashes that nobody knows but me. I'll track down some info and send it to your email. Then you'll have a bargaining chip.'

'Thanks again,' I said. 'I still have your Browning, by the way.'

'Keep it. I've got plenty of guns and that one can't be traced back to me. Just in case you need to drop it at a crime scene.'

'If you go back home, there are a few MP5s,' I said. 'I noticed you don't have any submachine guns.'

'Never know when you might need one,' he replied. 'You keep each other safe, hear me?'

'Loud and clear.'

Chapter 30

WE DROVE ON FOR SOME TIME in silence. A light snow began to fall. Not enough to make the driving bad, just a few flakes swirling in the glare of the headlights. I studied Sarah's face as she drove, facing resolutely forward. I couldn't read anything in her expression.

'You gonna be alright?' I asked.

'Probably not,' she said. 'Right now I'm just numb. And we need to think, to plan. I don't have time for a breakdown.' She shrugged. 'I don't know if I'm just putting it off, or for how long.'

'I'm so sorry,' I said. 'You're coping like a trooper. I've seen men break under a lot less.'

She gave a tight smile. 'Thanks. It helps that you're here. I feel safe with you. It sounds crazy, even to me. But I wouldn't have believed anybody could fight like you do. If I hadn't seen you beat these guys, I'd be a terrified wreck.'

'I'm glad you feel that way.'

'You know,' she continued, 'until I met you, I'd never seen a dead body outside of a funeral home. Now I've seen you kill eight people. I'm not sure if it bothers me. I know you had to, but you did it without a second's hesitation. I also know you can be gentle and charming. You just don't fit my idea of a cold-blooded killer.'

I didn't know what to say to that.

'Have you killed a lot of people? Have you always had a good reason?'

'Yes,' I sighed. 'And yes. I was a soldier for a long time. I killed men in combat. Most of them were strangers, and probably men I might have liked if I'd met them in other circumstances. Calling a battle a fair fight would be a stretch, but any man who shows up armed on the battlefield has to understand that he's accepting certain conditions and risks. I've never killed without a good reason. Before this week, I hadn't fired a shot in anger since Korea.'

'Is following orders a good reason?'

'Not by itself,' I replied. 'And for a guy who's spent so much time in uniform, I'm not very good at following orders. I've ignored stupid orders, pretended I didn't hear a few others. Just kinda shook my head at the squad when some lieutenant said something unacceptable and worked around it. I've never killed civilians or prisoners.' Not real prisoners anyway. That German machinegunner at Belleau Wood who took out half the squad and thought we'd forgive and forget just because he put his hands up when we got within grenade range—well, he didn't count. No point in bringing that up.

'Have you ever killed anyone to protect your secret?'

'No. I've left town in a hurry a few times, but I've never killed anyone just to keep them quiet.'

She drove for a while in silence. 'I guess I'll see how I feel about that when things settle down.'

I didn't know what to say to that, so I said nothing. I hoped she'd still want to be with me after this, but it wouldn't exactly be a surprise if she didn't.

I didn't think much about my reaction to killing. I'd gotten past the point where it bothered me. If it ever had. It wasn't that I didn't have a conscience, or that I was incapable of feeling guilt. I just understood that, sometimes, it was me or him, and, well, it was gonna be him.

I knew not everyone could be that way. I'd known soldiers who would shoot high, or just hide in their holes and not fire. I'd known men who fell apart afterwards because they'd killed people in combat. Maybe that's evolution. Maybe thousands of years of socialization has made resorting to violence more of a liability than an asset. I guess an oily, backstabbing speech from Marty is a more likely threat than a leopard dropping on you from the branches, or a longship full of axe-wielding Danes descending on your village. What used to be an essential survival trait is now a good way to get you jailed or, at the very least, fired.

I felt less guilty about shooting one of Doors' gang of thugs than swatting a mosquito. They weren't just men trying to kill me because we wore different uniforms. They crossed a line. After what they did to Tiffany and Sarah and Bob, I wanted an excuse to shoot more of them.

Sarah suddenly pulled off onto the shoulder, one of those areas on the side of the highway cleared so people could ooh and ah at the mountains without bouncing off a guardrail. She put the car in park and turned in her seat to face me.

'What would you do to me if I said I couldn't take this anymore?'

'To you? Nothing. I'd try to talk you out of it, probably beg and grovel and embarrass myself, but I wouldn't do anything to you. What makes you ask that?'

'If I said I was going to talk to the police or the papers, give a full statement in return for protection and immunity. You'd let me walk?'

'I'd be devastated,' I said, 'but I wouldn't try to hurt you or kidnap you. I understand this is a lot for you to take in. I'd just ask you to drop me at the nearest bus station. I know this is tough. I desperately want you to stay with me. More than anything. But if you want out, I swear I won't try to stop you.'

'What if said I was going to drive us to the State Police barracks right now and turn you in for a half-dozen murders? I'm a woman. Alone. Out in the woods. You have a gun, you're stronger, you know how to fight. You wouldn't do anything?'

'I'd use the full force of my charm, eloquence and smouldering male sexuality to convince you not to, but I'd never deliberately harm you in any way.' I put out a hand to touch her. 'I'd like to say you have nothing to fear from me, but that's kinda misleading, considering the danger I've put you in. But I'd never hurt you. I'd face jail or the FBI or Doors and his goons before I'd raise a hand to you.'

She looked at me for a long moment, her green eyes fixed on mine. I noticed that she was looking through her glasses rather than over them. My heart hammered worse than when there were guys shooting at me.

'I'm pretty sure I believe you,' she said at length. 'You're either very sincere, or the best liar I've ever met.'

'Can't a man be both?' I asked.

That brought out the ghost of a smile. 'Let's go,' she said. 'We'll get out of this mess. Then we'll have a talk about things.'

We drove for some time in silence, until we arrived in Twin

Mountain. Ski season in full swing, we had to look around for a bit to find a vacancy. We finally found a small motel with a room for rent. It stood back off the main drag, across the street from a convenience store, and wasn't exactly four stars, but was clean and cheap enough to survive on the overflow tourist trade from the big places.

Chapter 31

WE DRAGGED OUR BAGS INTO THE ROOM and I crashed on the bed. I'd been getting better, but the fight in the woods and rescuing Bob had set me back.

'I was thinking,' she began.

'Yes?'

'You and these teleporter guys inherited your talents from your parents—they've been passed down through the family. What happens if someone with a talent has a baby with someone who doesn't?'

'I'm not sure,' I said. 'Maybe it's recessive and the kid could carry it and never know, or maybe it could manifest in a small way. The guy who got me out of Doors Imports said something about not being pureblood so he could only go so far. Maybe that's why Bob can dowse, or why some people claim to have ESP. Maybe they have a tiny bit of the ability from some distant ancestor who could do really impressive stuff.'

'I always thought those guys were con artists.'

I rolled over. 'I'm sure most are. I used to think all of them were. That I was some unique freak. But I guess there's no reason there can't be more people like me, living in secret. I've done a good job staying out of the spotlight, maybe others have too.'

She thought for a while. 'It makes sense when you think about it. I just never bothered to think about it before.'

'No reason you should have. There're lots of rumors and myths and scams. I automatically dismiss faith healing as bullshit, and I can actually do it.' I paused for a long moment. 'There's been a time or two that people tried to burn me as a witch. Because I did things they couldn't explain. Lots of people did get burned, or hanged, and most were probably accused out of jealousy or revenge, but maybe some of them really did have special abilities.'

'More things in heaven and earth, Horatio.'

'Exactly. Lots of stories came out of Hungary and Romania where Doors and his merry band come from. Old gypsy legends, dark, scary tales.'

'You think the legends began with… with people like you and Doors?'

'I don't see why not.'

'Maybe you had brothers and sisters,' she said. 'Maybe you still do.'

That made me sit up and think. 'How about someone like Harry Houdini, or Rasputin?' she asked.

'The Mad Monk?'

'Sure,' she said. 'Think about it. He was the only one who could stop the Czarevich's bleeding. You could probably do that.'

'I probably could.'

'And when they tried to kill him, they, what? Poisoned and strangled and stabbed and shot him and then drowned him to finish him off, right?'

'That's the story.'

'Well, maybe he was your cousin.'

'I think I was happier five minutes ago when I didn't have any family that I knew of.'

'See, now you have an embarrassing relative like the rest of us.' She smiled. 'It humanizes you. Oh, I didn't mean…'

'It's OK.' I grinned. 'I know what you meant.'

'I think we need some booze,' she said. 'There's a little shop across the street. I'll just be a few.'

'You should stay here. We should lay low.'

'I need to think. I can't do that without sleep, and I can't sleep after a day like this without numbing things up and making myself relax. That means booze, a long hot shower and falling asleep in your arms.'

'I'm flattered,' I said. There wasn't much chance they'd find us here, and we needed a plan, which would be a better plan if it was made after a night's sleep.

I groaned as I sat up, reaching for my coat.

'You stay here,' she said. 'You've done more than enough moving around on that ankle for one night. I'll be fine. It's fifty yards away.'

'Then take this,' I advised, pulling the Browning from my bag.

'Paranoid.'

'It's gunmetal. It'll accent your boots nicely. Just tuck it in your purse. Please,' I said. 'If you don't, I'm gonna have to limp along. I can't help it.'

'Fine.'

I reluctantly watched her walk out the door. I could see the entrance to the store across the street, so I kept my eye on her as she walked over. I turned out the room light so I wouldn't get any glare on the window, raised the blinds and took out the MP5 I'd appropriated at Bob's place. Set to semi-automatic, it would be accurate as far as the store if anyone did try to grab her. I took up a firing position behind the bed, resting my elbow on it.

It was long odds they could know we were here, but I wasn't taking chances.

She soon emerged from the store and walked back across the street without being detained, tailed or kidnapped. Without getting into the jeep and bugging out on me either, which made me happy. I stashed the gun as she reached the door.

'I forgot about the liquor rules in this backwoods state,' she said, putting a bag down on the table and extracting two six-packs of beer. 'You can buy ammunition at a gas station, and beer and wine pretty much anyplace, but you can only get hard liquor at a State liquor store. Madness.'

'We'll make do somehow,' I said.

'I'm just going to have to spend more time getting drunk tonight than I'd planned on.' She opened a beer for each of us.

'It's OK,' I said. 'We have all night.'

She got halfway through the first beer before she started talking. Mostly about Uncle Bob, and she cried a bit. Then after the second beer she began to talk freer and faster, still mostly about Bob and old memories, but now with laughter. Eventually she treated me to a gloriously intoxicated, rambling monologue about her childhood, her life, her hopes and plans and dreams.

I mostly just listened. She needed to talk. I made reassuring noises when she paused, kept drinking so she wouldn't feel self-conscious about her own intake. She'd been through an awful lot the past week. She needed to talk it all out.

When we finally went to bed, she lay on her side, pressing against me, trying to get as much of her body in contact with mine as possible.

I think she needed to feel protected and secure. I curled around her, draping my arm over her and holding her.

That seemed to be enough. I felt her body relax against me and she soon began to snore. I thought it was a cute, ladylike drunken snore, but I may be biased.

The next day, I felt physically awful. I'd pretty much expected to, after my shootout in the snow and drinking too much. Sarah was at least as bad, shuffling around the room like a blonde zombie.

'Oh, God, my head,' she moaned. 'I haven't been this hung over since college. I need to go down to the desk and get us some coffee.'

'Drink a big glass of water first,' I said. 'You're dehydrated, and coffee will make that worse. Pop a couple ibuprofen too. I have a big bottle in my bag.'

'Can't you just heal the hangover?'

'Sorry,' I replied. 'There's no real damage, just dehydration. I can give your body a little jolt to help it recover, but you need some fluid first.'

She filled a glass from the bathroom tap and drank it down. 'OK, I need to throw some clothes on and go get us some coffee, or my brain will explode and leak out of my ears. I'll drink more water after I get some caffeine.'

'OK. You want me to come along? Help carry stuff?'

'Stay here, nurse the wounds. After we eat I need you to give me a head rub and undo the damage I did last night.'

She returned soon with two large coffees and a few pastries. The complimentary "Continental breakfast" that most cheap hotels think will fool anyone who hasn't been to the Continent. The pastry was fairly decent, and the coffee and burst of sugar would help the poor battered brain cells.

After the coffee, I did press Sarah to drink some more water, and gave her the promised head rub, quieting nerves, encouraging the cells to recover, and blunting the diuretic effects of the caffeine, since the last thing she needed was more dehydration.

'You're a liar,' she said.

'What do you mean?' I asked, trying to keep the horror out of my voice.

'You said you couldn't heal hangovers. I feel almost human.'

'You get used to it,' I smiled.

'Ha, ha. Anyway, you're sweet, even if you are a mutant freak.' She kissed me. 'Fortunately for you, I'm very open minded about that kind of thing.'

'What other kinds of things are you open minded about?' I wondered, pulling her close.

'Let's see about some real breakfast first. I can be only so open minded without something more substantial.'

We found a little breakfast place in town and ate a leisurely meal, letting the final effects of last night's drinking fade away. Feeling mostly better, we went back to the room. Sarah spent some time with her computer, and I tried to think of ways to turn some vague ideas into an actual plan. Planning ways out of things, I'm good at; planning quick and dirty squad level actions, I'm very good at. Planning confrontations, less so.

'Find anything new?' I asked.

'I don't know how relevant it is, but there's a commendation to one of Doors' family for his service in Operation Eiche in World War Two. When the German paratroopers sprung Mussolini from prison. Not surprisingly, he disappeared after the war.'

'Huh. Figures. Guys who can teleport would make good commandos. And the family's love of black leather trenchcoats. They'd never have been able to resist the Reich.' I thought for a minute. 'Hey, did he fight at the Bulge?'

'Doesn't say. There's not much else, just a copy of the commendation. I guess the clan is proud of that. Why do you ask?'

'Just wondering if I've shot at any of his family less recently than last week.'

'I thought you fought in the Pacific.'

'I did,' I said. 'I fought with the Marines at Guadalcanal. I got wounded in one of the Japanese night assaults on Henderson Field. We slaughtered them, but a few got in among our holes. One bayoneted me. More times than was necessary, the prick. One of the thrusts damaged my spinal cord. I was paralyzed.'

I winced at the memory. If old Manila John hadn't shot that bastard, he might still be stabbing me.

'Got sent home, discharged. I wasn't sure I'd heal, but in a few weeks I had feeling, and in a month I could walk, so I escaped from the veterans' hospital, changed my identity. That was in October of forty-two. By the next spring I was healthy, so I joined the army, went to Jump School, wound up a replacement in the 101st Airborne. Missed D-day, but not Bastogne.'

'You went back to fight after being paralyzed?' she asked. 'Are you just a slow learner?'

'The military is a good place to hide. And I'm good at soldiering. I knew I could make a difference, that more guys would make it home alive with less bad wounds if I were there. More of them could avoid getting shot in the first place with me to give them pointers. I wanted to go back in the Marines. Maybe be an instructor, but the Corps was too small a world, too many of the Old Breed would recognize me and wonder how I was walking around after that wound. As it was, it surprised everyone that I lived through the night.'

'Amazing.' She shook her head.

'I like the camaraderie.'

'You miss it?'

I took a long moment to compose my thoughts before answering. 'In the normal world, I'm alone,' I said. It shocked me to hear how hollow my voice sounded when I said it. 'So often alone. Friends, lovers, all go by in the blink of an eye. It's hard to get close to someone, and if I do they expect more honesty than I can afford. Deserve more honesty than I can afford. They start to wonder why I don't seem to look any older. They start to ask questions, and then it's time to move on.'

She reached out and squeezed my hand. I looked into her eyes and saw tenderness, sympathy.

'I can give other people a touch of immortality. Do a little maintenance at the cellular level, hold back the slow onslaught of time, but most people aren't ready to accept that. They'd have to choose to run or to watch their friends and family grow old in front of them. It's tough on people. On me too, but at least I've had some time to get used to it.' I shook my head.

I went on. It was important to me that she understand this. 'There's a closeness you feel in a combat unit. A closeness built of need, both for teamwork and for someone to lean on in what are probably the worst moments of most men's lives. But it only lasts for a short time, then guys muster out or get transferred. So for me, it's perfect. Closeness without anybody being around long enough to do the math and wonder why I don't look any older. I get pretty much the same bond working the ambulance. Especially in a busy city, working for a crap company. We back each other up, we trust each other and depend on each other, because we know we have to. Management sure as hell won't,' I shrugged. 'It's nice to get that closeness without the bad food, sleeping in a muddy hole, and constant physical danger. Or quite so much physical danger.'

She gave me a long look. Not keen and penetrating like before, but soft and gentle. Full of concern. 'I had no idea. I never thought of how lonely you must feel. You seem so well adjusted.'

'I've learned to adapt.' I smiled. 'Years of practice.'

She hugged me. Held me close. 'You don't tell this kind of thing to a lot of people?'

'You're the first,' I said. 'So far as I can remember.'

After a moment she drew back from the embrace. 'Why me?'

'I just feel differently about you. I think I love you. I'm not sure I ever really loved any of the others. Not the same way, at least.'

She took my hand and led me to the bed, then kissed me. Not with the fierce passion of previous times, but tenderly.

'I think I love you, too,' she said. I opened my mouth but she stopped it with a kiss.

'No,' she said after a second. 'No witty banter, no soliloquies, no comparisons to Mata Hari or Helen of Troy. Let's just be a man and a woman who've said the words. And meant them. Let's just pretend we aren't on the run, we aren't in danger and we really can spend the rest of our lives together, and that we both mean the same thing by that.' She kissed me again, her fingers moving to the buttons of my shirt. 'Just for today.'

Chapter 32

THE NEXT DAY, SARAH GOT AN E-MAIL from Bob. At least, *she* knew it was from Bob. I'd have deleted it, thinking it was spam; Sarah knew Bob well enough to spot hints in the subject line. The body of the message was just my name and a phone number I didn't recognize.

I dragged out the phone I'd stolen and dialed.

'Hello,' answered Bob.

'Hi. It's me.'

'Good. I got some info. Probably enough to buy you some forbearance. Maybe get the boys in Washington to keep out of this. Not send these drug smugglers any more intel or direct help.'

'That's good news.'

'I have to ask one question before I send this stuff over.'

'What's that?'

'This operation you were on,' he said, 'are you wanted for any of it? Legally? You AWOL or anything?'

'Long time ago and a long way away,' I replied. 'I'm clean with the US military. The guy that wants me has a personal grudge.'

'So if I call some people, all you're asking for is that they back off, let you go on your way, and you won't cause any trouble?'

'Well, I'll probably still be an insubordinate nightmare of an employee, but unless the CIA cares about ambulance company supervisors getting grey hair and ulcers, I shouldn't be a headache for anybody on the government payroll.'

'I can probably get them to go for that. Keep your head down. I'll show them what I have. It should be good enough.'

'What is it?'

'I'll send a copy to Sarah. You can look it over. If they know I don't have the only copy, they probably won't try to cut me out. I'll be in touch.'

'Can I call you at this number?'

'No. This phone is a throwaway. I'll get in touch if and when I have to.'

'OK,' I said. 'Thanks, by the way.'

'I owe you for coming for me.'

'I hadn't picked your place to hide out, there'd have been no need.'

'In that case, you can buy me another bottle of Scotch,' he said. 'Too dangerous for me to go back to my still until this blows over. Keep your head down.'

The line went dead.

'What did he say?' asked Sarah.

'He's got the info we need. Check your email. Says he's sending it over.'

'OK, I just got something.' She clicked and opened an attachment.

'That looks like a Nigerian money laundering scheme,' I said. 'You sure that's from Bob?'

'He used my middle name in the greeting. And you see these numbers across the top? Like an international phone number?'

'Sure.'

'It's code. The real message is in the Nigerian spam. The first number is 5, so you count five words in—'

'I got it,' I said. 'Like a book code but different.' I grabbed a pen and paper, and we started working on the code.

The attached file had a list of agents, active and retired, who had some connection to Afghanistan and to the poppy growers, and who seemed to live well on the salary or pension of a Federal employee. The CIA had had people in the area going back to the Soviet occupation in 1980.

There was enough info to make a lot of people very nervous. A lot of people who had access to guns and secure records and the skills to have people removed.

If a retired army vet, a college professor and a wiseass paramedic had to die to keep this stuff secret, I don't think many of the guys on this list would lose much sleep. That was nothing in the scale of things in the thinking of the intelligence community. Just a little collateral damage from the people who brought you the Bay of Pigs.

The flip side was that this might be enough info to buy the forbearance of those same people. If they knew that our deaths would result in this info coming out, they might just become invested in our continued good health. That kind of accommodation was also nothing that would make a spy blink.

'That might buy us some security from Doors' buddies in Washington,' I said. 'Now we just have to get him to drop a blood feud.'

'So how do we do that?' she asked.

'I take a page from Conrad,' I said. 'I just hope Doors doesn't read as much as you.'

'You think he'll go along with it?'

'He almost has to. If this challenge is delivered so that any of his men hear about it, he has to take it up or lose face. If he refuses the chance to fulfill his oath in an honorable duel, he's done as a leader.' I shrugged. 'He'll probably be excited to do this. He's cocky. He's good with a foil or an epee, and he's been raised as an aristocrat. This is the kind of thing they drill into them from birth.'

'But he's not a nobleman now. He's just a smuggler. Last I checked, they aren't all that hung up on honoring promises.'

I rubbed my chin, tried to think how to explain. 'He was raised as a nobleman. He believes it. It's hard to explain to an American.'

'We're not exactly a classless society,' she said.

'No, but the American upper class is based on money or power. A family blows that, they become just any old family. A penniless Duke, on the other hand, is still a Duke. The title matters to him—especially if he's lost his estate and the title is all he's got. He's been raised to believe he's better than the rest of the population.

'The thing is,' I continued, 'Doors has proof he's better than everyone else. He didn't just inherit a birthmark and a signet ring. The guy has a superpower.'

'So that makes it OK?'

'No, but it makes it understandable. Look, I saw it in his office. It's not Eurotrash steel and glass and abstract sculpture, it's not drug-lord bling, it's old-world hand-carved woodwork. He has photos of himself fencing, riding, doing all those upper crust things. Diplomas from good private schools. Look at the weapons they use. Knives, not guns. Gangs love to show off their guns. Even the knives aren't new, carbon steel. These are either old and handed down or, at least, they're hand-forged in the old style. Those symbols mean something.

'You know he's a thug. I know it. On some level, even he probably knows it. But deep down, he'll have convinced himself he's a knight. Avenging the family grudge is his chance to live out that fantasy, to prove he's not just some drug pusher.'

She chewed her lip as she thought about it. 'It does make sense in a way. I hope you're right.'

'Me too.'

'Thanks for putting my fears to rest,' she laughed.

'I live to comfort.'

'You think you can beat him?'

'Age and guile, my sweet. Age and guile,' I replied. 'And while he's done a lot of fencing, I've done a lot of fighting. Looking over this list you put together, I know about half his coaches and trainers. Most of the masters I studied with are dead.'

'That probably sounded more reassuring in your head,' she pointed out.

I smiled, 'OK, yeah, that did sound bad. But most of them died in advanced age in their beds. Or someone's bed, at any rate.'

'So what do we do next?'

'Well,' I said, 'I'm gonna need to contact him and set up a meeting. I'll probably need to find a second. Then I'll need a little something to get me back on my feet and in condition to fight.'

'So we hang and rest up?'

'Yes, but not here. They may still be looking in the area.'

We headed back South, past Philips Mills, down Route 114 to Middleton and the Moonlight Inn. I knew it from doing a few ambulance calls there. It turns out you really shouldn't mix your cardiac medicine with Viagra. But, if you have to die of something…

The Moonlight had amenities like hot tubs in the rooms, mirrored ceilings, theme rooms, that kind of thing. It was the kind of place you went on your honeymoon, or your anniversary, or to rekindle the cooling spark of your relationship, or cheat on your spouse.

It was the kind of place that understood if you didn't want to put this on the credit card. I paid for the room in cash. Three nights. I tipped lavishly, since it was money from the pockets of the thugs I left cooling up north. The clerk smiled and handed me the key, not commenting on the fact that we were the third Mr and Mrs Smith to sign the guest registry that day. So, while he would assume we were hiding, he would assume it was from my wife or her husband or both, not from a bunch of knife-wielding Eastern European drug dealers.

The only other way to get a room without showing a valid credit card or photo ID would be in the flop houses in the city, and I guessed we'd be safer among the adulterers than the junkies.

Plus, the Moonlight had in-room hot tubs.

We settled in, and I set the bags down and spent a long, shaky half-hour lying on the bed, groaning as my injuries throbbed.

Sarah raided the mini bar and sat beside me, handing me a few fingers of whisky. 'It's a blend, so I poured it over some ice,' she explained. 'It should still dull the pain.'

'You're too good to me.' I sat up and rolled the cold glass across my sweating forehead before sipping.

'So, now what?' she asked.

'Get out your laptop and pull up the website for Doors Imports.'

When she did, I leaned over her shoulder. 'Do we have a phone number for Doors Imports? I don't want his personal phone. I want the low-level guy at the front desk to know I called. The better known this is, the more incentive he has to play it straight.'

'Call him out at high noon?'

'Something like that.'

I dialed the main number for Doors Imports, and waited through the recorded list of options until instructed to hold for an operator.

'Doors Imports.' A voice finally came on the line, flawless English. No accent, but too precise for a native speaker. 'How may I help you?'

'I'd like to speak to Mr Toren, please.'

'I'm sorry sir?'

'Ah. My apologies. Mr Doors. You can tell him this is Mr Danet. He and I need to discuss an old family obligation.'

After an extended pause, the voice came back, a trace of agitation under the polished tone. 'One moment, sir.'

I smiled as I waited. By the time I got off the phone, everyone in Doors' organization would know that I'd thrown down the gauntlet.

At length, someone picked up.

'Hello.'

'Mr Doors?'

'Mr Danet. If that is how you call yourself. I have waited long for this day.'

'I haven't exactly been looking forward to it myself,' I replied.

'I must say, this call surprises me. I expected you to run. That seems to be your strength.'

'If I thought your men posed a real threat, I might have,' I replied, trying to put enough aristocratic arrogance in my voice to rankle him. 'I'm calling you because I find your attention irritating, not frightening.'

'And your recent... visit?' I could hear the words forced through clenched teeth.

'I had to be sure who you were,' I said. 'I suspected, but I had to know. Now I do. In fact, I know an awful lot about your... activities.'

I let that sink in. With his connections, he'd escape from any drug charge easily enough, but I could get his US operation shut down. Force him to relocate, spend a lot of time and money to get it up and running somewhere else. Get a lot of his contacts in trouble. That kind of failure would erode confidence in his leadership. It wasn't something he could allow.

'So,' he said, keeping his voice level with some difficulty, 'what do you propose?'

'I think perhaps you and I could settle this like gentlemen.'

'You? Propose a duel?'

I shrugged with an affected nonchalance of which Oscar Wilde would have been proud, then remembered this was a phone call. 'I do. That way I can stop killing your men and you can stop inconveniencing young ladies of my acquaintance.'

'I will take the greatest pleasure in finishing this old business, believe me,' he snarled.

'I find it distasteful, but I do look forward to putting this behind me. What would you like to choose for weapons? Knives at midnight in a dark alley?'

'Swords,' he snapped, ignoring my taunt. 'Saturday. Noon. The renovation project in the old Exeter Mill. Bring a second.'

The line went dead.

'You should have a little pencil-thin Errol Flynn mustache to stroke when you talk like that,' Sarah said. 'This is a new side of you.'

I shrugged, with much less disdain this time. 'I know how to speak arrogant nobleman. I don't like to. As far back as I can remember, I've been a humble outcast and I've lived and worked as a soldier, or a medic. The thing is, if I want this guy to deal with me, he has to think of me as an equal. If I'm a social inferior, he can lie to me, have his men rough me up or kill me without feeling any stain on his honor. If I'm a member of a noble family, however disgraced, he owes me some basic courtesy.

'It's crap, I know, but it's like dealing with a different tribe or a mob of baboons. You need to know the signals. Observe the social niceties.'

'So, no portraits of noble forebears on the walls of the Danet dining room?'

'Do well,' I said, 'and you have no need of ancestors.'

'Voltaire,' she said. 'I'm impressed.'

'I am a well read peasant, at least.'

'That's OK.' She smiled. 'I never really wanted a prince to ride in and carry me off.'

'A short, underpaid ambulance jockey will do?'

'Seems to be working out at the moment,' she replied. 'How do you think the call went?'

'Well, the fact that he wants to do this on Saturday gives me three more days to heal, which is good. Now I have to get hold of a second and some lidocaine.'

'So many conversations I never thought I'd have.' She walked toward the kitchenette. 'I need a cup of coffee. I imagine you do too. Then you can tell me all about seconds and lidocaine.'

Chapter 33

I DIALED PETE'S NUMBER.

'Yo!'

'Hey, man. It's Sean.'

'Dude! What happened? We wondered where you got to.'

'I had to check up on somebody,' I answered. 'How's Tiffany?'

'Better than we expected. CAT scan was clean, no damage to her eyes, no teeth missing. Bad bruises, some broken fingers.'

'Thank God.' I released a long breath.

'So what's up with you, man?'

'I need a favor.'

'Money, an accomplice or an alibi?' he asked without hesitation.

'An accomplice,' I replied. 'You know the guy who was asking about me? The guys who attacked me and Nique? They're the same guys who beat up Tiffany. I have a line on them, but I need a little help.'

'I'm in.'

'It might be dangerous,' I warned.

'Danger is my middle name. Of course, that means "Dodging" is my first, but if you ain't running for the hills, it can't be that dangerous. I'm in.'

'You wound me,' I said. 'But thanks. Meet me at the Moonlight Inn. Soon as you can get here.'

'What are you doing there? This isn't a ploy to take advantage of me, is it?'

'You've seen through my cunning ruse. Just come on over, OK?'

'Will do. Oh, call Monique. She's worried. Doesn't want to lose her best girlfriend.'

'I will. Thanks again.'

'See ya in a few hours,' he said. 'I got some stuff to finish up, then I'll head over.' He hung up.

Sarah walked back in with a cup of coffee in either hand. She offered me one.

'Who was that?'

'My second, probably,' I replied. 'His name's Pete. He's a medic.'

'So now what?'

I took a long sip to buy time. 'I need to call Monique.'

'I see.' Her tone was neutral. No anger, nothing I could detect.

It scared the hell out of me.

'First off, she's worried about me. She's a good friend and deserves a call back. Second, I need another person to pull this off. Someone I can trust. That's a short list. And last, I think it's time you two met.'

After a long pause, she forced a smile. 'OK,' she said, 'maybe it's time to put a face to the name.'

I squeezed her shoulder. 'You've been amazing, you know. You gave me enough new perspective on this for me to try to solve this mess, and being with you is the motivation I need to actually stick it out and do it. I don't know who took you for granted, or how, or why, but he was an idiot. You have no reason to be jealous of anyone. If heavily armed thugs who can teleport can't come between us, do you really think I'd let another woman?'

The tight, forced smiled thawed into the twisted grin I'd come to love. 'You're right. How bad could it be? She's not gonna beat me up.'

'Probably not,' I returned the smile, 'but try not to make any remarks about her having a bimbo name.'

'It was her bimbo *voice*,' she corrected. 'She has a *stripper* name.'

'Ah. That'll make it OK, then.'

'But like a stripper who would work at an expensive place, not a cheap dive. Or maybe an escort service. Oh, that's it! She totally has an escort name.'

'This'll be fun,' I muttered as pulled out my cell and dialed Nique's number.

'Sean!' she exclaimed as she picked up. I'm still taken aback by the fact that people know it's me before I say anything. I have adapted to technology slowly. 'Is everything alright?'

'I'm fine. How's everybody?'

'Tiffany's doing much better. Nobody else has been hurt. We were all worried when you took off. What happened?'

'I had to run and check on Sarah,' I replied. 'She was trying to research some writing on the knife I took from those guys who jumped us. Tiffany got attacked after she gave us the demographic sheet on the guy we brought in when all this started. I figured they might go after Sarah too.'

'Oh my God. Is she OK?'

'She's fine. And, thanks to her, I've made some progress tracking down the guys who did all this.'

'Really? That's great. You going to the police?'

I grimaced. 'It's a bit more complicated,' I said. 'In fact, there's a favor I need. Can you meet me today?'

'I picked up a shift. I'm actually on the truck now. I'm out at seven tonight, though.'

'You know what? If you're working, there are a few things you could pick up for me.' Shopping from the ambulance supplies is pretty much illegal.

'Sure thing,' she answered brightly. 'What can I get you?'

It's also pretty much a constant.

So long as you only steal a little bit, and you don't touch the narcotics, which are strictly tracked, you can outfit a small personal clinic.

I gave Monique my laundry list and we said goodbye. As I hung up the phone, Sarah gave me what I can only describe as a *look*.

'Tiffany? Really?'

I shrugged.

'Hey, you wouldn't let me run away from the guys with knives. I say we stay and face the peril of the girls with stripper names.'

She sighed in theatric exasperation. 'You're lucky you're a good cook.'

I killed time going over and over the plan in my head. It wasn't the craziest plan I'd ever been involved in. I'd seen worse plans work out. I'd also seen better ones go to hell, but I didn't dwell on that.

What gave me that weightless, falling sensation in my stomach was that this was different for me. This wasn't me hiding out in uniform, trying to put myself in the absolute minimum danger to avoid totally disgracing myself or betraying my companions. This was leading a group of civilians I cared for into harm's way to confront *my* problem. In theory, I'd be the guy in danger, but how much faith did I really want to put in Mr Doors' sense of honor?

Much later, the welcome sound of a knock on the door interrupted my fretting. 'Hello?'

'Hi!' came a cheery voice, which, to my dismay, would be all you could ask for from an escort. 'It's Nique.'

'Come on in.' I gave Sarah a quick smile, saw her take a deep breath in preparation.

I opened the door to Nique's sunburst smile. She gave me an enormous hug. As she released me, she turned to Sarah, who was doggedly maintaining a frozen grin.

I'd not have thought it possible, but Nique cranked up her smile by a few thousand BTUs.

'You must be Sarah,' she beamed. 'It's so nice to finally meet you. Sean can't stop smiling since he met you.'

See, a good partner always has your back.

Sarah's reserve melted in the face of Nique's greeting. Stronger men had fallen before. Nique was just about impossible to dislike, even for the new girlfriend who's just discovered what her boyfriend's partner looks like.

I limped to the mini bar for drinks, and by the time I got back, the two women were chatting like old friends. I heaved a sigh of relief and marveled at Monique's ability to charm. Drop her with a tribe of headhunters in the jungle of the Amazon basin and a week later she'd be thanking them as they carried out her luggage, and they'd be smiling that she let them.

Pete eventually showed up, introduced himself, got an eyeful of Sarah and practically dug his elbow in my ribs and high-fived me. I tried to enjoy it, but I was sure he'd work the whole thing into a new gay joke by week's end.

After the introductions and small talk, I felt it was time to address the matter at hand.

'Thanks for coming, you two,' I began. 'As you know, there have been a series of attacks on me and people close to me recently. It took a while, but with some help, I've put together who it is and why. Sarah finally helped me figure out how to fix this. But this is a strange story, and I'm gonna ask you to take it on faith. I had no idea these guys were looking for me, or that it put any of you in danger. I never would have taken a chance on that.'

I was happy to see nods all around. Even Pete didn't make a wisecrack. Reassured, I pressed on.

'A long time ago, I did something to piss these guys off. I basically disobeyed an order that never should have been given.'

'You?' asked Pete. 'Get out of town. Mr Sorry-the-radio-is-cutting-out decided to ignore an order? No fuckin' way.'

I looked to Nique for support, but she just shrugged eloquently. 'He's not wrong.'

'I took the punishment and got on with my life,' I continued. 'I guess my colleagues weren't so quick to forgive and forget. Now that we're all mustered out, they want to settle the score.'

'You were in the military?' asked Pete. 'That must've been after "Don't ask, don't tell".'

'Well, I hadn't met you yet, so I had nothing to hide.'

'Where did you serve?' asked Nique, rolling her eyes as she tried to drag us back to business.

'It's not important,' I replied. 'It was a long time ago and a long way away. Let's just call it service to a foreign power.'

'Dude! You were a merc? No way!'

'Oh my God,' exclaimed Nique. 'Were you in the Foreign Legion?'

'No I was—wait, why the Foreign Legion?'

She shrugged. 'I've heard your French. Your accent isn't Québécois, like you say. My Memère is from Montreal.'

Huh. I had thought I'd done a better job with my cover than that. I wondered if all the women in my life were smarter than I was.

'Something like that,' I offered. It wasn't completely a lie. I did spend some time in the Legion, but that was unrelated to this mess. So far as I knew.

'So, anyway...' Sarah prompted.

'Right. Anyway, I have some information that would be embarrassing for these guys. They've agreed to meet just me to settle this, and lay off my friends in return for me not leaking this. The thing is, the boss is a bit... well, traditional. He wants to settle our differences the old fashioned way. A duel.'

'Are you shitting me?' Pete asked, pretty reasonably.

'Sean, you can't be serious,' Nique said. 'Why can't you just go to the cops?'

223

'It's complicated. The info I have would be bad for them, but it wouldn't end this permanently. And you guys have seen what they'll do. Remember the ambush at Dugan's? The attack on Tiffany? They'll be out for revenge, and I can't have that.'

'So you're gonna *duel* this guy?' asked Pete incredulously.

'Yep.'

'You can hardly walk,' said Nique. 'How are you going to fight?'

'That's where your shopping spree comes in.' I took the bag she'd brought and tipped it out on my coffee table.

'Some lido and syringes?' asked Pete. 'What's that gonna do?'

'It's going to numb my ankle and wrist so I can fight. Think Schilling in 2004. Game six against the Yankees.'

'You're going to inject an anaesthetic into a damaged joint so you don't feel the pain of the incredibly bad idea of running around on that joint?' Nique demanded.

'Sometimes you need to do what you need to do. And I heal fast.'

'Sean, I really think you need to think harder about this.'

'No.' Sarah put a hand on Nique's shoulder. 'He's right. This will work. I've seen him in action.'

Nique gave her sad but tender smile. 'Sweetie, I know Sean is a great guy, and I suppose he's a decent fighter, but he needs somebody level headed to watch out for him. He's not big on details.'

'I'd noticed,' Sarah replied with a grin. 'We're working on that.'

The two women seemed to have bonded. I wondered if that would be good or bad for me in the long term. For now, it was a relief.

'OK, for the sake of argument, let's pretend this isn't a stupid idea,' Nique continued. 'This guy isn't the Count of Monte Cristo, he's a drug lord. Why would he agree to this? Why wouldn't he just have his thugs kill you when you show up?'

'He's an aristocrat. There are forms that must be observed.'

'Yeah, but if he's dealing drugs, isn't that already violating his code?' asked Pete.

'Not really,' I replied. 'How well do you know your history? Look at the Opium Wars. British merchants were basically pushing drugs on the Chinese, and it was OK, since it was just on the Chinese, not real people who mattered. It was so OK that the Crown sent a fleet and a few regiments over to China to force a treaty to allow the Opium trade.

The take-home point is you can deal all the drugs you want, so long as you watch where you do it.'

'So why keep his word to you?'

'I have... connections,' I replied. 'I've worn the Old School Tie. I know not to pass the Port to the right. He has to treat me by the rules.'

'So why do you need me?' Pete asked, suddenly suspicious. 'I left my pistols in my other suit.'

'I need you on the off chance I'm wrong about the whole "obeying the rules" thing,' I said. 'We'll be dueling with swords but, as my second, I'll need you to be ready for anything.' I reached into the bag at my feet. 'I'll provide a pistol. This,' I held up the weapon, 'is a Colt .45 automatic. Ever shoot one?'

'Nothing that wasn't attached to an arcade game.'

'OK, quick lesson. This is the magazine. It holds seven rounds. You slot it into the butt of the gun like this. Pull the slide back like so. That cocks the hammer. This is a single action pistol. It won't fire if the hammer isn't back. That shouldn't matter if you chamber a round, but just know that. This is the safety. Leave it in this position until you decide you want to shoot, then disengage it with your thumb. It's positioned to make that easy. As far as sights, you want to line the front blade up in this back notch. Aim at the biggest part of the target and squeeze, don't jerk the trigger. It's an accurate weapon, but it has a decent recoil, so after you shoot, let the weapon come back down before you shoot again. Here,' I opened the slide and handed it over, 'it's empty. Now, push that, the slide release. Yeah, right there.'

He did, not flinching as the slide closed, which made me happy.

'Now hold it in your right hand, and support your right hand in your left, like that. Good.'

'So, apart from doing my best Dirty Harry, what does a second do?'

'You're there to observe for me, make sure that the rules are obeyed and the duel is conducted honorably. I think it will be. The thing is, when I win, if his second gets any ideas, I need you to watch my back. Don't pull the gun unless things go to hell, and don't shoot unless you feel confident you aren't going to hit me. But once you decide to shoot, finish the job.'

'Got it.'

'What about us?' asked Nique.

'I think they'll play the duel straight, but I want you two someplace safe where you can look out for one another. Stay together, and keep this.' I pulled a second pistol from my bag, 'This is a—'

'Browning Hi-Power nine millimeter,' Sarah answered matter-of-factly. 'What? My dad was an MP in the Army. My uncle collects guns. I used to go shooting with him.'

I digested this fact for a moment.

'You ever shoot an M1911?'

'Yes. It's been a while, but I'm sure I can still shoot a six inch group at ten yards.'

I paused for a moment, then took the .45 from Pete, handing him the 9mm instead. 'This,' I told him, 'is a Browning nine millimeter. It's similar to the Colt—'

'Wait,' he protested. 'I get the little gun? Why?'

'It's got less recoil than the .45, so it's easier to control, and the magazine holds more bullets, so you can shoot more before you need to reload. It's a better gun for a less experienced shooter.'

'It matches your mascara better, too,' Nique observed.

Chapter 34

THE NEXT FEW DAYS WERE EERILY QUIET. I laid low, recuperating, and keeping an eye on the news as well as checking in with Pete and Nique.

In a way, the lull made sense. We had agreed to a meeting, and any action before that would look bad, and hurt the very family honor that my enemy was trying to avenge. If he was planning some treachery, I had promised to show myself at a known time in a secluded location, so it was probably a safer bet to strike then rather than risk making a move earlier.

I had Sarah take Pete to a local pistol range and let him shoot a few rounds. If the meeting did go to hell, I didn't want it to be the first time he'd ever fired live ammo. I wasn't expecting to turn him into Sergeant York in a few days, but I'd feel better if he got acclimated to how the gun felt and sounded when fired. I'd have felt a lot safer with Bob standing behind me, but it was better that he not be there. Doors' black ops buddies would know that Bob was out there with incriminating info; they'd want him to play this straight. If both Bob and I were at the scene, then removing both of us would look very tempting.

While I had my little friendly brush with death, Sarah and Nique would be at the Harp. It was public, and sure to have a few off duty Philips Mills cops in it at any given time. They all knew Nique from working the street, so they'd all keep an eye on her. The fact that she'd be drinking with another attractive woman wouldn't hurt on that front either. And Sarah had my pistol in her purse. All those factors would probably keep them safe.

By Saturday, I could walk on my ankle without much more than a twinge. My wrist was stiff and sore, and I winced if I lifted anything heavier than a ballpoint, but it was better than it had been, and it wasn't my sword hand. With the lidocaine, I was pretty sure I could get through this.

The fact that somebody would be trying to shove a foot of steel through me would probably give me enough to worry about without thinking of some minor aches and pains. It's amazing how imminent death can focus one's concentration.

Pete, acting as my second, called Doors and confirmed the details. Smallswords. Doors would provide a matched pair, I would choose one. We would fight to a mortal wound.

Exactly what I hoped for.

Which is odd, considering it made me vaguely nauseous to think about it.

It's one thing to face danger, to face the chance of dying. You can always rationalize it away and, generally, the real, scary moment when you *could* die comes on so suddenly that you deal with it in a mad rush of adrenaline and it's over. To plan a brush with death for just after lunch next Tuesday, for example, sounds insane. And it is. Human nature doesn't work that way. The rush of good old fashioned fight or flight chemicals is short acting and on a hair trigger. Keep them flowing too long and you get short tempered, queasy and irritable and have a hard time eating or sleeping. The sympathetic nervous system is designed to handle a leopard leaping down on you from a tree, not one sending you a note to meet him at sunrise.

I tried to tell myself that this would be an end. That after this, I would be free.

Of what? my stubborn self preservation instinct demanded. Could I print up some business cards saying Sean Danet, Immortal Faith Healer? Could I stop running every few years? Settle down with a good woman and trade her in for a newer model once she got wrinkles and osteoporosis? And, assuming that everything did actually go according to plan, which is hardly ever a given even when there isn't a swordfight on the agenda, on what was I basing my faith that the Doors clan would actually follow through on the deal if I did win? I was risking everything, and for what? A few more years at a job I enjoyed with a few short-lived friends.

And Sarah.

Was this in any possible way worth it?

Yes, I decided.

The sheer flat certainty of my answer surprised me. It came from somewhere deep and primal. More innate even than my knee-jerk self-preservation instinct. I hadn't realized that I had a more ingrained motivation.

Being a man of science and reason as well as instinct, I felt the need to analyze my decision. It was a decision, as emphatic and final as any I'd made, of that I had no doubt. I just wanted to know, as a wise man had once put it, the cause in which I was expected to die.

What was it about this woman that made her so much better than a million others? Well, part of it was the year of her birth. Vast improvements had been made in the field of young women recently. For most of western history, they had been considered subservient to men, and while I'd certainly enjoyed the company of a number of them, and my tastes had always run toward the least subservient of the bunch, it certainly colored how they saw themselves.

Then, very recently, when women had begun to make strides, there was a tendency to have a bit of a chip on the shoulder. Again, nothing I wasn't willing to work around.

But it was refreshing and exhilarating to meet a generation of women who truly felt that they were equals, who took it as a given that they deserved to be treated as such. That quiet expectation delivered results far beyond what any strident demands could have.

In a way, Sarah was the epitome of that new mindset. She didn't just wait to be pursued or seduced; she was equally willing to take the lead or follow mine when I seemed on a roll. She was even helping me in my current situation, doing a lot of the mental heavy lifting.

Could that be it?

In a way, Sarah was a comrade in arms. We were sharing a foxhole, shoulder to shoulder in the line.

I hadn't ever done that with a lover.

My world had always been segregated. There were girlfriends and squadmates and never the twain shall meet. I expected different things from each, and thought of them differently.

Did that make me sexist? I wondered. Probably. For most of my long life the world had been pretty clearly divided into what men did and what women did. I was still adjusting to the times.

I think I've always treated women well, but had I treated them as equals? Not usually, I had to admit. I mean, I respected them, cared about them, I was thoughtful and generous. I tried never to take them for granted or lie to them more than I had to, to keep my secrets, but had I ever felt that bond of shared trust? No, I had to say I hadn't.

Well, except for Nique, but she was—

Standing beside me in the line. I had mentally sorted her into the category of other men, since men served beside you and shared one kind of reliance, and women—

Huh. Maybe that was one reason I hadn't felt any strong sexual attraction towards Nique. You cared about your buddies. Cared deeply. But you didn't fantasize about sleeping with them.

OK, so how did that explain my feelings for Sarah? Was it that I'd lusted first, trusted second? Maybe. Whatever the reason, she, pretty much uniquely in my life, stood in both camps: a lover and a partner.

Which made her someone I wasn't about to walk away from.

I hoped Doors didn't kill me. It would be such a waste to have made this journey of personal discovery and not live to use any of it.

Chapter 35

PETE AND I DROVE OUT to the Essex Mill complex. As the erstwhile epicenter of the American textile industry, Philips Mills was full of abandoned mill buildings. Now most were just massive, empty brick shells, filled with pigeons. In place of the dirty, unsafe, exploited labor of the weavers of the industrial revolution, it now saw the dirty, unsafe, exploited labor of prostitution and drug dealing.

Developers were planning to turn the old buildings into condominiums, shops, and restaurants. The theory was that it would attract wealthy homeowners and shoppers to the city, creating legitimate prosperity.

The dealers and hookers would survive. Some would find other slums, some would sell better drugs and cleaner girls to the new arrivals, enjoying the new prosperity.

The Essex Mills had been one of the biggest complexes. Four long, narrow four-story mill buildings formed a quadrangle a hundred yards on a side. The enclosed space was littered with small outbuildings that had served as guard shacks, warehouses, and carpenters or machinist shops back when the mills were active. Now, they stood empty.

The area also held a good deal of construction equipment and trailers. Perfect for an ambush. Not that I thought they'd try that, given how he'd want this done right, and how he'd have to expect all my careful blackmail info to come out if he tried something, but a paranoid survivor streak can't help but notice.

A trenchcoated heavy waved us to a corner of the yard where a trailer screened a small cleared space off from both the worst of the wind and casual view.

We parked and got out. Pete checking the placement of the Browning in his pocket and then slinging over his shoulder the jump kit that he had borrowed from one of the spare ambulances.

Doors stood at the far side of the space, three men behind him. I couldn't see any weapons, but they all wore those stylish long black coats, so I was sure they were packing something. A table stood to one side. A case containing the swords lay open on it.

The man himself stood out from the rest of the crowd. Like me, he wore a white shirt under his long coat. This was part of the custom. It was easier to spot blood on a white shirt; too much blood, and the seconds could halt play.

If he was as nervous as I, he didn't show it. There was an intensity etched on his lean face, a glint of predatory anticipation in those steely grey eyes.

Pete set the big jump kit on the table, made sure he had some bandages and IV supplies ready. We were only a block and a half from the hospital, and Pete had the numbers for today's ambulance crews in his cell, so if I did lose, and nobody got too ugly, I might have a chance. I'm not sure just how lethal a wound it would take to kill me. I'd recovered from some bad injuries, but never anything that would be instantly fatal to a lucky man in good health. I hoped this wouldn't be the day I'd find out.

Doors' second indicated the case on the table. I looked in and saw an exquisite matched set of dueling swords. Narrow, pointed blades, triangular in cross-section. Stiff, sharp and deadly. No edge to speak of, just a swift, wicked needle to puncture a man's vitals. As far as I could tell, they were identical. I lifted one out and gripped it, feeling the heft and balance as it settled into my hand.

Holding that weapon would make Ghandi want to pick a fight.

It was perfect. It was a first kiss, a nine-minute guitar solo, the first cup of coffee on deck on a brisk October morning, a twelve-year-old single malt, a lover's satisfied sigh. It felt light and alive in my hand, an extension of my fingers and wrist and arm and thoughts. *Forget the Manhattan Project,* it purred seductively, *forget John Moses Browning. I am the most sophisticated instrument of death ever forged by the hand of man.* Just making a quick parry and thrust with it I wanted to fence the world, impale the heavens and spill an ocean of blood.

It was a very nice sword. I nodded approval.

Doors took the other sword, twin to the one I held, and we saluted, then came *en garde*.

I took a deep breath and blew it out through pursed lips. I felt the roiling in my stomach subside, the energy of fear channeled into imminent action. My reactions felt keen, my step light, my senses sharper. I felt the electric surge humming through my body, the exhilaration of the moment.

That's why men skydive and race horses and fight bulls. The addictive rush of adrenaline, the thrill of feeling life's fleeting and fragile nature made it that much more precious. After the clean, sharp taste of life on the edge, some men found it impossible to return to the drabness of an ordinary existence.

For myself, I'd have been happier with a pint in my hand and a pretty girl on my knee, but I was grateful for the pick me up.

I took a careful look at my foe. His form was textbook. Knees bent, back erect, right foot pointed at me, left at a precise ninety degree angle. His body was turned almost sideways, his left hand out behind him to provide a counterweight to his extension and lunge. You could have drawn a line through both of his heels to me. Perfect for Olympic foil.

I kept my own stance just a bit more open, my body a shade more forward, my left hand out to the side, not behind. All that would shorten my lunge a bit, but gave me more lateral mobility. Here, we weren't confined to a strip. We could circle, and while it probably wouldn't make a difference, fending off a thrust with my left hand was better than taking it in the body.

When the judge gave us the command, Doors sprang forward, slapped my blade aside and lunged. I scrambled back, parried by a whisker. I began a riposte, but he stopped it almost before it started. He kept moving forward, testing my guard, throwing firm, quick attacks at me. I gave ground, circling to my left, keeping my guard close.

Damn, he was fast.

He was aggressive, but not rash. I hoped he would overextend, but he disappointed me, not leaving himself open for a sneaky counter or swift riposte. Fast, strong, and skilled. All that I could handle; but he was also smart, and obviously trusted on his talent to bring him victory so long as he didn't make a mistake.

Good as he was, he was very orthodox. I held him off less by speed or skill than by instinct, reading where he intended to attack, subconsciously knowing where, thanks to centuries of practice and training and masters who had discovered that it was the right attack to make. That and the fact that actual dueling swords were just a bit heavier and stiffer than the sporting weapons he'd won medals with. That little difference that slowed his reactions just the tiniest bit. It probably kept me alive.

When I thought I had his measure, I threw my first real counter. He deflected it with a flick of his wrist, beat my blade to the right, then disengaged under my parry. I leapt back, reversed my blade into a circular parry in *sixte*, deflected his thrust and made a riposte to his chest.

With a speed he must have kept in reserve, he counterparried and drove his point back at me. I frantically backpedaled and parried, barely catching it in time. His point actually ripped through the sleeve of my shirt and I felt the cold steel slide across my shoulder, but doing me no harm beyond raising goose-bumps.

Seeing me almost impaled on my first real attack, he smiled a cold, predatory smile. More a baring of fangs than an expression of happiness. He increased the speed and power of his attacks, and I held him off with difficulty, straining to my limit.

I was fencing better than I ever had, but he was so fast and I was tiring and my bad ankle was starting to feel stiff. Sooner or later—no, sooner—I would stumble or lose the rhythm and it would be over. I shoved down my growing fear and focused.

What did I have that he didn't? He was at least as skilled, he was faster, he was stronger, he was younger.

Younger.

And trained to compete.

My coach's words came back to me. *Nobody fences Italian anymore.*

I increased the extension of my sword arm, started making wider parries. Doors' smile grew. I must have looked tired. I let my point drift just a hair's breadth too far to the right, giving him an opening he couldn't resist.

His lunge was like a lightning bolt. He threw his whole body into the attack, extending his arm and launching himself explosively forward. His back leg, his shoulder, elbow, wrist and the point of his sword making one straight line toward my heart.

My blade was a bit high and right of his attack. Instead of sweeping my arm and weapon across to my left, I twisted my wrist in and down, catching the middle of his blade near the guard of my own weapon. Keeping my elbow at a slight angle out to my right, I guided his point down and to the side while driving my own toward his body. I advanced into his lunge, robbing him of the split second between his realizing what I'd done and being able to do anything about it. His body offered almost no resistance to the sharp, narrow point. I felt the blade slide along something solid, a rib maybe, or his spine. He gave a startled gasp.

The combined movement of his lunge and my advance brought us very close. His right foot actually landed on mine and I looked into his eyes from less than a foot away. The guards of our swords butted together, his point far out to my right, half of my blade buried in his body.

His face registered surprise more than pain. A tiny, strangled cough forced its way past his lips, and the sword dropped from his hand. I put my left hand on his chest.

'Everybody stay right where you are!' Pete shouted. I had no attention to spare him, I just hoped he'd keep the situation under control and didn't squeeze the trigger by mistake.

I sent my awareness deep into my enemy's body, exploring the wound. The sword had entered just below his right breast, passed through his right lung at a slight downward angle, piercing his descending aorta and going out just to the left of his spine.

I looked him in the eye and gave him a smile. 'This sword is through the biggest blood vessel in your body,' I told him. 'When I pull it out, you'll bleed to death in less than a minute. You could fall backwards onto an operating table and the best surgeon in the world couldn't save you. I think we can call that a mortal wound.'

I whipped the blade free. Blood surged out behind it, spattering thick and warm on my knee. I sent some energy quickly through to seal the hole in the great vessel, stopping the loss of the precious fluid. Once I was satisfied that the blood loss was staunched, I repaired the lung, then finally the connective tissues and skin, leaving only a matched pair of scars, front and back, for him to remember me by.

When I was finished I stood, stepped back and spoke, clearly enough that all potential witnesses would hear.

'By every rule of single combat your life belongs to me. That does not mean that I want to take it now.' I spoke the words that Conrad's pen had put in General D'Hubert's mouth. The words that Sarah had pointed out held the one loophole in this mad vendetta. I tried to plagiarize with a straight face.

'What do you mean?' he demanded.

'By right of combat,' I said, 'I hold your life in my hand. As a gesture of good faith to your family, and to mend the rift between us, I will not take it. But I insist that in light of this meeting, you consider yourself, in all matters concerning me, a dead man.'

A bit formal, but it seemed to fit the occasion. I saluted, reluctantly placed the sword on the table and walked briskly away.

I didn't look back. I just projected the absolute confidence that nobody would try to stop me. That's one of the secrets to effective leadership: if you don't believe it, nobody else will.

Plus, I wanted to get out of sight so I could resume limping and panting.

Chapter 36

THE FOUR OF US WALKED BACK to my apartment, laughing and joking in the hallway. I had my good arm around Sarah, who was still clinging to me, and Pete had my keys. Pete opened the door and stepped in, reaching for the light switch.

There was a sudden rush of motion; Pete started to step back, and there was a silver blur as he reeled back into me, blood spraying from a cut throat. I shoved Sarah aside as a man came at me, bloody blade driving toward my chest. I grabbed the wrist, instinctively using my left hand. Block with the left, attack with the right had become ingrained.

In this case it was a mistake. The man swung his arm, banging my broken wrist against the doorjamb. The pain was literally blinding. The well placed punch I was going to deliver to his throat got lost somewhere and he drove a much less sophisticated but brutal fist into my ribs.

I staggered back, gasping. He yanked his knife hand free of my grip.

I stepped in and tried to swing at his body, to keep too close for him to use his knife, but he blocked my punch, and stiff-armed me.

I saw him poised, light on the balls of his feet, his knife held low, ready to strike. I ran through my options, unarmed, injured and taken by surprise. Against this guy, the only hope I had was to try to trap his knife, in my body if need be, for long enough so Sarah and Nique could do something.

Like escape.

Looking at him, I felt a rush of fear—fear of the pain of being knifed and the oblivion of death; for the women behind me; for Pete who was bleeding out in my doorway. But most of all I felt that this just wasn't *fair*.

I had taken a Hail Mary of a plan and made it work, and now I was probably going to die here, when it should all be over.

When he made his move, I sidestepped, deflected his wrist with my good hand, and tried to catch him with an elbow to the neck, but he put his chin down and I only grazed him, then took another punch in the ribs for my pain. While I was busy sucking wind and feeling nauseous, he kicked my legs out from under me.

I went down in a heap. Whacked my head on the doorjamb, wrenched my bad ankle. I was waiting for either a boot in the gut or a knife blade when I heard the world explode.

I smelled burnt powder, and a hot brass shell casing landed on my neck as the .45 roared again.

'Put your hands up!' Sarah yelled.

My assailant turned away from me, took a step toward the hallway. I wrapped my left arm around his ankle and rolled into him, tripping him. He twisted around, drove his knife at me. I caught his wrist with my good hand this time, holding on for dear life.

'Get out of here!' I yelled to Sarah and Monique.

'No!' Sarah screamed. 'Drop the knife or I swear I'll shoot you!'

The thug ignored her, struggling to get his hand free. I held on with all my strength, but I was at the end of my stamina.

I felt the whole thing coming apart. My world collapsing. Sarah was screaming and sobbing, refusing to run. Pete spilling his lifeblood in my doorway, and a younger, stronger, bigger man than I straining to shove his blade into my vitals. My strength draining away, darkness swimming at the edges of my vision. My attacker loomed over me. I could smell his breath and see the sweat standing out on his brow and feel the pulse pounding in his wrist.

His pulse.

I wondered—

I reached out, feeling my way through his body, seeking any weak spot, just like I'd search for an injury in a wounded patient. I found a weak wall in one of his intercranial arteries.

I'd never done this before, but I applied a bit of force to the spot, weakening the bonds between the cells, letting the adrenaline push his pressure higher, until something...

Had...

To...

Give.

I felt the arterial wall part, the blood escaping and choking off the brain cells, the pressure in his cranium becoming unbearable.

I pulled myself out as fast as I could. The man stopped pushing, began to twitch and shudder. I butted my forehead into his face, wrenched the dagger from his failing grasp and drove it in between his ribs, just beside his sternum.

He jerked backward, leaving an artful spray of blood drops on my woodwork.

I rolled over, emptying my stomach on the floor. I heaved and retched myself dry. Trying to expel the taint of what I felt, what I had done.

I dragged in a ragged breath and checked the attacker. He lay spread eagle on the floor, a gash in his chest, just to the left of his breastbone. He wasn't breathing, *per se*, but air made a rasping, gurgling sound as it escaped from him.

'Are you alright?' Sarah's voice reached me, muffled by the fact that my ears were still ringing from the unexpected gunfire so close. My head was pounding, but I think that had as much to do with the way I'd... abused... my gift.

'Mostly,' I said. 'You should have run.'

'Sorry I couldn't shoot. At first, I had to wait for you to get out of the way, but even when you did, I... I just couldn't.'

I decided not to tell her that my whole strategy was to stay in the way so she could make a getaway. I hadn't done a very good job anyway.

'No shame,' I said. 'I think a reluctance to resort to violence is nice in a girlfriend.'

'How's Pete?' Nique asked, straining over me to see for herself.

I crawled a foot or so to where I could see, and shook my head.

'Can't you fix him?' Sarah asked.

'What do you mean?' Nique demanded. 'He's a good medic, but we're not superheroes.'

'Sean can heal wounds,' Sarah said. 'Oh, do not look at me like that,' she warned. 'I gave you a pass on the escort name and the fact that you look like you do and spend more time in a week with my boyfriend than I do, but if you look at me like I'm *crazy* right now I swear—'

'OK, OK,' Nique raised her hands; she'd dealt with enough agitated patients to let the escort comment slide. 'But what do you mean he can heal wounds?'

'After that other girl got beat up. Crystal or something—'

'Tiffany,' Nique corrected.

Sarah tossed her head in dismissal. 'After that, I was attacked. Some of those bastards beat the hell out of me. Sean stormed in to the rescue, killed them and healed me.'

'Doesn't matter,' I cut in. 'His heart's stopped. He's dead.'

Nique looked at me like I was an idiot. 'Can you patch up that hole?'

'Yes. Don't ask how, but I could, if he were alive. I can't get dead cells to work, and I can't make his heart beat.'

'Jesus, Sean,' she shook her head. 'I know it's been a long day, but you can stop thinking like a pirate and start thinking like a medic. Death isn't an event. It's a process. His throat hasn't been cut for more than a minute.' She pushed into the room, slinging the heavy kit off her shoulder. 'Fix that hole. We have enough saline in here to top him off and enough epi to give a steak a heartbeat.' She unzipped the bag and began assembling IV supplies.

I shook myself into action. I'd never tried this before. In theory, his cells would still be alive, just a bit oxygen deprived. The blood loss we could maybe reverse, maybe get a rhythm back.

I supposed it could work.

If I still could.

I felt slimy. Sick. I'd killed people, but never like this. I'd never used something I held so sacred to harm.

Enough of that, I told myself. *Suck it up, Marine.*

If I hadn't taken out the enemy, I'd be dead. Sarah and Nique would be dead. Nobody would be around to try to save Pete. So, fight the demons later, but dig deep and do this thing now.

I gingerly sat beside Pete, placed my hand on the gaping gash on his throat. I'd never tried to repair a body with no pulse. I felt the extent of the damage. The trachea was lacerated, the right exterior jugular was severed, but the carotid was intact. I sent a trickle of energy through to the tissues, prodding them to knit.

It was... odd. The cells responded, but lethargically. Like they were drunk, disoriented. Hypoxic.

Which they were. Anthropomorphism aside, the cells were alive, still vital, but they had been without circulation for long enough to begin to feel the effects.

I poured more energy through, pulling the ends of the blood vessels together, sealing the cut. I closed the tear in the windpipe next.

'IV's in,' said Nique.

'OK,' I replied. 'I got the cut closed. Fill him up.'

Nique opened the IVs, hanging the bags on my coat-rack. She had started two large bore lines in Pete's left arm, one in the antecubital space inside the elbow and one in his forearm. Pete was a young, healthy guy, so even flat from blood loss, he had some nice big veins.

She dragged a chair over and lifted his feet onto it. Move all the blood he had left to the core, where it could do some good.

'No pulse?'

'No,' I replied. 'I think we have an empty tank.'

'We need a defibrillator,' she said. 'I'll call 911, get a truck over here.'

'Wait!' I put a hand on his chest, feeling my way down to his heart. What should have been a beautifully choreographed symphony of contractions was chaos. The cells were all in business for themselves, firing impulses randomly. Fibrillating, to us medical types.

'We got fib now,' I said. 'How much fluid we got in?'

She quickly looked at the two bags. 'Six hundred cc's between the two.'

'Good enough,' I replied.

'He needs a shock,' she said.

'I got this,' I informed her calmly.

'You gonna walk across the carpet in your socks and touch him?' she demanded.

'He doesn't have time to wait for a defibrillator! Just bag him and trust me.'

She paused for a second, then nodded and assembled the bag valve mask, falling into the support role like a good partner, even when confronted with the unexplainable.

I sent some energy to calm the impulses. Quiet the disarray, to create a moment of electrical silence so that the natural pacemaker could resume its control.

People think a defibrillator restarts the heart. It doesn't. It stops it. Any cardiac cell can create its own impulses. Generally, they follow the lead of the sinus node, which sets the pace, but if it fails, any cell can take over. When the cells get irritated—for example if they're asked to beat an empty heart, deprived of nutrients and oxygen because somebody cut your throat and let all the blood out—they stop acting like a well drilled marching band and start acting like the patrons of an Irish bar at last call on Saint Patrick's Day.

The shock of defibrillation silences it all.

Like the sound of a bottle of Jameson's being opened.

Then, in theory and sometimes in practice, the sinus node resumes calling the pace and a productive heartbeat resumes.

I was hoping to achieve the same result without burning my friend by sending two hundred joules of electricity searing its way through his chest. Even supposing he could wait that long—which he couldn't.

I quieted the jumble of impulses, the same way I would still the pain of an injury. After a short delay, the cells responded.

I held my breath, hoping the heart would come back online. After a long, long second, I felt the cells contract in glorious sequence, atria then ventricles, a beautiful, rhythmic *ba-boom*.

'Sinus rhythm!' I shouted. 'I am a GOD!'

Nique pressed two fingers into the side of his neck. 'Pulses,' she said. She gave a little shrug. 'Rapid and weak, but it's a pulse. I guess you are good for something.'

'You're too kind,' I replied. I focused my attention on Pete, assessing the damage. There was no more trauma; the lethargic, disoriented hypoxic taint in the cells was fading, the saline that was pouring into his veins was replacing the volume spilled on the floor. Saline didn't actually deliver oxygen, mind, but it gave the remaining blood enough volume to prime the pump. Like when the ice melted in your drink. It wasn't a very good drink any more, but it was better than nothing.

I nudged the marrow to speed up production on blood cells. 'Stop bagging for a sec,' I said. Nique, being a medic and thus able to follow directions from someone without bugles on his collar, did so.

After a few seconds, I saw Pete's chest rise with a deep breath. Once I was certain this was becoming a trend, I relaxed. He looked horribly pale, but he had a pulse, he was breathing, it was just a matter of time now.

I sat back, nursing my throbbing wrist and trying to think what to do next.

I'd never before used my powers to resuscitate someone although, in fairness, I'd been healing broken bones for centuries before I ever took a cardiology class, and *quieting* the heart of a dying person isn't really intuitive.

The sound of a cell phone cut into my thoughts.

We all froze for a moment, before I realized the sound was coming from the dead man's pocket.

I dug out the phone, a sleek new model, and pushed the green button. 'Ja?'

Chapter 37

'K ARL!' DOORS' VOICE BARKED OVER the phone. 'Get back here immediately. I do not authorize this. I will not have my word questioned. Do you understand?' A long pause, 'Karl?'

'Karl can't come to the phone,' I answered.

Another pregnant pause. 'Mr Danet. I trust you are well?'

'I am. Karl is less so.'

'I apologize for any inconvenience he may have caused. I assure you, this was done without my consent or authorization.'

I actually believed him. His tone was embarrassed. Exactly what I'd expect of an aristocrat in this position. He wasn't sorry I'd been endangered, or upset at what might have happened to his man; he was ashamed that his orders had been disobeyed.

'I assume you will take steps to control your people in the future?' I said as arrogantly as possible.

'I will see that they all take Karl's example to heart,' he replied, an edge to his voice. 'I would like to pick up my employee.'

'You know where he is?' I asked. I wasn't going to give him my address if Karl was the only one who knew it.

'I found his message.'

I thought for a moment. 'You come alone,' I decided.

'Agreed.'

I put the phone down. 'Doors is coming to collect the body. Sarah, keep the .45 and put your back to the wall there. Nique, help me get Pete up on the couch in the living room.'

'He's coming here?' Sarah asked, shocked. 'You agreed to it?'

'It's not like he can't come in if I don't invite him. He's not a vampire,' I grunted as I looped my arms under Pete's shoulders. 'He's coming alone, we have two guns.'

'So, we're going to take the murdering drug dealer at his word?' Nique asked. 'There's no chance we'll regret that.'

'One, two, three,' I counted and we lifted Pete and carried him to the couch, propping his feet up on one of the arms. 'Well, if we say no, what's to stop him showing up anyway? If he wanted to surprise me, why ask? Now we're alerted. He knows I'm armed and dangerous. And you need to think like an aristocrat. Or a gang boss. If it gets out that he's broken his word, who's gonna deal with him?'

As I talked, I retrieved the Browning from Pete's jacket. I checked that there was a round chambered and took up position near the wall, facing the doorway where the body lay. I leaned back against the wall, taking my weight off my injured ankle. I took a deep breath and forced myself to concentrate. There would be time to lie down soon enough.

One way or another.

'Nique,' I said, 'if Pete's vitals are stable, you and Sarah probably want to get out of here. I got this.'

'No chance,' said Sarah.

'Don't count on it,' said Nique. 'You need her to back you up with that gun and you need me to remind you you're a medic. Partners look out for each other.'

I smiled back. 'Thanks. That means a lot. Just don't complain when I'm wrong and he shows up with eight henchmen and they kill us all.'

'You always know what to say to a girl.' Nique shook her head.

'That's why I love him,' Sarah put in.

At that moment, there was a knock at the door.

The three of us jumped. Fortunately, the safety was on and my finger was outside the trigger guard or I might have put a round through my floor.

'Already?' whispered Nique. 'How'd he get here so fast?'

There wasn't time to explain teleporting and I'm not sure it would have been a good idea anyway, coming so soon after the revelation of my superhuman healing ability. Nique was cool, but even she probably had her limits.

'Long story,' I replied. 'OK, if you're going to stay, get in the bedroom, out of sight. We'll move Pete there, and you can keep an eye on him. If you hear anything scary, call 911 and hide, alright?'

'OK, but if he kills you, your last thought better be how I was right this is a bad idea.'

We got a blanket and carried Pete into the bedroom on it. I gave Nique the most reassuring smile I could come up with and closed the door.

'Mr Danet,' came a now-familiar voice. 'May I come in?'

I didn't know when he'd picked up a polite streak. I glanced at Sarah, who nodded. I settled the Browning in my grip, aimed at the floor in front of the door, where I could whip the gun up and fire in a split second but he wouldn't walk through to see a barrel pointed at his face. That makes some people twitchy, and twitchy is never good.

'It's unlocked,' I said. No point in asking if he was alone. Either he was honest and came alone like he said, or he wasn't and he'd just lie again. I still didn't know how many of his people were able to teleport, plus he seemed genuinely concerned about keeping his word, so I guessed he was flying solo on this one.

The door opened slowly and the man stepped through. He looked well enough after our meeting, if a little pale. Considering the length of steel he'd had in his guts a short time ago, not a bad deal.

He looked down at Karl's body. His eyes hardened a bit, but his face remained set. I wasn't sure whether he was upset at Karl for breaking his word, or at me for Karl's death, or at Dame Fortune for leaving him for another man. Probably a bit of all three.

'I apologize for this attempt on you. I had no knowledge of it.'

'How did your man know where to look for me?' I asked. 'Come to think of it, how'd you know where to come tonight?'

'We have been looking for you for some time. Since our first meeting.'

'When I earned your ire for fixing that ankle?' I let a bit of acid into my tone.

A muscle on his jaw twitched, but he didn't rise to the bait. 'It took some time to locate your address, and by that time you had gone to ground. As that seems to have been a skill of yours over the years, I thought we might not see you again. I was a bit surprised when you showed up for our meeting. I wondered if it was just to buy you some time to run.'

'I thought about it,' I admitted. 'But I didn't think my vanishing would make you lay off my friends.'

'This I do not understand at all,' he snapped. 'My ancestors did not understand it. Why do you choose these creatures over your own people?' If he noticed Sarah in the room, he made no indication of it. 'If they discovered what you are, they would hunt you like a dog. With your powers, you could have been a lord over them, even without remembering that you were born a prince among men. Instead you choose to live like this.' His gesture took in the apartment, which was about what one would expect on paramedic pay after drink, food and women had taken their cut. The art on the walls of Doors' office could have furnished my place three times over.

'I'm not going to try to explain that one to you,' I replied. 'If you don't see humanity around you, I can't make you.'

He shrugged dismissively. To him I was a traitor, but more than that, I was an oddity. In his world, we were different from other people. Better. A species apart. I'd seen enough men who shared his perspective. Those aren't *people*, they thought: those are Irishmen or Indians or Zulu or Orientals. It was the disconnect that lets men do so much of the evil that men do.

'Regardless,' said Doors, 'I think we must clarify our arrangement. As you requested. As is your right.' He grimaced as though the word tasted bad. 'I swear that I will "conduct myself as a dead man" as far as you are concerned. And I shall see that those of my household do likewise. But I must know if you plan to tread on my business activities. I need to know that you will not sally forth from your Fortress of Solitude to thwart me.'

The reference surprised me at first, but it made sense Doors would have been a Superman fan.

I shrugged. 'If you don't deal drugs, someone else will. I'm not going to applaud you, but I'm not naive enough to try to fight that. That's a job for the police, anyway. You lay off me and those close to me and I'll turn a blind eye. You can tell your friends at Langley the same applies to them.'

His lips drew back in a cold smile. 'So, you are not the spotless crusader. You have simply gone native.'

With that, he reached into his coat. I tensed my grip on the Browning until he drew out a small bag, opened it and spread some dust from it on the blood pooled in my entryway. He dropped a towel on it, planted a foot on the towel and reached down to his fallen employee. He brushed some hair back from the man's forehead, almost affectionately.

'Karl was young and foolish. He had yet to learn that there is more dishonor in a lie than a defeat.' His voice became clinical again, as though he felt the need to show he was all business, even as he stooped over a dead friend. 'I'd have thought he would have surprised you. You are a bad man to underestimate.'

'He is.' Sarah spoke for the first time since Doors had entered. I spared her a glance. Her green eyes were hard, her expression set.

Doors' tight smile widened, but there was no mirth in it. He turned to me and said, 'You make interesting choices. I would say I wish you joy of them, but I will not be so dishonest.' He lifted the lifeless Karl, stood on the towel. 'I leave you, now. Not to your Fortress of Solitude, perhaps. No, I leave you to your dances with wolves.' He smiled at his own wit, then closed his eyes in concentration. Along with the corpse, the towel and the blood beneath it, he shimmered and vanished.

Now I knew why the police didn't have inconvenient questions about Sarah's apartment.

I let out a breath and engaged the Browning's safety. Sarah slumped back against the wall and shook. I walked to her, took the Colt from her hand and held her. She stiffened for a moment, then melted against me, letting out shaky, ragged breaths.

'It's OK,' I murmured in her ear. 'Everything will be OK now.'

I hoped that was true.

Nique came out of the bedroom. Stood silently, watching me.

'Now what?' Sarah asked, her voice muffled against my chest.

'Well, Doors and his thugs won't run me off,' I said. 'I'm hoping you won't either.'

She shook her head against me. Then looked up into my eyes. 'I want to keep you around. You saved my life, you know.'

'After I put it in danger.'

'You had no way of knowing that,' she said. 'I'd given up on the knight in shining armor. Maybe too soon.'

'The old armor is a bit dinged and scratched,' I said. 'I want to be with you, as long as you'll have me, but don't fall for an illusion. The apartment that Doors sneered at is me. The noble duelist he cut a deal with shows up on rare occasions when cowardice and my natural charm have failed me.'

She shrugged prettily. 'I like everything I've seen so far. And I think you sell yourself short.'

I kissed her. 'If you'll have me, I'll be had.'

I turned to Nique. 'How about you? You feel OK about all this?'

'We don't throw our own under the bus. You could have skipped, but you stayed and saw this through. You did something to patch up Pete and Tiffany, and you took as much risk on yourself as you could. You're a good friend. I won't dime you out. Besides,' she smirked, 'I have you almost trained. I'm not breaking in a new partner just because you're some inhuman freak.'

'You sweet talker, you.'

'But if any more guys with knives show up to hassle me, I will absolutely kick your ass.'

CHAPTER 38

Bob sat at my kitchen table sipping a large Scotch while I peeled and chopped potatoes at the counter.

'Thanks for having me over,' he said. 'Sarah says you can cook, but that's not a very high bar.'

'Hey,' she said, entering the room with a bag of groceries. 'Just because I don't know how to cook doesn't mean I don't recognize talent when I see it.'

'Glad to have you,' I said. 'I owe you for your hospitality, and for that info you got me. That's probably what kept Doors' buddies in Washington off my back and made this possible. The drug trade made a lot of intelligence people rich, and lots of them are actually good at finding and eliminating people. They'd have helped Doors get rid of me to protect their source. Threatening to release that info if anything did happen to me would make them think twice. That's the kind of thing that would have ruined careers and reputations and put spooks in jail.'

'You don't owe me a thing,' he replied. 'And you swing a pretty good sword for a guy with as many injuries as you had.'

'I'm sure the reports of my prowess were exaggerated.'

'My eye don't exaggerate.'

'What do you mean?' I asked.

'Watched you guys through the scope of my aught-six,' said Bob. 'Couldn't leave you hanging after you came for me in that hotel. Wasn't gonna give them a shot at both of us by turning up next to you, but I figured I'd best be on hand.'

'Where were you?' asked Sarah.

'In the clock tower of that old mill, just below the face.' Bob paused for a drink. 'Once I heard where you guys were meeting, I did some recon. Set up a hide in the best spot I could find. If things started to

251

look hopeless, or if those goons got rough after you beat him, I'd have reached out and touched a few.'

Sarah shook her head. 'I'm still not used to hearing how calmly you two talk about killing people.'

'It's probably a sign of a damaged psyche, but every so often, decent, well adjusted, solid citizens need a few head cases like us,' said Bob.

'I'm just wondering how a white guy as big as you managed to sneak into a building in this town with a gun as long as that,' I said.

Bob smiled and sang a few bars of the Green Berets' hymn: 'Silver wings. Upon their chests.'

I shook my head. 'You call us Marines crazy, but you brag about your willingness to jump out of perfectly good airplanes.'

'No such thing as a perfectly good airplane,' he replied.

The doorbell rang and Sarah buzzed Nique in. 'Thank God it's you.' She greeted the other woman with a hug. 'The testosterone was getting thick in here.'

'Welcome to my world,' Nique replied with a weary smile.

Pete arrived shortly afterwards, and the five of us sat at the kitchen table in my apartment. Sarah, Bob, Pete, Nique and I. I had marinated and pan-seared some pork tenderloin and finished it in the oven. The whole place was warm and filled with the happy aroma of roasted meat infused with garlic, thyme and rosemary. I love using the oven in winter.

'So that asshole gets to walk?' Pete demanded around a mouthful of mashed potatoes. A week had passed, and he was still a bit pale and easily winded, but he was on the mend.

I shrugged. 'Pretty much. There really wasn't another way to stop the violence.'

And because none of my friends had died. If Pete or Sarah or Tiffany had died, I don't think I could have settled with Doors.

Pete shook his head.

'It doesn't seem right,' Nique offered. 'I mean, their drug operation is still up and running. He really didn't lose anything. After what they did to Tiffany and you guys. Where's the justice?'

'In this life, my dear,' I paused for a sip from my beer, 'there is no justice. There is only accommodation. He's been beaten, and publicly—for a narrow definition of the public—agreed to drop his feud. He knows that I know enough to sic the police on him, and he knows that if anything happens to me, it will all come out. And heroin isn't going away. If we put Doors out of business, then some other thug will run it, and they'll be every bit as brutal.'

'So what, exactly, did he give up?' asked Pete. 'I'm only asking because I got my throat cut for it.'

'You got better. Anyway, what we got out of the deal is a bit of security. You don't have to worry about your safety just because you know me.'

'Knowing you is kinda punishment enough.'

'It has its moments,' Sarah said, flashing me her twisted smile and a meaningful look over the top of her glasses.

'Easy for you to say,' Pete mumbled.

After that, things went back to normal, for a given value of normal. Bob came out of deep hiding into mere hiding. We had some long, boozy arguments about politics and cooking and Scotch. Nique stayed the most reliable partner I could ask for, and rather than inspire jealousy in Sarah, the two formed an alliance designed to keep me in my place. I didn't mind. It was a nice place.

Pete recovered, and may have viewed me with some trepidation for a while. It was a week before he went back to gay jokes or offered to step in and show Sarah what a real man was like.

For her part, Sarah decided to place her trust in a man who lived by aliases, made his life a pleasant fiction, and had cut and run more often than a pair of cheap nylons. I feared she might be shaming me into being a better man.

I had a lot to think about. I'd stood and fought to stay with a woman instead of running, and that was new. I'd revealed myself to a handful of people, and that usually meant running. I'd pushed my talents into a dark area where I never had before. And, for the first time in a long time, I knew who I was, where I came from, and which family I'd been born to. Maybe there were family members out there right now. Who knows—maybe there was a cousin, or a brother, or a great-great-great nephew who shared the same powers as me…

The cynical voice in the back of my head cleared its throat, demanding attention. Things were happy now, but what about tomorrow? Next year? Four people knew I could heal. Four at least. They were people I trusted, but what if one of them got sick? What if Nique's fiancé crashed his truck, or Pete's mom threw a clot? Would they ask me to help? Could I refuse? My secret was out, how many people could know before I'd have to move on?

And Sarah. I was thrilled to be with her now, but how would she deal with the onslaught of time? I had the power to shore up and renew her cells, keep her healthy and beautiful, but would she want that? Want to remain forever young as her friends and family grew old before her eyes? She might choose to age gracefully. How bad would it be when she started to show her age and I still looked the same, and the company kept on hiring freethinking twenty-year-old EMTs to work the trucks? Could she trust me? Hell, could I trust me?

And what if she did agree to my help? How long would she want to stay with me, and how much would that be for me, and how much would be the seductive addiction to the energy of youth?

I forced my misgivings back, focusing on the present. I wasn't any more vulnerable than I had been, and none of these worries was anything that hadn't been a concern for ages. And now, I felt truly connected. I was with a woman without hiding behind any secrets. That removed a weight I'd become so used to that I hadn't noticed it in centuries.

Despite the uncertainty, life was good. I still worked too many hours for too little pay, subservient to supervisors like Marty, in a city where the drunks, gang members and junkies knew me by my first name. But things could have been a lot worse.

I could have wound up like Doors. Living a solitary life on a pedestal, ruling over people I though of as servants or cattle, rather than sharing the love and respect of friends and equals.

My life had to be better.

Sarah went to the fridge for another beer. She looked at me with a smile. I raised my empty glass and she got me another bottle too. She leaned over my shoulder to put the beer on the table, kissing me on the cheek. I smiled up at her, feeling a happy glow at the warmth of her smile, the mischievous gleam in her eyes.

This was better.

I slipped my arm around her waist, pulling her close. Grinning as I felt her soft curves settle against me. I kissed her cheek and her smiled widened.

Revealing some tiny, tiny lines.

This was better.

Wasn't it?

PATRICK LECLERC MAKES GOOD USE of his history degree by working as a paramedic for an ever changing parade of ambulance companies in the Northern suburbs of Boston. When not writing he enjoys cooking, fencing and making witty, insightful remarks with career limiting candor.

In the lulls between runs on the ambulance—and sometimes the lulls between employment at various ambulance companies—he writes fiction.

You can find more of it at http://inkandbourbon.com/

Also Available!

Available at Amazon from Firedance Books, Summer 2012…

THE WALKER'S DAUGHTER BY JANET Allison Brown.

When her mother dies at the hands of a silver-haired figure in black, six-year-old spirit-walker Cora Bloux hides out in her own body. Twenty years later she's still there, fiercely maintaining an outwardly stable, conventional life.

But when her own daughter is hit by a car, Cora is forced to spirit-walk again—and discovers that the spirit world has been waiting for her.

In the extraordinary, fast-paced world of spirit-walkers, body-swappers, rock bands and second chances, Cora must discover her true self and learn the ordinary lessons of courage, trust and love.

To see the world as it really is, sometimes you have to close your eyes and… walk.

Available at Amazon from Firedance Books, Summer 2012…

EXPECT CIVILIAN CASUALTIES BY GARY Bonn.

Jason has spent the last six years living wild on beaches. Now he's seventeen and a feral girl walks into his life.

A girl with no name.

He calls her Anna. She's fun, she's kind—and she's the most dangerous person in the world.

The most unusual love story, and a truly strange war story… Expect Civilian Casualties turns how we see the world upside down.

Coming to Amazon from Firedance Books, September 2012…

TALES OF THE SHONRI: CITY OF LIGHTS by Stephen Godden.

Darkness never falls in the City of Lights.

Ruled by the brutal creatures of the Magi, the people of the city fear the dark, but the Magi fear only the Shonri.

Legendary warriors who cast off the shackles of slavery, the Shonri fight in the dark places, in the hidden places, of this shattered world. A slow stuttering war against the power of the Magi, with the roles of hunter and hunted always in doubt.

The witch Medina dances a perilous path between the Shonri and the Magi. Loyal only to herself, she gives the Magi the means to destroy the Shonri once and for all.

The world's last defence against a dreadful future, the Shonri must enter the city to safeguard their very existence.

And, under the streets of the city, something begins to stir.

Made in the USA
Charleston, SC
01 October 2012